Mother Wode

Dev Gualtieri

Tikalon Press
http://www.tikalonpress.com

ISBN-10: 0985332506
ISBN-13: 978-0-9853325-0-1

Cover art based on a photograph provided through the courtesy of the Cornell University Library, A. D. White Architectural Photographs Collection (Accession Number 15/5/3090.00927).

AUTHOR'S FORWARD

Mother Wode is a novel set in the near future. The year is not explicitly stated, but the time period has many elements similar to the first decade of the twenty-first century, intermixed with an extrapolated future. Computers are much faster than today's computers, but computer scientists and computer programmers behave about the same. Also very similar to their present day counterparts are the corporate and academic cultures in which these people work. The human condition has not changed much through the years. Love, and the desire for a secure lifestyle, are still prime motivators. There may be people routinely working on the moon, but there are still bad guys back on Earth, and everyone would like more money.

A corporate computer scientist, a computer science graduate student and a computer hacker stumble upon evidence of a conspiracy to control worldwide financial transactions. Their curiosity fuels their attempt to discover the source and purpose of this conspiracy.

▬

This book is dedicated to my wife, Anne, who has had to live with a pastiche of some of the characters for many years; and to my son, Michael, and daughter, Marianne, who read the final draft and noted improvements.

▬

CONTENTS

1 MOTHER WODE

Michael Martelli was not the type of student who ran from place to place. His life's motto was that all things happened at their own rate, and speeding through one task would just make you arrive at the next task too early to do something useful. However, today was an exception to his life's rule. Today, Michael Martelli was running for his life. He must not be late for today's interview, since the entire future course of his career might depend on its outcome. This would be the first face-to-face meeting with a representative of his future employer, and folklore stressed that first impressions are crucial. In this case, Michael wasn't going to act contrary to tradition. As he walked past the familiar university buildings on his way to the distant student parking lot, he began to reminisce about his student career and the university in general.

The structure of universities started to change in the early part of the twenty-first century. Universities had become increasingly dependent on industrial support, and the successful research universities began to grow at the expense of the smaller private and public schools. Finally, all pretenses were dropped, and university programs became just another profit and loss center of large corporations. At first, the faculties were resistant to the change, and cries of lost academic freedom were widespread. But the most successful professors had been "on the take" for years, and they rather enjoyed the liberation from the bloated academic bureaucracy that had developed around the money sources. Finally, the authority to grant degrees was wrested from the universities themselves and given to Chartered Academic Guilds. The original argument for establishment of the Guilds was to reign in all the shady "distance learning" enterprises that had sprung up out from the original Internet, but the changes transcended mere accreditation. The professor-student relationship was shifted to a master-apprentice model, and all this had worked to the benefit of the large corporations.

East Wodenstumpf University had been on the fringe of this restructuring. It had been too small to be a real research university, but too large to be ignored completely. One thing that Mother Wode had was location. It was close to several powerful corporations. Not only that, but several top names in Computer Science had decided that the Atlantic beaches and friendly neighborhoods of East Wodenstumpf were preferable to the Pacific beaches and very highly priced neighborhoods of most West Coast universities.

The biggest enigma surrounding East Wodenstumpf University was its name. Yes, there was a city called East Wodenstumpf. It served as logistical support for the university and habitat for most of its employees. College students were still fueled by pizza and Chinese food and the occasional risqué cinema, and there was an abundance of purveyors of these in the many small establishments within walking distance of the campus. The enigma was that there was no Wodenstumpf; nor was there a North Wodenstumpf, South Wodenstumpf, or West Wodenstumpf. Most records of the city's founding were destroyed by a fire at about the time of the Civil War, but some explanation was pieced together from other sources. It seems there was a falling-out of bothers (Wodenstumpfs, of course) that led to an East-West split in the town. Over the years, East Wodenstumpf prospered and expanded. West Wodenstumpf faltered, and finally disincorporated. The records of the matter are hazy, but some fiscal malfeasance in the city administration appeared to be the root cause. When the West Wodenstumpf town hall caught fire, it didn't help that the fire department was ill equipped because its funding had been siphoned away over a number of years. There were reports that the town hall fire was arson, done to burn the records of some scandal. It was all downhill from that point. With the demise of their western rival, the citizens of East Wodenstumpf had the opportunity to shorten their name. However, the expense of making new signs, or merely chopping away parts of signs, was voted down, so it's been East Wodenstumpf for more than two hundred years.

Michael Martelli was at Mother Wode because of the fearful combination of chance and the prepared mind. He had been a curious and precocious child. Since he liked taking apart his toys to see how they worked, his parents decided that he would enjoy the converse activity - putting things together - so they showered him with kits. These were at first models of automobiles, aircraft and rockets. Later, there were electronic kits for radios, door chimes, and finally simple robots. Robots were a turning point in his life, not merely because he could race them around the house to the occasional gasp of family and friends, but because they were programmable. This was liberating for a young boy who was always taking orders from others. Now, he was the master! He could give the orders!

After he had exhausted the limited instruction sets of his first programmable robots, Michael found network sites with instructions on how to "hack" his robots. He thought that the word "hack" was apropos, since the first step was to cut something open, typically with a hack saw. In reality, the earliest computer programmers coined the word, "hack," to refer to the quick fixes they sometimes did to existing programs to make them work in a different way. The word eventually became applied to the clever application of computer code to a specific problem, and later to the modification of consumer appliances to do odd things; like a coffee maker with a built in steam whistle to signal when the pot was ready. Hacking his robot kits allowed Michael to do things not usually seen in any household, such as dancing pairs of robots that responded to the beat of the music. By the time he had reached middle-school, his knowledge of programming was at a university level.

At the age when every other secondary school teenager was struggling to write acceptable computer programs, or at least programs of the type required to get a passing grade, Michael was spending most of his time on mathematics. He excelled in mathematics, and it's the ability to apply mathematical and logical reasoning to data structures that separates computer scientists from mere programmers. For one science fair project, he calculated pi to a million decimal places using the computing power of his computer's graphical processor chip and Machlin's arctangent series. Since the graphical processor couldn't do both its display tasks and his algorithm at the same time, Michael's computer chugged away for days with a blank screen. It was only when the computation was finished that he could check his results with another program that calculated just the few digits of pi around its millionth digit. He won that science fair not just because of his ability, but also for his showmanship. He printed the results on a ribbon of paper that he pasted around the high school gymnasium.

After secondary school, Michael Martelli became a willing participant of the University-Industrial complex. He enjoyed computing, so it was an easy decision to continue in computer science at a university. East Wodenstumpf University wasn't exactly a Mecca for the computer literate, but it was nearby, and he didn't like the "Distance Learning" concept. If he must be apprenticed, then it would be at a brick and mortar university. Besides, the social life would be better. A computer geek could only hope.

Although he was more prepared than most students, his university career was not a romp. There were other things required of him than his mathematical and computer skills. He was expected to be somewhat literate, an armchair historian, and a philosopher. Furthermore, because of the intimate link between computing and its primary application in the sciences and economics, he was forced to take introductory courses in many topic areas he would choose to ignore. At times he was tempted to leave without a degree and get a programming job, possibly with some startup company where his innovative talents would be appreciated. But the "A"s in his computer and math courses balanced the "C"s in his other courses, so he stayed at the Mother Wode. Michael's computer science skills did not go unnoticed among the Mother's faculty. When he had completed his undergraduate training, he was quickly apprenticed to one of the more eminent Master Professors of computer science. At that point, his education accelerated, since it was all computer science with none of the cocktail-party-conversation subject areas he had detested as an undergraduate.

Michael reached his car, carefully parked in a student slot at about 6:00 AM that morning. He had gradually become an early riser when its advantages became apparent. Most of the undergraduates still tried to postpone their first class to as late in the morning as possible, and they struggled with traffic and parking as a result. Few cars were on the roads when he traveled to the university in the morning. Few students were apparent on campus at 6:00 AM, so he got his pick of parking slots. There were other perquisites, such as fresher coffee at the campus eatery, Wode's End, and time to think before the hubbub of civilization filled his campus building.

As usual, his windshield was festooned with leaflets about one event or another. Michael laughed that the "Save the Trees" people would doom so many trees to spread their word. He popped the door of his car's trunk, and tossed his mobile computer onto a pile of soft debris sitting there. "I've got to do something about this mess," he thought, "But at least it serves as impact protection for the computer."

Settling into the driver's seat, he felt exhilarated as he started his engine.

2 HAEMATITE

Michael had seen the industrial campus before, but it never ceased to impress him. Here was the corporate realization of the Robber Baron mansions of the last century. There were flowing fountains, manicured lawns, abstract sculpture, huge windowed facades, and plush carpets. There was even a human receptionist at the front desk and not just an automated help center. What impressed him the most was the parking. As a student at Mother Wode, he was required to park in lots at the distant perimeter of the campus and trek at least ten minutes to his office. Haematite, the corporation that had funded his education, had a parking lot right at the front of its building, and his walk to the front door was less than a minute. In the rain, he might not even need an umbrella.

The receptionist invited him to sit in a huge, overstuffed chair, while she buzzed the University Liaison Office. After a few moments of tapping his feet to the latest elevator music, an attractive young woman arrived to escort him into the offices of the inner sanctum. He was supplied with coffee and an exotic tropical flavor snack bar while waiting for the Director to finish a call. The snack bar was so good that he pocketed the wrapper in the hope of finding the brand at the food market at a reasonable price. He didn't discount the possibility that it was a custom foodstuff designed for this particular corporation.

Robert Moses, the Director of University Programs, was a somewhat plump man in his early fifties. He had a ready smile, firm handshake, and considerable people skills; in short, the perfect man for the job. Moses directed him to a chair across from a small round table and sat across the table from him.

"Michael, I've heard such wonderful things about you from Master Professor Sterba! He says that your progress has been superb, and he's about to recommend you to the Guild for certification as a Doctor Philosophiae. You know what that means!"

"That my sheepskin and thirty dollars can buy me a good cup of coffee?"

Moses laughed. It was a sincere laugh, although that ability could have been a prerequisite for his job.

"You must get out more often. It's more like fifty dollars, now, for a better cup. But that goes to the heart of what I meant. It's time for a real job! With a job, you can pay those outrageous coffee prices, hook-up with a nice girl, buy a house - all that normal living stuff!"

Michael knew before Moses' speech that this was the purpose of their meeting. His university days were ending and his indentured servitude was about to begin. It was time for Michael to settle down.

"Of course, you have the option of working anywhere," Moses suppressed a chuckle, "But we would like you to work here."

Michael could understand why Moses chuckled. Yes, he had options. They were required by law. He could repay the corporation for all the years of his training and move on. But another corporation would never pay for his freedom for the privilege of hiring him. Beyond all the unwritten rules of the game, there was no tax incentive in such a transaction, whereas Haematite Corporation had been getting a terrific tax break for funding his apprenticeship all these years. The only viable option for buying his freedom was paying the bill himself, which was not at all practical. As all the other apprentices before him, he would take the only viable route and sign on with Haematite.

Moses continued. "Haematite has some interesting ongoing research you could be a part of. I'm not a technical person, so I really can't explain it, but I've arranged for you to meet with Dr. Sandra Webb, one of our Computerati, so she can explain. I understand that you would be working for her." He shuffled through some papers. "I see that your Non-Disclosure Agreement is in order, so you and she can talk freely about what you can do for Haematite. Let me buzz her."

While Moses stroked his transceiver, trying to reach Webb, Michael had time to study the office. It was spacious by most standards, but sparsely furnished. He read once that an executive's importance was in inverse proportion to the number of items on his desk. By this standard, Moses was quite high in the corporate food chain, since his desk had only a transceiver and one other display. The display cycled through family photographs, and Michael speculated that this was the primary purpose of the display, if not its sole purpose. There was no keyboard, but most non-technical people used voice recognition almost exclusively. Keyboards were only needed when someone needed to scratch out some equations, or do programming. The wall hangings were photographs of early industrial settings. They were probably images of Haematite's early history.

"Dr. Webb will get you in a few minutes. She's finishing something... or starting something... whatever it is, she said it won't take long." Moses extended his hand, and while they were shaking hands, he steered Michael to a seat in the outer office. The pep talk and interview were over.

When Sandra Webb blanked the transceiver, she nearly launched into the usual string of expletives she reserved for times when management interrupted her work. In this case, she realized she had mixed feelings about the call, since this newbie might become a useful assistant. It was only two years ago when she herself had been the newbie, so she was able to muster some empathy for him. Her only concern was that he was just another average performer from East Wodenstumpf, Haematite's local nursery. She grabbed her dress whites - a lab coat rarely worn, but useful in hiding whatever crumpled mess she was wearing at the time - and walked down the corridor to the executive wing.

Sandra Webb, Ph.D., had apprenticed at Stanford with a Master Professor who would have won a Nobel Prize if the Alfred Nobel Foundation hadn't gone bankrupt and out of business several years prior. She certainly wasn't sponsored by Haematite. She was sponsored by a much more prestigious corporation, Tressor Systems. Unfortunately, the smaller Tressor was acquired by Haematite in a hostile takeover. Her management left *en masse*, but she was transferred like all other property to Haematite, and Haematite promptly relocated her here. Sandra was married to her work - no close family, no boyfriend, not even a cat - so the relocation didn't affect her lifestyle at all. At times she missed the temperate weather, but that was about all. She was actually starting to enjoy a real passing of seasons, but winter driving still made her nervous. Blizzards typically meant an overnight in her office, but she didn't mind. Sandra had come to the realization early in life that she was defined by her work.

At Tressor, she worked on autonomous agents that scanned local area networks for unusual traffic. This could be caused by hardware problems, or, more likely, malicious attacks by competitors. This was an outgrowth of her apprenticeship, and it was important enough to be funded now by Haematite after the Tressor takeover. At first, she resented the takeover as much as Tressor's management did, but she was doing the same sort of research, so a name change didn't seem to matter. As a benefit, Haematite seemed to have more financial resources than Tressor. Slow, but steady, really did seem to win the race.

Moses' secretary identified her on sight, and introductions were made. Sandra led Michael to her office, not by the same long corridor through which she had come, but by a more impressive "Scenic Route." There was, of course, the obligatory view of the clean room, a Class 1-50n facility in which only one particle larger than 50 nanometers per cubic meter of air was tolerated. It was a great place to work if you have allergies, but for a different reason than you would expect. All the workers breathed through air supply tubes, since one breath into the room would shut down the operation for days. The operators' white suits were specially coated so they would not shed particles or fibers when rubbed, and there was a near cyclone of filtered air flowing from ceiling to floor, sweeping any rouge particles out of the system. Electrostatic precipitators handled particles too small to be filtered.

The clean room personnel were working on standard electronic circuits with a few nano-mechanical twists. Many decades ago, quantum computation was touted as the holy grail of computation. Laboratory tests on small computation cells were impressive, but when people actually started building practical-sized circuits, they discovered fundamental problems they should have realized much earlier. First, quantum states cannot be maintained indefinitely. They tend to spontaneously disappear by a well known process called spontaneous symmetry breaking. Also, as useful functions were built from the standard cells, the physical size of the device necessarily increased. Through the fundamental properties of quantum mechanics, the electron wavefunctions spread out to encompass the entire device. This increase in spatial extent resulted in calculation errors. All this was related to the Heisenberg Uncertainty Principle, which states, in effect, that you can have peanut butter, or jelly, on your nano-sized slice of bread, but not both.

After the quantum roadblock, physicists had to devise physical shortcuts to achieve rapid computation of important functions. As usual, they were helped by some very old research. Ernest Chladni, a French physicist at the time of Napolean, had discovered the strange acoustical modes of vibration in irregular plates. He sprinkled sand on thin metal plates, and when they were excited by a violin bow, the sand would settle into a pattern in places where the amplitude of the vibration was small. After a while, the mathematicians got into the act, and they were able to analytically describe how these vibration modes related to the irregular boundaries of plates. In effect, you could simulate a mathematical function by a properly shaped plate. When nanotechnologists were able to make very small plates that would vibrate at high frequencies, Chladni Computation, the rebirth of analog computers, was born. It was most useful for signal analysis and filtering of data streams.

After the scenic tour, Sandra's office must have been a let-down, but Michael didn't seem to notice.

"Is this where you do your work? Nice place."

"Well, Haematite would probably like it that way - low overhead, and all that. As you know, we Computerati don't require much more than a display panel and keyboard. However, when I relocated here from Stanford, I insisted that as a scientist I needed a laboratory. I'll show it to you later. I keep up the scientist charade by wearing this coat."

They both laughed. Sandra was starting to warm to this character.

"So tell me about your work."

Michael started the elevator speech, but Sandra seemed genuinely interested, so the description dragged out into a half hour. There were dueling scribbles between Sandra and Michael on the white board, and Michael pulled-up some of his published papers on the panel. At one point, he forgot a link path to a publication, and he needed to search for it. Sandra was impressed when a keyword search on just his name yielded hundreds of page hits. This guy may just work out. When the conversation wound down, Sandra led him to her laboratory. The laboratory was small, but not cramped, and it had white boards filling three of the four walls. In one cozy corner was a desk with two large display panels and a keyboard.

"Watch this," said Sandra.

She poked at a wall switch, the lights dimmed to a restful illumination, and there was the sound of breaking surf off to one side.

"The sound can be changed. I sometimes use a setting called Forest Murmurs, but Surf Sounds is my favorite - probably imprinted on me during my California days. The sound is necessary to drown out the low level hum of the clean room machinery. Conducive to Deep Thought, wouldn't you say?"

Michael was awestruck. If this was servitude to Haematite, he could get used to it. Sandra took the chair at the desk and offered him another. Now that she was acquainted with Michael's work, it was her turn to present.

"Haematite's foremost and most successful business is electrical futures. As you must know, there are nearly as many industrial generators of electricity as there are users. Everyone is doing co-generation from their waste heat sources, updraft turbines, solar converters... things like that. Along with the power transmission grid, there is a shadow communications grid where users bid for electrical power, and the generators set asking prices. It's like a specialized stock market, and it works like the stock market. Everyone wants to buy low and sell high, but there are many parameters involved, one of which is transmission cost."

"Although the superconducting backbone transmission lines are lossless, this efficiency comes at a cost; namely, amortization of the physical plant, maintenance of the cryogenics, vacuum systems, etc., so there's a per mile cost for transmission of electrical power. You would like to buy your power close to where it's generated, but sometimes that's not possible. However, there's a complex grid of other buyers and generators of electricity between you and some intended power sources. With appropriate calculation, you can offer a lower price to some of these buyers, a higher price to their generators, take your power off the top, and make some money on the deal. The problem, of course, is that these computations aren't easy to do, but you need to do them fast. The market moves in microseconds, and there are so many players that it's hard to find the lowest price, and find it before someone else does."

Michael interjected. "A perfect job for intelligent agents, but these autonomous programs can't be allowed on the same network. It would turn into a battlefield."

"Precisely. You need to follow the rules of the game. You can query individual suppliers for prices, or put out a bid, but you aren't allowed to host intelligent agents on the network to collect information on all the transactions. So, what you can't do in software, you do in hardware. That's where Haematite comes in. Haematite has its own shadow network of computational nodes that tap into the power network at various points. These nodes act like small users or generators of power, and they send out bids and offers just like everyone else. The trick is this - each of our nodes knows the existence of the other Haematite nodes and what they're doing, but no one else does. That way they can get the same data an intelligent agent would if it were allowed to roam the network, although not as efficiently. A little more expensive, yes, but the stakes are high in this game."

“It's a very interesting computational problem, but the whole thing sounds illegal.”

“It isn't illegal. It's a fairly old game the economists call arbitrage. We play by the rules of the game, just like everyone else. We make money because we're smarter than everyone else. The problem is this: other companies may be attempting the same thing; we don't know. We need to somehow analyze the data to determine whether they are, where they are, and how to defeat them. We need to make constant improvements to our network and our algorithms.”

“And this is what you would like me to do at Haematite?”

“One of the things. Our staff Computerati at a satellite location have most of the power thing fairly well covered, and it shouldn't take too much time to write some code to do some analysis of transactions to find whether we're getting any competition in this. Although this search for competing agents and improving the optimization algorithm are interesting problems, the rest of the power thing is rather mundane stuff. Ph.D.s shouldn't do the mundane. Haematite, of course, is a diversified corporation and does a lot of different things, like the clean room stuff, for example. In order to survive, Haematite is always looking for other things to do, typically variations on things it has done before. That's why I'm here, and that's why Haematite sponsored your apprenticeship at Mother Wode. We work on the research end of all this, here.

At this point, Sandra paused. Perhaps for emphasis, or maybe because it was one of those things you don't blurt outright.

"What Haematite wants is to do the same thing with the stock market. Actually, the commodity market at first, since it's a simpler case."

"Wow! That's either the best idea, or the worst idea, in the world! Playing the stock market has led to the ruination of many a poor soul. And then you have to consider the fact that by trading stock you're changing the same system you're studying. You could get yourself into a non-linear area, things start to oscillate violently, and you wipe yourself out!"

Sandra smiled. Michael's last point was the first bullet point on her risk presentation to management. This guy really did know his stuff.

"Exactly right on all points. But there are a few things to remember. First, they pay our hefty wages because the things we do are not easy. Next, the testing phase will be extensive. We'll throw some neural networks at it to check for robustness... things like that. This will definitely not be launched before Haematite is thoroughly convinced that the risk/reward ratio is where it should be. At that point, Management will take the blame for failure, because it's their decision, not ours. How's your schedule for the next few months?"

Michael was excited to finally apply his knowledge to real problems, and he also understood his obligation to repay Haematite for his education. If he remembered right, built into his contract was a transition period between the time his dissertation was drafted and finally defended in which he was expected to start working for Haematite. His dissertation was essentially "in-the-cache," written, pretty-printed, and sent out for comments, but his Master, Professor Sterba, had a few more papers for him to write.

Sterba was coauthor on all these, and he had an extreme vested interest in having these submitted before Michael was out of his grasp. In fact, Michael's dissertation defense would not happen until all were submitted for publication and Sterba could handle things from there. Sterba was a stickler for details, so all this would take time.

"Doctor Webb, have you ever met Professor Sterba?"

"Call me Sandra. No, I haven't, but I did hear him present something at a conference about two years ago. The paper was well crafted, but he seemed like the European Proper Professor type."

"You've got that right! You can understand that I have quite a few loose ends to handle before Sterba will schedule my defense."

"What about two days a week at the start, ramping to full time after your defense. When you start working full time, you'll be salaried at the appropriate level. Until that time, any work you'll do will be based on that salary, pro-rated on the number of hours you work. Just a little incentive to get the most out of you. Sounds fair?"

More than fair. From starving student to employed Computerati. He could buy that new display panel he had been lusting after for months and upgrade his wardrobe. Still not enough money for a girlfriend, but he didn't have time for that right now. You give up a lot for your craft.

"Yes, that's fair. Can I set my own days? You know, things will change from week to week."

Let's make Tuesdays a definite, with another floating day during the working week. I'm often here on Saturday, so you can consider that a working day, also."

"Doesn't your husband mind?"

"No husband or significant other. At this time, I'm married to my work...," Sandra thought she shouldn't give the wrong first impression, "...Not that I'm disinterested. No opportunities have presented themselves."

"Sounds like a copy of my life, but I'm still a student."

Bad choice of words! He didn't mean to offend. At least from her expression, she didn't seem to react, so he got off easy.

"Yeah, that's the Burden of the Computerati. Next Tuesday, then?"

"Sure."

A few minutes later he was exiting the manicured beauty of Haematite Corporation back to the granite buildings of Mother Wode. As he drove, Michael rehashed the visit in his mind. Haematite's physical plant was impressive, everything from the landscaping to the walnut paneling and original artwork in the reception area. While in the reception area, Michael immediately recognized what must be a very expensive serigraph by Robert Rauschenberg. He realized that all this wasn't there just to give the employees a nice working environment. Such a show of conspicuous consumption was there to impress Haematite's customers. Only a corporation making a good profit could afford such amenities. And then there was Sandra.

First, Sandra as the computer scientist. There was certainly nothing unusual about a female computer scientist, since the genders were split fairly evenly in his field. In the last century, when women typically avoided mathematics, and computer science was decidedly a subset of mathematics, his field was dominated by men. When the sociologists decided to study this phenomenon, they discovered that math aversion in schoolgirls was more a product of subjective factors than a difference in brain function. After some government sponsored programs, a few girls actually surpassed the boys in their classrooms in math ability, and the visibility of these role models acted as a catalyst for the eventual equalization of the genders in all technical fields.

Then, there was Sandra, the woman. During their brief conversation, as Michael became more comfortable with her, he started to assess her possibility as a sex partner. He didn't feel at all guilty about this, since he had learned from the youngest age that this activity is hardwired into a man's brain. The locker room argument was that if men didn't behave this way, the human race would have gone extinct a long time ago, so men should feel guilty if they *didn't* think that way. The formal argument, which he learned later in a philosophy elective course he had taken, was called the Categorical Imperative. Sandra was rather attractive. Michael's question about her supposed husband's complaint about her work hours was the first step in a sequence of logical statements that would refine the probability of his success. At this point this probability had barely crept ahead of zero, but at least some progress was being made. As for now, though, it was best to concentrate more on his driving, since traffic was starting to pick up.

3 TOWARDS THE PRIZE

The rest of the week ran smoothly. Professor Sterba was out of town, at a meeting of the editorial board of a journal for which he was editor, so Michael could do a lot of work without interruption. While drafting one of the papers, Michael found a gap in the analysis that was too wide to ignore. He went back to the original data, and after some serious number-crunching on the Mother's central processor, he was able to produce a graph and summary table to support his conclusions. It was likely this type of attention to detail that encouraged Sterba to bring him on board in the first place.

This first paper was nearly finished, and he had taken some care in his writing. First, he tried to anticipate any objections the old professor might have and to flesh-out the text accordingly. Next, he scanned several of the current papers in the Journal of Autonomous and Intelligent Agents, the place where his paper would appear, to subsume the look and feel of the type of paper that was accepted for publication in that journal. Finally, he produced his final version of the draft to mimic exactly the format of that journal. Having a draft look exactly like a published paper sent a subliminal message to the editors and referees that this was publishable material. He was reminded of a story he had heard as an undergraduate about an astronomer who sent his friends copies of a paper on a controversial topic. The draft was prepared in a style that exactly mimicked that of a prestigious journal. This was long before desktop publishing - he actually had to have it typeset and run off by a print shop - so everyone believed it had been published in that journal. The end result was that there was serious talk about his controversial theory before the circumstances were revealed. This was exactly what he wanted, to get people thinking. Michael didn't know enough about astronomy, or the history of the matter, to know whether the theory was found to be true. It was a good story, nonetheless.

Rogue scientific papers had run rampant on the networks. There was a plethora of junk science out there that couldn't be published otherwise. A skilled scientist could usually sort the wheat from the chaff, but all this got the established journals very nervous early on. With the help of their own Computerati, they devised a digital signature system that not only identified a paper as a true scion of their journal, but verified that it had not been subtly changed. Each paper was associated with a lengthy number. When you fed the content of the paper and the code number of the journal into a certain algorithm, you would get the code number of the paper if the paper were genuine. Some cryptographic scheme made all this work. Michael had only a rudimentary knowledge of cryptography and had to take this on faith. He knew that there had been many attempts to break the algorithm, and all had failed.

His first day at Haematite was about what he expected. He spent a long time in an office filling out personal information forms. This was information that he had supplied earlier, during his internship, and he was amazed that they couldn't pull everything together from existing databases. But he was a Computerati, not a bureaucrat, so he just wasn't thinking straight. He was retinal-scanned, fingerprinted, voice-printed, and otherwise-printed. He was reminded of days past when young women would shed their underwear, hike up their skirts and scan their backsides on the primitive copy machines of their era. At least he wasn't required to do anything like that, but he was certain that several of his MRI full body scans resided on some Haematite computer, somewhere.

Michael was given a biometric ID badge, and he was issued several passwords. Sandra set him up in an office, and then ignored him most of the day. Apparently, Sandra's laboratory was her personal hideaway, and she wasn't about to cede space to a potentially annoying intruder. Michael passed the time by catching up on current papers and ordering his own lab coat. He chose a pale blue color to offset Sandra's white, but he doubted he would use it much. Maybe Sandra would require it at meetings with the management as a way to separate the scientists from the bureaucrats. Sandra cut a fine figure in her coat, but he doubted he would turn any female heads wearing his.

Professor Sterba had returned to Mother Wode, jet lagged on the first day - he had scheduled his meeting for Vienna, of course - and didn't even say hello. However, his second day back was a different story. When Michael opened his calendar, he saw that he was five minutes late for a meeting Sterba had set up the night before. He raced to Sterba's office and found him engrossed in a call. He stood outside the office door for several minutes before Sterba logged off and invited him in.

"Mr. Martelli, sorry for the delay. I've been patching loose ends nonstop since I've arrived back from my trip. I've read a message that you've started the transition to Haematite."

"Yes. It's just two days a week at the start - not too taxing. I haven't really accomplished much."

Sterba continued, "You won't let your work schedule interfere with what is required of you at East Wodenstumpf, will you? After all, these last few weeks are the culmination of all your efforts here. It's no time to become too distracted."

Michael, of course, had anticipated this query. It was classic Sterba.

"My transition to Haematite hasn't really affected my final tasks here. If you check our file cache, you'll see a draft of the first publication, the one on stochastic network automatons."

"Excellent! Exactly what I had hoped to hear! You must remember that apprentice contracts work both ways. Haematite has an obligation to you, and secondarily to me, to facilitate your dissertation defense and these exit tasks. Although you have an obligation to work for Haematite for the next few years, there's the future to consider. Haematite may not be interested in publications, but it is important for you to publish and establish yourself in the field. Otherwise, your future options will be limited, and you may be stuck at Haematite." He paused for a second.

"Not that Haematite is all that bad, of course. They've been very good to both of us over the years."

Money, especially big corporate money, has a way of cementing friendships.

"No, I have no complaints. I'll start work on the next paper. You should see something in a few weeks."

"Oh, don't drag things out that far. Let's see how it looks in two weeks. I'm sure that won't be a problem, will it, Mr. Martelli?"

A rhetorical question at its best. Once again, classic Sterba, with a dose of Frederick Winslow Taylor.

"No, I think I can pull things together by then, but it might be a little rough around the edges."

"That's expected, but as they say about that journey of a thousand miles, it's good to make that first step, but then keep things moving along."

As Michael exited Sterba's office, his mind was already spinning a schedule for the next two weeks.

The next day, Saturday, was his last chance to do his second working day of his first week at Haematite. That is, if you counted your week starting on Sunday, and not Monday. Calendars tended to go either way, since there was still no universal consensus on which day really started the week, although Michael was partial to Monday. After all, why were Saturdays and Sundays part of the weekend if they weren't both at the end of the week? He forced himself to bed by midnight the night before, so he wasn't too much of a zombie the next day. When he arrived at the Haematite gate house, he startled the guard out of a very deep reverie, or perhaps it was outright sleep. The guard seemed surprised to see anyone on Saturday, especially at such an early hour. Michael proffered his badge. When the guard saw his Computerati tag, he mumbled, "Oh, yeah," and let him through.

He hadn't really planned arriving on Saturday, but he thought a Saturday might be a good day to interface with Sandra. No one else would be around, and she might be more available. He needed to get some background and direction from her - at least pointers to some relevant documentation - or he would be spinning his wheels. Michael did not like spending time uselessly. It was against his nature, and it was possibly another trait that Sterba admired about him.

Sandra was in neither her office, nor her laboratory. He had nearly written off the day until he spotted her in a corridor with a cup of coffee. The coffee aroma was wonderful.

"Michael, I wondered whether I would see you again this week."

"Hi, Sandra. Two things. First, good morning. Second, where can I get some of that coffee?"

"When I have the building to myself, I use the executive coffee station. Tastes much better. It must be a better blend, or maybe their assistants actually wash the pot once in a while."

On the way to the coffee, Michael explained that Sterba had him jumping, but not any more than usual. He was right about working Saturday. Sandra was much more relaxed and friendly. More importantly, she sat with him in his office, bookmarking several important documents for him, and giving him enough work for the next few weeks. She retreated to her laboratory after offering to take him to a local restaurant for lunch. Although she didn't say it, there was a tacit understanding that she needed to work undisturbed until lunch.

As he surveyed the documents, he realized the size and complexity of the operation. Haematite's shadow network had thousands of nodes, distributed among all the US states and the Canadian provinces. As he pulled data into graphs, he saw that the node distribution was in close proportion to population density, and, by implication, to power usage. Each node was a custom built computer with two wide bandwidth optical pipes - one to access the power marketplace network, and the other to connect to the Haematite hidden network. Because of the large number of nodes, the capital expense of the network ran into tens of millions of dollars. There was also the recurrent expense of the interconnecting network. The Computerati who did the initial installation had used a Traveling Salesman optimization on the network connections to both minimize cost and maximize speed. If a competitor decided to compete with Haematite in this game, it would take at least a hundred million dollars and more than a year. It proved both the adage that it takes money to make money; and, that time is money.

In the back of Michael's mind was his original idea that what they were doing was illegal, or should be illegal. It seemed as if Haematite was making a lot of money by tricking power generators into selling at an artificially low price, and then tricking the power users to buy at a higher price. He was reminded of a twentieth century scheme to corner the silver market. At one point, a small group held claim to half the world's silver, but the attempt failed with disastrous consequences to everyone involved with silver.

Immersed in his work, Michael lost track of time until Sandra arrived at about 12:30.

"Sorry I'm a little late. I guess most people expect lunch to be at noon. Are you ready to roll?

"Sure. I'm really starting to understand things now. I'll have a few questions for you over lunch."

Michael blanked his display, and they exited to the parking lot. Sandra led him through a shortcut he hadn't learned. The building was cavernous, and he was certain it would be many months before he had toured every wing. When they arrived at the parking lot, he was surprised to see Sandra's vehicle. It was a late model, two seat, sports convertible, sans roll bar. Rapid-deploy carbon composite roll pivots, an innovation to replace the unsightly, but government mandated, roll bars, did not come cheaply. His general impression of Sandra as a lab rat with no social yearnings was starting to change.

Anticipating his question, Sandra said, "I got a great deal on the wheels. The car was previously owned, but in mint condition. I think the owner had one for every day of the week. Haematite pays its employees well, but usually not well enough to afford such luxuries."

The restaurant was only a few minutes from the site. It was quite large, but there were few cars in the lot, and few people inside. The place was designed for the Monday to Friday crowd. Sandra and Michael were seated in a window booth in a somewhat secluded area. Michael got the idea that the hostess thought this was a romantic lunch for a couple that didn't want to be noticed.

Sandra started the conversation as they paged through the menus on the tabletop displays and keyed their selections.

"They get a lot more business during the usual work week. Not only the Haematite crowd, but there are quite a few other corporate sites in the area. So, what do you think about your first little project at Haematite?"

"After reading the docs, I can't say that this is a little project. This is serious stuff. I guess it's not unexpected that I had no idea what goes on in the real world. I knew Mother Wode was a sheltered environment, but I didn't realize how sheltered it was. There I was, running simulations on how Grandma's electronic messages are routed to her grandkids, and millions of dollars were zipping around underfoot! It's a whole different world."

"Yeah, it takes a while to get used to the scale of things, but at the code level, it's all the same."

"I'm still concerned with the underlying ethics of this venture. You said it's legal, and I'm sure the Haematite lawyers checked and double-checked things before it was implemented. There are likely teams of lobbyists out there steering the laws to ensure that the status quo holds. But the base idea is that we're using trickery to broker transactions. In economic parlance, it's not a level playing field. We've tilted it in our favor."

"Nowadays, almost all money is made that way, at least in brokerage. The smart trader is the one who wins, and we just use our technology to increase our smarts. As for social implications - stealing money from orphans, and stuff like that - what we do may even help society. The money Haematite makes isn't just thrown into a hole. We hire new employees, and we use it to buy goods and services from other companies who hire new employees. It's the same argument for increased government spending. That single government dollar changes hands so many times, the government gets back more in taxes than what it spent in the first place."

Michael thought for a moment.

"Hmmm... the dreaded second-order effects. The simple analysis does not apply. OK. I'll take it on faith at this point."

The waitress arrived with their orders. Michael steered the conversation to personal matters in an effort to understand this intelligent and attractive woman who was now his immediate supervisor and quite a change from Sterba!

"You said you were from Stanford. A rather impressive place. How did you end up in the area?"

Sandra recounted the acquisition of Tressor Systems, her initial misgivings about Haematite, and her acceptance of a new reality.

"I really enjoy my work. Sure, there are a few interruptions - calls from management, monthly progress reports, project reviews, stuff like that - but I'm usually happy when I'm in my laboratory. Everyone seems to understand, and they leave me alone. I can get away with it, because they know I produce, and dollar signs are what these guys understand. It doesn't hurt that we're highly-compensated employees. A Ph.D. is a professional employee, just like a corporate lawyer. Everyone else gets a cubicle, and we get an office. "

"Yeah, the perks are good. There's also what someone said once about physicists and baseball players - They both get paid a lot of money for doing something they enjoy. It applies to Computerati as well."

"Our game was so good that the physicists tried to capitalize on it in the late twentieth century with the rise of the 'Quants.' Sure, they made it seem like what they were doing was applying arcane statistical physics principles to the stock market, but in the end it was just data mining and algorithms, just like what we're doing now."

They were talking so much that they had ignored their food. Sandra had ordered a tuna sandwich which was still in its pristine state, but Michael had ordered a hamburger and fries, which were now cold. He decided to eat just the meat part of his hamburger, and he only picked at the fries. Sandra and he finished their meals at the same time, and as the check arrived, Michael wondered about the payment protocol. Was it the peer-to-peer protocol in which they split the bill? He certainly didn't think it would be the male dominant protocol in which he paid the whole tab. Sandra diffused the problem by putting it on her company card.

"Every new employee deserves at least one welcome lunch, or what's a company for?"

On their return to Haematite, Michael spent the rest of the afternoon organizing his office, which principally meant customizing the look and feel of his display panel and loading some favorite applications. Most of his application programs were free. These were user-supported software packages built up over generations on the network. He had himself contributed a few snippets of code to some of these. This was something that made him proud, although his contribution was likely only a tenth of a percent of each application. The pride came because his code did something useful, and it was fully vetted by his programming peers. His name was there, somewhere in the source code, and perhaps it would remain for a century or more, becoming more hidden as programmers expanded the code. Haematite was automatically billed for the few applications that didn't interest a sufficiently large cadre of coders to have a free version or were bundled with a specific network database.

It was nearly six o'clock when he decided to end his first working day. As he drove home, he realized that his work at Haematite would possibly be enjoyable. No one bothered him, Sandra was pleasant to work with, and the hefty paycheck had its own appeal. Perhaps he could finally buy a new car, stop renting, have his own home and buy a few appliances. He could even support a non-working wife, but for that he would need to solve the girlfriend problem first. And then there's the mother problem - Mother Wode, that is. His new life depends on Mother's approval. Michael's mind snapped back to reality and all the tasks laid out for him by Professor Sterba. He needed to jump through a few final hoops before he could fully enter the next chapter of his life.

When he arrived back at his apartment, Michael did something that he rarely did. He wrote a task list. He generally maintained a task list in his head, shuffling priorities as the need arose. He didn't worry about forgotten tasks. As he had read in many articles about time management techniques, any task not important enough to be remembered should be dropped from even a written task list. His mind acted like the bookmarking agent on his computer - most accessed information was at the top of the list, and things not viewed in a long time were relegated to the archive. Now that he was being pulled in several directions at once, he needed a task list to give both Haematite and Sterba their due. Otherwise, one or another would be shortchanged, and Michael couldn't offend either.

His required work out of the way, he grabbed a quick sandwich for supper and decided to kick back and watch a video. After all, it was Saturday night.

4 BAD STATS

As Michael pulled into his usual space at Haematite, he started to realize that his life was becoming routine, but it wasn't a bad routine The routine of a regular, and hefty, paycheck was welcome. At the turn of the twentieth century, there was a saying, "Another day, another dollar." Towards the end of the that century, because of inflation and currency devaluation, the expression was true for a hundred dollars. Now, "Another day, another thousand dollars," was more like it, at least for a Computerati with a Ph.D. Ten dollars today purchased a loaf of bread which sold for about a penny in the early 1900s. Of course, it wasn't possible to buy a display screen in those days, so progress of some sort had been made in the quality of life.

There were those who thought that display screens, and Computerati in general, had been responsible for a decrease in the quality of life. These new Luddites, or Noviluds as they were formally called, yearned for a simpler yesteryear that probably never existed. The true irony was that they used the technology of the present age, like network postings, to protest technology. Several decades ago, there had been some violent demonstrations, and there had even been bombings of some computer fabrication plants. In one case, an obvious inside job, a smoke bomb had been placed at a strategic air intake, closing a plant for months while contaminating particles were scrubbed from a clean room. Such violence had scared away many followers, but a vocal core group still remained. Michael himself had been accosted on campus by a group of young Noviluds who saw him leaving the computer building. Fortunately, it was mid-day, and all he suffered were a few verbal barbs.

The environment at Haematite was quite different than Mother Wode's campus. Either Haematite's personnel were more tolerant towards each other, or they were indifferent. Michael thought it was the later. Everyone was immersed in their own projects, so there was no time to even think about others on a personal level. There was certainly no Novilud sentiment here - everyone was living high off the technology pig, and enjoying it. He imagined the Haematite father coming home to find his children wearing shirts embellished with Novilud slogans purchased with his money.

Michael's near-term data-mining task for his second project, applying Haematite's shadow network to financial transactions, was somewhat routine. While his computer was chugging away in the background, amassing a huge data set, Michael was programming filters in the foreground, trying to make sense out this data fire hose. A fire hose was a good description, since the number of financial transactions was huge. Most were brokered by autonomous agents, each looking to attain a few pennies advantage in arbitrage from currency fluctuation or some emerging newsworthy event. Then there was the undercurrent of corporations buying back their own stock in huge quantities, either for employee bonuses, or just to reduce the cost of their dividend. Way down the list was the individual investor who thought the banks were in business to rip-off the little guy, and he would get a higher return on his money than the banks offered by eliminating the middle man. These people were generally deluding themselves, since they were fighting a war against ultra-fast machines armed with mathematical models honed through many similar battles. Michael didn't understand most of this, nor did it matter. Numbers were just numbers. Temperatures in South American rain forests, or insurance mortality tables - they were all the same. Although the specific task at hand was unique (or, at least, Haematite thought it was unique; business intelligence was never perfect), he had done similar things repeatedly in his student career, so he wasn't over extended by any stretch.

As data were harvested over the course of days, an expected pattern emerged. Looking at all transactions in any given period, the dollar amount of the transaction plotted against the number of transactions gave a power law distribution. This was a consequence of the simple fact that large transactions happened infrequently, and smaller transactions happened more often. Such behavior exists in many natural process, such as the number of species per genus in a given geological period, and the intensity of solar flares. A power law also describes many man-made processes, such as the frequency of words in novels, the number of followers of religions, and the number of deaths occurring in wars. It was as if we humans, despite all our culture and civilization, could not really distance ourselves from Nature. Large nuts go in this pile, and small nuts in the other. The existence of a power law distribution didn't tell Michael anything other than his dataset was accurate and complete.

This data harvesting exercise was getting boring, so Michael was spending more time at Mother Wode, polishing up his manuscripts. When he decided to check his data again, he noticed something odd. The distribution of transactions was still following the definite power law trend, but occasionally there would be a data point quite a bit out of place. Early in the analysis, Michael had noticed this, but there wasn't enough data to be concerned. One rule-of-thumb in statistics is that errors are in inverse proportion to the square-root of the number of data points. What this means in practice is that you need a lot of data to prove anything. In the case of a power law process, where you're looking at data over a large range of magnitudes, this proscription is that much more severe. But now, he had enough data to fit the power law and look at the residuals, the deviations from the fit. Some points stuck out like sore thumbs.

It's not as if such an occurrence was unusual to a computer programmer. It typically meant that he made an error in his code - Things like counting from one instead of from zero when accessing a data array, or a poorly constructed logical expression. Crap! Writing code is easy compared with debugging code! Michael had flirted in the past with some of the available error-checking programs, but the entire process still defaulted to the programmer scanning his own code, line by line, with a skeptical eye. Fortunately, his data harvesting programs were relatively simple. It would be a distasteful exercise, but it wouldn't take that long. Time for a cup of coffee.

As he went for coffee, he realized that the building was quite empty. A glance at a clock told him why. It was 6:30 PM, and his programming reverie had masked both the passage of time and the hunger pangs from his stomach. He passed Sandra's office and lab, hoping for a dinner companion, but she wasn't around. He decided to head home for a quick meal and tackle his debugging task the next day.

The next day started somewhat late. Sterba had sent him one of his infamous "need for speed" e-mails, the contents of which reminded him that they were working in a competitive field and asked for a copy of the most recent draft of a particular paper. Michael had been neglecting his writing duties while working on the Haematite data mining project, so he spent the evening actually doing a first draft of the paper, which he posted to Sterba at about 2:00 AM. He didn't awaken until late in the morning, and it was nearly noon when he arrived at Haematite. Fortunately, professional Computerati weren't on the clock. In any case, his after-hours effort the prior day easily erased any guilt he may have had.

The debugging effort went quickly, primarily because there weren't any bugs. The exercise did give Michael an opportunity to add some much needed comment lines in his code, something he often neglected to do in the heat of programming. Comments would prove invaluable if he needed to modify the program later, or reuse parts of his code. He thought that debugging would be a problem, but he was left now with a bigger, and more fundamental, problem; namely, why did these few transactions fall so far off the expected curve? Were the agents, whether human or machine, who posted these transactions making errors? The money involved was too great, at least from his starving student perspective, to allow such errors.

He did some searching to see whether this was a known feature in financial markets, perhaps attributed to the phase of the moon, or the times the Congress of European States adjourned for lunch. He wasn't able to find any corroboration.

Most of the Haematite regulars were starting to leave. Although he felt guilty about arriving at noon and leaving at five, he was in a rut and needed time to think. That's what they paid him for, deep thought, twenty four hours a day, seven days a week. That's the lot of the professional. He's always on the clock because his mind is always active. This didn't apply to just waking hours. Analysis of a dream had often led to an important scientific discovery, such as the chemical structure of benzene.

Michael didn't drive directly home, since his cupboards were bare. They had become more barren than usual with his double shifts at Haematite and Mother Wode. There was simply no time to shop, and even if he did shop, there was no time to cook. The other home dining options, zipping ready-heat bagged meals or calling out for pizza, left much to be desired. He stopped at Miguel's, a Mexican restaurant near the campus, for a satisfying plate of burritos, corn chips and salsa. He ordered a Mexican beer as something to both relax and stimulate his mind. The restaurant was nearly empty, since the usual student clientèle dined much later in the day.

As he watched a boisterous group of all male students at another table, Michael remembered his first meal at

Miguel's, when he was a freshman at Mother Wode. He had been part of a group of students that went on an impromptu field trip to attend a late night lecture by a Computerati superstar at another university. It was nearly midnight when they had returned to Mother Wode, and someone suggested a stop at Miguel's for food and beer. Michael wasn't yet of drinking age, but he had learned that if he was in the company of older students, no one bothered checking age when the drinks were served. It was a memorable night, not just for the alcohol, but also for the sage advice of the upperclassmen. He learned which professors were most respected in their disciplines, and which professors you should avoid when choosing a senior project; what computing fields were hot, and which were in decline and should be avoided. And, importantly for a poor student, where to get the best deals on the latest hardware. It was the information gleaned at this table that steered him towards working with Sterba.

That trip to Miguel's was one of his few group activities. He enjoyed them when they happened, but he was generally a loner. He had several friends, but he would see them infrequently. There were the occasional celebratory parties for graduation and the like, and he had even had his own graduation party with a dozen of his associates. It was just beer and snacks in his apartment, but that was their usual definition of a party. Some brought their wives, but there were no girlfriends. He wondered how there could be wives without there first being some girlfriends, but that was one of the mysteries of the universe best left to the physicists. He was never a gamer. He would see quite a few of his fellow students sleeping through their morning classes because they had been awake most of the night participating in multi-player games. These were computer students, so he could be fairly certain their stupor was from gaming, and not from wild partying.

Michael brought some printouts with him to Miguel's, and he spent some time examining his data analysis over the last few sips of beer. The sheer amount of data was enormous. Haematite had huge pipes to the network, and he was one of the few in the corporation who could take advantage of these. The one trouble he faced was that the tail was wagging the dog. Unlike physics, in which theory guides experiment, he was sorting through the experimental data looking for the theory. He had read once about the clash of cultures in physics that occurred while the Italian physicist, Enrico Fermi, was just starting his career. Italian physics at that time was divided into two camps. One of these advocated a shotgun approach for the experimental discovery of new phenomena, along the lines of switching the positive and negative battery terminals to see if there was any change. The other camp, the one to which Fermi subscribed, thought random experiments were a waste of time, and they allowed theory to guide them. In the end, Fermi's camp won, and their battle ribbon was Fermi's 1938 Nobel Prize.

Michael decided to call it a night. It was either the beer or the late hour, but he was having a hard time concentrating. He would present his findings to Sandra and get her advice. It was her project also. Luckily, it was just a short drive from Miguel's to his apartment. He didn't think he was driving in an impaired state, but he was extra cautious on the short drive.

Michael arrived at his office the next morning earlier than usual. He collected his results into some easily understandable graphs and tables, and he went in search of Sandra.

It was mid-morning, so Sandra was in her laboratory. She smiled when Michael entered. He hadn't seen her in a few days. Was she genuinely happy to see him? He forced himself to subsume the student fantasy and concentrate on the work.

"Sandra, I've got some results here on the data mining. Something strange is going on."

Michael explained his results, emphasizing his code checking. After all, he was a professional now, wasn't he? There should be nothing left to chance.

"OK. I'm convinced, and I have no idea what's going on. Maybe it's time to call in an expert."

"An expert? You and I are the experts. What can someone tell us about computation that we don't know already?"

"No, not a computer consultant. Someone in finance and economics."

Sandra flitted along her display screen, accessing a company database.

"It looks like we've got an expert on retainer. Well, at least we're contracted with a knowledge company that has him on retainer. Malcolm Flory, Master Professor of Economics at Princeton University. Judging from his rate schedule, he's one of the best. The comments say he apprenticed under some Nobel Laureate. He might be our answer man. However, there's one bad thing about Professor Flory."

"Has the Old Man been shacking up with a graduate student?"

“No, nothing that bad. You could say he's eccentric - possibly Old School is the better term. He refuses to teleconference. He only communicates face-to-face. When you're as distinguished as he is, you can get away with it.”

“He sounds almost like a Novilud. So, what do we do?

“You get to file your first expense report. You and I are traveling to Princeton.”

5 LONG TAIL

Professor Flory's assistant set up an 8:00 AM meeting on Wednesday, just before Flory's first teaching responsibility. Sandra and Michael chose to travel by bullet train, the best option for any travel within the Eastern Locale. Even this efficient transport would require them to awaken at a uncomfortable early hour if they chose to travel on Wednesday. Instead, Sandra arranged for rooms in Princeton, and they left from work at mid-afternoon on Tuesday.

The train hugged the coastline through Connecticut, giving them a fine view of the Atlantic Ocean for the first few minutes of their trip. Then it was an endless urban landscape as they traveled just north of New York City, took a left turn somewhere north of the border with New Jersey, and then proceeded generally south in New Jersey in the general direction of Philadelphia. New Jersey still maintained the slogan, "The Garden State," and it still seemed to be true. The scenery was all trees, punctuated by an occasional outcropping of roadway. From his vantage, the state appeared to be unpopulated. Just short of Philadelphia, their rail car was automatically detached from the train, and shuttled up a slower branch route that finally terminated a little south of Princeton.

As they disembarked and waited for a cab, Sandra said, "We're very near an historic site. Just about a mile in that direction... " she pointed out into the distance, "... The Martians landed on Earth." Michael looked confused, so Sandra continued, "That's Grover's Mill, where the Martians landed in the Orson Well's version of War of the Worlds. There's even a plaque that marks the spot. Imagine if an archaeologist uncovers that in a few thousand years, and history has forgotten Orson Wells!" A cab came quite quickly, and soon they were within sight of the university.

Several decades earlier, the artificial distinction between Princeton, the town, and Princeton, the university, ended when Princeton University became manager of all its surroundings. Princeton had evolved from a minor whistle stop for trains out of New York into a major New Jersey suburb by riding the coat tails of university expansion. Through the end of the twentieth, and the beginning of the twenty-first century, Princeton University had become a research behemoth with new buildings being erected on an annual basis. The surrounding areas were enriched by spin-off companies established through university start-up funds. The municipal government had evolved into a rubber stamp for the university, and it was finally subsumed by the university through a ballot proposition.

Nassau Street had remained the historical main street in Princeton. Not surprisingly, the Nassau Inn had remained the preferred accommodation because it was within easy walking distance from the university. When Michael noted the room rate, overlaid with a hefty 30% tax, he was happy he was on an expense report. The view from his room was unremarkable. He could see nothing except for the office building across the street, a few stray pedestrians, and others on bicycle. The street was likely closed to vehicular traffic. The younger people all looked like students, and the older ones all looked like professors.

Sandra had suggested that they meet for dinner at about 7:30, so Michael spent his time showering and viewing the news on his room display. There was the usual - A hurricane off the coast of Florida; a workers' rebellion somewhere in South America; some religious leader ranting about declining morals in the world, but especially in the US; a vignette about scientific studies at the International Lunar Base; and dedication of a nuclear reactor in California, the third reactor that year.

Thankfully, Sandra knocked on his door a few minutes before 7:30. He was getting hungry. When he opened the door, he was surprised by what he saw. He had never seen Sandra in anything except pants, and here she was in a very flattering dress. Her breasts, usually hidden at work under a lab coat, were half exposed by the spaghetti strap top. If he didn't know better, he could believe she was coming on to him. Then again, maybe she was. The age difference wasn't that much - she was likely only two or three years his senior - and they certainly had common interests. Michael started to imagine the possibilities, when Sandra snapped him out of his reverie by pointing to the clock and shuffling him out the door. She had inside information about a great Indian restaurant within walking distance. As they left the hotel, he wondered whether she had noticed his aroused gaze when she had first appeared at his door.

The restaurant was just a few blocks away, and it was a step above the Indian restaurants he frequented near Mother Wode. He was encouraged by Sandra, who said, "Don't worry, we're on expense report! We deserve a little combat pay for this trip." The restaurant was about half full, probably because of the late hour and the fact that Tuesday is not a typical restaurant day. They lingered a few minutes over the ice water, and then the waiter took their orders. Michael selected the Lamb Korma. Sandra, who was more adventuresome, ordered Chicken Vindaloo, which was a little too spicy for Michael's taste. They also ordered a Vegetable Pakora appetizer and Aloo Paratha as a bread accompaniment. Michael started the conversation.

"Do you travel much for Hamatite?"

"I try not to travel more than four times each year. Haematite has me visiting some of its other locations about twice each year. There are always some problems that demand some professional firefighting on location. Generally, I'm just someone from headquarters they pull in to demonstrate that their site is not isolated from corporate attention. The other two times are for professional conferences. I try to present a paper at one of these, at least. It gets a little difficult to do this, sometimes. The Haematite lawyers need to sign-off on my work, and they think we're giving away too many secrets, etc., so that's why I do some after hours stuff and work on Saturdays. I have to remind them that publication often works in the company's favor, since it prevents others from patenting the idea and forcing us to pay royalties for our own work."

"That's really different from my situation. I need to publish, and publish a lot, or Professor Sterba will be all over my case. There's an unwritten rule that you need three papers, either published or in-press, to get your Ph.D., no exceptions. It's probably a good rule, but don't ask my opinion just yet!"

"It was the same in my day. Professors need a hefty list of publications - publications in the right topic areas - to get corporate funding. It's like preventative maintenance for an old automobile."

The Pakoras arrived, and the conversation morphed from a philosophical discussion between Ph.D.s to sounds of gustatory delight. A Princeton Pakora apparently needed to live up to its name, and these did. The remaining dinner was just as good. When they arrived back at the hotel, Michael's after dinner fantasies were deflated when Sandra's only parting comment was "See you for breakfast in the morning, 7:00 AM sharp." Either she had passed beyond the college fantasy stage, or it was time for him to make the passage himself. One thing about hotel video displays, there's always some programming to aid in the release of male tension, so Michael slept well that night.

Sandra knocked promptly at 7:00 AM. Michael remembered how prompt Sandra had been the previous night, so he was ready a few minutes early. Sandra was familiar with much of Princeton, since she had attended a workshop there in her student days. Her choice for breakfast was an apparent throwback to that earlier time, since she zeroed in on an egg and bagel bar overrun with students attempting to get a quick breakfast before their early classes. He had eaten bagels before, or what were called bagels at Mother Wode, but they didn't resemble the bagel he bought, either in size or taste. These were true New York bagels, trucked in from the city in the early morning hours. The Princeton crowd would be satisfied by no others. Sandra and Michael ate breakfast out of bags while sitting on the window ledge in front of the store - a far cry from the elegant dinner the night before.

There was an enjoyable walk to Professor Flory's office at Fisher Hall, and they arrived right on time. Flory, as befitted a professor of his stature, had an inner office fronted by an assistant's office. The assistant was not there, but Flory was, and he motioned them into his office. He was a cheerful older man, probably late eighties, with a ready smile.

"Sorry that my assistant wasn't here to greet you. Helen must be tending to her morning coffee. If I had the choice of a decaffeinated Helen, always at her desk, or a sometimes absent, but caffeinated, Helen, I would always choose the later. You must be the Haematite people. I'd better start my stopwatch to capture all those billable minutes!"

Flory laughed, and so did Michael and Sandra. It would be a billable hour, whether they stayed five minutes, or fifty minutes. After introductions, Sandra got down to business with a brief overview of the data mining Michael had undertaken. Although Flory must have been under a non-disclosure agreement, Sandra was careful not to state the purpose of the data collection. Then it was Michael's turn to speak. He pulled out printed copies of his analysis graphs. He had made printed copies, since he remembered Flory's aversion to teleconferencing, and this possible Novilud might object to all displays. Michael highlighted the discrepant data points, and Flory was quick to respond.

"So, you're hunting Black Swans."

"Black Swans?"

"Black Swans are the unexpected events that disagree with the simple probability distributions we've grown to love. Everyone knows that swans are white, but there's always a very slight probability that a black swan will appear. If our models expect white swans only, they may be unstable at the appearance of a black swan. A famous example is an equation that was used to price derivatives many years ago."

Sandra decided that Michael shouldn't take the full brunt of their ignorance, so she asked the question.

"What's a derivative? I assume we're not talking about the mathematical variety."

"A derivative is essentially a bet on the occurrence of certain conditions. It's gambling, pure and simple, so most types of derivative trading have been outlawed for years. As an example, an early winter in the US Midwest would be expected to lead to a poor wheat harvest, so the price of wheat is expected to increase. Householders need heat, so energy prices would be expected to rise under the same conditions. If you were a betting man, you would probably accept a bet from someone who says that the price of wheat will actually decrease when energy prices increase. Since it's such an outlandish position, you could be persuaded to give that man some rather high odds, say ten-to-one. You don't really care much, since in your mind it's easy money. But then the Black Swan appears, in the form of the cash-strapped European States dumping wheat on the market for one reason or another. The contrarian, the man who said that wheat would decrease in price makes a bundle of money. There were fancy formulas for calculating the odds, and everyone patted themselves on the back for discovering derivatives. The problem was that the odds equation was based on statistics that all too often ignored the Black Swan."

"Your transaction distribution, as you've noticed, is a power law distribution. It's also called a fat tail distribution, since it has more transactions at the extreme end than a bell curve would. A true power-law distribution is a straight line on this sort of graph, but people never have as much data as you have here to really show a good straight line. That's why your Black Swans are so evident. The overall power law happens because there's a continuum of big agents and small agents, all interconnected, and, on the average, they do the same things. Since they do the same things, no matter how large or small they are, the process is said to be scale-invariant, a physics term, or scale-free, a term used mostly by computer people."

"Economists thought that financial processes could be modeled on such natural systems, such as statistical mechanics and thermodynamics. They were making the incorrect assumption that people were like molecules of gas - not predictable individually, but quite predictable in the ensemble. They soon found that humans transactions are not always as predictable as gas molecules. Human nature needs to be considered, like the rate that information diffuses and the idea that information might not be complete or accurate. There's also the widow who keeps her stock certificates under the mattress. The result of all this is that some of the smaller transactions don't happen in a timely fashion, and you get excess area under the tail of the curve. Your fit to the data is obviously not a pure polynomial, since the fat tail slopes upwards slightly, likely representing all those widows and all those mattresses. Whatever function you used seems to do this quite nicely."

Michael responded, "I can't take all the credit for that. I used an evolutionary algorithm. The computer picked the curve."

Flory smiled.

"Both of you did a nice job. Now, as for your particular Black Swans, there's no obvious reason why they're there. People have talked about them for quite a while, decades, in fact. In the past, there were too few examples to build up a pattern. I think people lost interest in this and moved on to other things. However, no one has had the resources or the interest to harvest as much data as you have. I'm as much in the dark as you are at this point, but you now have the advantage. My one observation is that, although you have a huge quantity of data, few of these data are the Swans. Collect as many Black Swans as you can, and do further analyses on just the Swans. Something might pop up. You might be able to get their DNA and clone your own Black Swans if you wanted to."

They had come here thinking their ignorance arose from their not being economists. Now, Flory was telling them that even eminent old school economists like he had no clue. It seemed that Haematite's money was well spent. It meant, also, that there was more work ahead. Without pinning down these Black Swans they had no hope of doing Haematite's planned market prediction.

Flory had a further warning.

"You seem to be following along the same tracks as the physicists of the last century. Physicists were at first confident that they could make big wins in the financial markets. It seemed all too obvious to them. First, financial transactions are uniquely specified by a set of numbers, and physicists love numbers. In the simplest case, where you're looking only at one specific item, these numbers are the cost of the transaction and the time of the transaction. The physicists were spurred on by several factors. First, you didn't need to be right a hundred percent of the time, you just needed to be mostly right. Second, you always worked with a mixture of financial instruments, so, by the law of large numbers, things should average out. You would never take too big a loss on one bad prediction. Finally, you just needed to be smarter than the next guy. With a phalanx of computing power behind you, it's easy to start to believe that this is true."

"What the physicists found in the end was that the financial markets were quite unlike the natural phenomena they were accustomed to study. Their models had some fatal axioms carried over from physical systems. One axiom that I described earlier was the idea that people were rational agents who always acted to maximize their financial worth. But markets do not act that efficiently. The most worrisome axion was that the market behaved like a thermodynamic system and things followed a normal distribution. In actuality, price trends are typically slow on the up-tick, and fast on the down-tick. There's no bell curve here, and the market knows that. There's a thing called the "volatility smile." The volatility smile is a graphical representation of the fact that bets on price decreases have lower odds than bets on price increases. You make money more easily on betting that the financial markets will go down in any time period."

Sanda interjected.

"So, in the end you have scale-free behavior of the kind Michael found. There will be more outliers than the bell curve predicts; that is, more billionaires than you would predict from the average income."

"Yes. So the physicists tried to work that into their models, as well. Soon, these models appeared to be somewhat like the Ptolomeic model of the solar system - a patchwork of epicycles that made predictions but gave no knowledge of the underlying system. Of course, their models were found to be less and less predictive, and all this work was abandoned. The lofty idea that the financial markets could be expressed by a nice equation was abandoned. Don't fall into the same trap."

"Thanks for the warning," said Sandra. "Fortunately, Haematite's interests here are completely different."

Since their technical discussion was at a close, Michael saw the opportunity to ask another sort of question.

"Professor Flory, now that we are familiar with each other, can I ask you a somewhat personal question?"

"A man my age is hard to embarrass. Ask away!"

"Why do you dislike computers?"

"Yes, that must be a mystery to a Computerati like you, and the fact that computers seem indispensable to every field of intellectual endeavor, including my own field of Economics. Economics is very mathematical, and large data sets are *de rigueur*. I used computers extensively when I was a student, although what we called computers in those days are considered toys, today. I found, especially when transferring my handwritten notes into a publication quality piece for my dissertation, that I was no longer doing Economics. I was acting more as a secretary or an assembly line worker. I wasn't the master of the machine, I was its servant. I didn't like that at all, so I leave the servitude to others. I try to just think. After all, that's what a professor should do, isn't it?

Michael had heard it all before, although not from someone so advanced in his field, so he spun out his stock response.

"Things have changed from those days. The user interfaces are more developed. There's speech recognition, and computers that evolve their interfaces to match a user's style. I think computers are definitely the servant. You might want to give them another try."

Flory smiled.

"Old men have a habit of spouting aphorisms, so here's mine - You can't teach an old dog new tricks."

Helen was at her desk, sipping her morning coffee, as they were shuffled out of the office and into the mix of students and professors on the street. It was only 9:30 when they arrived back at the hotel, so they decided to chock out, catch an early train and get lunch at home.

On the short train ride, Michael had one nagging question.

"Sandra, when we were talking with Flory and he warned us about the physicist's failed attempt to model the financial markets in the last century, you told him that Haematite wasn't trying to do the same thing. In my mind, it seems as if we're trying to do a variation on the same thing. Are all our efforts doomed to failure, even without the Black Swans?"

"No, what Haematite is attempting is arbitrage, not speculation. Just like in the energy futures markets we're in now, we're using speed to take advantage of small price differentials between different markets. If we're faster than the other guy - and in this case we're throwing a lot of hardware behind our need for speed - we'll always win. Sure, the net amount of any given trade will be small, but we're doing many trades, so the money should add up to a tidy profit. Our immediate goal is to verify that the profit does justify all this hardware expense, and that's why we need to understand these Black Swans, as Flory calls them."

It was just a little past 1:00 PM when Michael and Sandra arrived back at the East Wodenstumpf station, so they faced a decision. They were hungry, and they weren't expected back until late in the evening, which was effectively the next morning. Should they be loyal employees and head back to Haematite, or have a leisurely lunch and an afternoon holiday. Sandra's vehicle was at the station, so she asked Michael if she could drive them to her place for lunch, and then take him back to Mother Wode. Her condominium was about ten minutes from the train station. Michael's stomach agreed, and he was also curious to see how she lived. After all, he was about to adapt a similar lifestyle in just a few weeks, and a tutorial would help him make the jump. Knowing Sandra, he didn't expect to find too many feminine touches about her place. Her place would likely be more masculine than even unisex.

Michael was suitably impressed when they arrived. It was a secluded community of condominiums with a pillared entrance drive, and Sandra's living accommodations were palatial compared to his student digs. Her place had a split-level floor plan. A marble tiled entry way lead to a spacious living room with fireplace on the right, and a spacious kitchen at the top of a short stairway. Stairs to the bedrooms continued off to the left, and the kitchen led to a small dining room that overlooked the living room. Sandra was not shy about colors. The living room was rose with canary accents, and the dining room was teal. The kitchen was wallpapered with a finely detailed floral print. The wallpaper, and possibly the choice of living room colors, were the only marginally feminine aspects of her interior decoration, but he hadn't seen the bedroom. Perhaps he would never see the bedroom, and that would be in keeping with Michael's history with women.

Sandra rifled through the freezer chest and came away with two food pouches.

"Well, it's either Beef with Broccoli, or General Tsao's Chicken."

"I'll take the chicken, but only if you don't have a preference."

Sandra pulled the rip cords that mixed chemicals in sealed pouch compartments so they would react and heat the food that surrounded them, a useful consumer spin-off of military technology. She plopped the pouches in plates before they got too hot to hold. In a minute, they had opened the food pouches and were having a Chinese dinner with White Zinfandel. Michael started the conversation.

"So, what do we do next?"

"I thought a light movie on my entertainment display, maybe a comedy. Want to join me?"

Finally, a slight movement in the direction of Michael's fantasy! He decided to play it cool, and not let his imagination run rampant.

"Sound's good to me, but my question was actually about the project. We need to completely understand these Black Swans. Flory convinced me that an uncertainty like that in our model can't be tolerated. Things would look good for a few days, then the whole thing would shatter.

Haematite's margins on the stock transactions would be thin, at best, so even a small perturbation will lead to losses. Management would be upset. I think we need much more data."

Sandra sighed, "More data are not always useful. You need to look at the statistics, and see whether we might have enough data already. One thing I remember about Economics is this thing called Marginal Utility - you might be working too hard for too little gain. You might find that you do have enough data. Then again, maybe you need ten times as much data, in which case we need to rethink the whole model. We may need to convince Haematite to scrap the whole idea. At this point, we just don't know."

"Yeah, I see what you mean. No use spinning our wheels for nothing. I'll start the analysis tomorrow to see whether the data are sufficient. Now, as for your suggestions about the rest of the day..."

He purposely dropped his voice in a semi-seductive manner, waiting to see her reaction. There was none. OK. Perfect serve, but no follow-through. He could blow off the afternoon, so he decided to stay. In the end, he was glad he did.

6 YES, YOU!

Sandra hadn't given much thought to men since moving from Tressor to Haematite. She was a solitary individual, as were most scientists. It wasn't as if she was married to her work, but they did have an exclusive relationship. Suddenly, Michael appeared, and she started to reassess her position. He was smart and reasonably good looking. Was he already in a relationship? Was she attractive to him? She would need to tread lightly, especially since they were coworkers.

Women scientists did not achieve parity with their male counterparts until the turn of the century. Women in science were a rarity a few hundred years ago. A few wives, daughters and sisters started as assistants to their scientist kin. When the Old Boy died, many of them continued their work, sometimes publishing still in the man's name, or finding another established scientist who would promote publication in the woman's own name. There were some outstanding exceptions. The work of Caroline, the sister of the astronomer William Herschel, was so essential to her brother's observations that she received a small salary from King George III. She was awarded a gold medal from the Royal Astronomical Society.

Towards the middle of the twentieth century, woman began to infiltrate the biological sciences and chemistry. Male scientists would joke that chemistry appealed to women because it was so much like cooking. Women were rare in mathematics, but after a while they quickly infiltrated computer science, which was considered a branch of mathematics at the time. Women in physics were extremely rare until the first part of the twenty-first century. Women at the top of their fields were rarer still, and the ones who did succeed seemed to have succeeded because they adopted a male persona and merged into the sea of their peers.

The outward signs of this persona was non-feminine dress and an aloofness that deflected any sexual overtures. There was a wall between male and female scientists that was hard to scale, and nearly impossible to break down. That was essentially a synopsis of Sandra's relationship with Michael up to that point. It was the same type of reception that Michael got from the girls at Mother Wode, and, fantasies aside, he didn't really expect anything different from Sandra. That's why he was so surprised when it happened.

The whole thing had started simply. Sandra excused herself to slip into her house clothes. Michael sat on the couch, sipping the remainder of the White Zinfandel, when she returned. Sandra's house clothes principally consisted of a lacy bra, fully shown, with some loose pajama bottoms. She snuggled alongside Michael so closely that his only option was to put his arm around her, and for a time they both feigned interest in the video. Michael finally turned to her and brushed his lips against her cheek. She responded by turning to touch her lips to his, and it was automatic pilot from that point forwards. They migrated to the bedroom, and Sandra chose the top. After a few minutes, she stopped and shuddered. This was was his cue to finish, which took only two additional slow strokes. They lay together, interlocked, for about half a minute, and then Sandra rolled off him. He was not familiar with any company rules about office relationships, but if there were, he and Sandra broke all of them in the span of fifteen minutes.

They lay together on the bed for a short time, side by side, but it was just mid-afternoon, so they returned to the living room and, this time, actually watched the video. They clung to each other on the sofa, rehashing the moment and contemplating how it would change their lives. After an initial intimacy, things sometimes become awkward. What to say? How to react? But they were genuinely comfortable with each other, and Sandra asked whether he could stay the night.

"I'm a man of very few needs. If you can find another food pouch in your freezer chest, that and your company will get me through the night."

When morning arrived, Michael remembered that he had his travel bag from the Princeton trip, so he was showered and dressed at the time Sandra summoned him for breakfast. Sandra pecked him on the cheek.

"So, how's my favorite travel companion this morning?"

"Well rested, and feeling rather good about myself. Geeks like me don't usually score with such beautiful women."

"Get used to it. I think we're committed. But there's the work thing..."

"What? There's a rule that I'm not allowed to bang the boss?"

Sandra slapped him with the dish towel.

"First, we're colleagues. I'm not your boss. Second, we're not just consenting adults, we're highly-educated consenting adults. Neither one of us is taking advantage of the other in any way. From where I sit, that would be impossible, actually laughable. However, the people we work for have a general one-size-fits-all policy that makes things difficult for us."

Sandra paused for emphasis.

"Under no circumstance should anyone at Haematite have any suspicion that we have a relationship. It could mean our jobs."

"OK. No necking in the laboratory, and no locker room bravado. It's all that much easier since Haematite doesn't have a locker room."

"You're wrong. There is a locker room at Haematite, but it's where the clean room personnel change."

After breakfast, Sandra drove him to his apartment so Michael could get his car and they could drive separately to work. He killed a few minutes in his apartment so there would be a decent interval between their arrivals. He cleaned his bedroom a bit, since there might be a time when Sandra would stay the night; but his was a student's apartment, and it seemed to him that he would be spending most of his time at Sandra's. He had heard that women were more comfortable having sex in their own bed.

After a few days, their relationship started to seem very natural. Because of their irregular work habits, it wasn't that hard to give the appearance that they were just distant coworkers. At times when they were both free, Michael found himself at Sandra's condominium.

Sterba was out of town more often than not, so Michael had a lot of time to continue his analysis of the transaction data set. Flory had convinced them that they should be hunting Black Swans, so he filtered the dataset to select just the Swans, and he set up a program to work in the background to harvest any new Swans as they appeared. As each new Swan was added to the dataset, his display would beep and flash up a statistical summary. Each time that would happen, he would look for an emerging pattern, but no pattern was emerging, and Michael was getting frustrated. Finally, he did what he should have done in the first place. He programmed a genetic algorithm to evolve to find a pattern. His program randomly generated thousands of potential pattern-finding algorithms. These were tested against the dataset, and the ones that were clearly the bad performers were eliminated from the gene pool. The best performers were allowed to "mate" to replace the algorithms eliminated from the population. This mating would tend to preserve the best properties of each parent and give an opportunity for a precocious offspring. There were some random mutations programmed as well, the Hand of God in the machine. Unfortunately, genetic programs take a while to run, so he left for a cup of coffee.

Michael's work routine had been fairly insular. He kept to his office, occasionally walking to Sandra's lab. He and Sandra avoided too much contact at work, for obvious reasons. Since he had time to kill, he wandered the hallways aimlessly, taking in the sights. One floor was populated with the cubicle dwellers who tended to the financial operations of the corporation. It reminded him of a beehive, since everyone was active, and there was a background noise of transceiver rings and people talking that sounded like a buzz. The most interesting floor was the fabrication facility he had seen on his first tour of the building. Now, he was able to linger in front of the double-glazed windows to watch the workers making the specialized computing circuitry required for Haematite's operations. Michael noticed that in each area of the clean room, there was one guy doing the actual work, one guy who seemed to be looking over his shoulder, and another standing at a distance taking notes. This hierarchy seemed to be true for any factory, not just the Haematite clean room. It was like the old joke about the ten person row boat with one rower and nine managers.

When he arrived back at his office, his population of pattern-finding algorithms seemed to have converged on a solution. When he pulled up the summary, he had a hard time understanding it at first. Michael stroked Sandra's name on his transceiver shortlist.

"Webb, here. Oh, it's you, Michael."

"I think I found something you should look at."

"OK. I'll get a coffee and be at your office in a minute."

When Sandra arrived, he flashed his screen onto the wall display.

"At Flory's suggestion, I confined my analysis to the Black Swans. Since we're in a big money game, I figured that we needed to look just at Black Swan transactions above a certain monetary value, but what value should we use? Actually, that step was easy, since there appears to be a diploid distribution of transaction values; that is, there's a market for the big money traders, and then there's a market for everyone else. Then, I needed to decide at what place on the distribution I wanted to start looking. We want to look at the fat tail events, only, but where does the fat tail start? Once again, Flory was a help. Since the distribution should be scale-free, I just looked for the point at which the self-similarity breaks down."

Sandra stared intently at the graphs on the wall.

"OK. That makes sense, but how did you calculate where self-similarity breaks down? Would you do a curve fit and see where the data departs from the curve? That seems somewhat crude and open to interpretation."

"Exactly. That's why I normalized the data according to the scale-free model, and then did an autocorrelation. The breaking point is very apparent."

"OK, Mr. Math, I'll take your word for it. What did the analysis show, once you decided where to look in the distribution?"

"That's where I had a problem. I couldn't see any pattern, whatever, so I programmed a genetic algorithm. These Black Swan transactions are not out of place. They're out of time. They all make sense if the transactions happened an hour or two prior to the actual transaction time. Not only that, but if you plot the distribution of these errant transactions, they follow an almost perfect Gaussian distribution, a bell curve. If I were a betting man, I'd say that all this is the result of some sort of fixed process. It might be some subtle error in the network software, a periodic bug that shifts some bits left or right, or maybe someone is cooking the books. In any case, this is deterministic. It has a definite cause, and based on the distribution, it has one definite cause."

"It reminds me of the saying that anything that can go wrong will go wrong faster with computers. It could be a wrong line of code, but that line of code gives a predictable outcome. Sort of accidentally, on purpose. We need to know more about the internal workings of the network. Our model of the network as just something that moves data reliably from one place to another seems to be flawed. It's just as fallible as any other piece of computer code. Do we need to see another consultant?"

Michael thought for a moment, and then he had an answer.

"I think I know the perfect consultant for this, and he's local. He works at Mother Wode."

"A professor?"

No, probably better than a professor. Let me make an initial overture."

7 BASIL

It was time to call on Basil.

Basil had been a student at East Wodenstumpf many years ago, and then his sponsoring company went belly-up, leaving Basil out on a limb. He was from some Eastern European country - his accent gave him away - but he was always reticent about specifying exactly which country. You got the idea that Basil had done some unconventional things with computers in his homeland, and he wanted to keep a cold trail. Formal degree or not, Basil was a genius and a Computerati of the first rank. He was so useful that he had been kept on at a small salary by the university for all these years. Basil didn't complain about the money, and no one complained about Basil.

It was easy to find Basil's office, although it was often hard to find Basil in his office. First, Basil kept odd office hours, typically arriving as everyone was leaving, and leaving when everyone was arriving. Second, his office was so overloaded with junk and old beverage bottles, that Basil was well hidden. You could find him in his office anytime from late-afternoon through dawn - he freely admitted that he preferred night hours when no one else could disturb his concentration. There was an old joke about a Computerati who was asked to attend an 8:00 AM meeting. His response was that he didn't stay up that late. The joke could have been written about Basil.

Michael zipped down the basement stairs of the computer center and found Basil in his office. The only light was from the display, and it projected onto Basil's face in a way that reminded Michael of a villain from an old video. Basil didn't hear Michael's approach, and Michael was careful not to startle him. Michael retreated slightly outside the door and gave a gentle knock. No response. Another, louder knock. No response. Was he asleep? Michael knocked again, and between the first and second rap, Basil responded.

"OK! OK! Give Basil a second, here!"

Basil tapped out a few commands on a keyboard and swiveled around in his chair.

"That compile should take about fifteen minutes, so you caught Basil at a good time. You've got fifteen minutes, maybe more if you're entertaining!"

Basil pointed towards a chair, but thought better of the idea, since the chair was piled high with books. The paperless office, years in its coming, was still years into the future.

"It's Michael, right? You wouldn't mind standing, would you? Basil hears that you'll be leaving us in a few weeks. You do good work. Basil will be at your public defense."

"Basil, I'm honored. The reason I'm here is for some advice - about network routers."

"Ha! You came to the right man! Basil had some experience with these back in his home country during Gymnasium days - what you would call high school. Routers don't change much - standards and all that. They try to sell them on speed nowadays, not features. So, what about routers?"

"I think there must be some software bug in network router code that nobody knows about. They seem to unexpectedly drop packets here and there, then let them through at a later time. Sometimes the later time is an hour or two, which might indicate the limit of the store and forward capacity. I hear that the manufacturer will not release the code, for obvious reasons, and I won't even try to get them interested in this problem. The problem is too small, and they know that fixing it would likely cause a more serious problem somewhere else. As a Computerati, I understand their position, but I still need to know. By the way, there's some money in this for you. This is for Haomatite."

Basil's face perked-up at the mention of money. He probably had a list of tech-toys posted somewhere in the office. Where exactly in the many piles of paper was anyone's guess.

"Good to hear about the money! Money makes risky things much more acceptable to Basil! So, you want to see the router code, maybe disassembled for easier reading. Not too hard to do. Speedy code must be short code, well written. Plus, there's the standard network protocols. The code almost writes itself. If anything is out of place, Basil will find it. But not here! Too easy to trace, but Basil knows a place. You come, too. No copies of this - we read it straight from the display and then erase the buffer! Easy in, easy out!"

Basil outlined a few scripts he would need to write to disassemble the code into a human readable form after he cracked into the system. The cracking part was all in his head, where it had resided since high school days. That part would not be committed to any script file - it would be Basil playing a symphony at his keyboard. Basil wrote Michael directions to an apartment on the outskirts of East Wodenstumpf and told him to arrive at about 2:00 AM the next day.

Michael had never been in that section of East Wodenstumpf before. It was a marginalized area that was bypassed years before by the major transport systems. As a consequence there were few merchants and the few residents who could stomach the tortuous commute to work in the more developed areas. Although he was out of his milieu, Michael wasn't concerned about his safety. Petty crime had ceased to be a problem after repeal of recreational drug criminalization. The monies saved on drug interdiction were funneled with great success into educational programs in primary and secondary schools. He remembered the addict videos he saw in elementary school, and these images still made him shudder.

He arrived a few minutes before two. The building looked strangely dark even for 2:00 AM, but he proceeded to walk up the front steps.

"Michael! Here!" Basil called to him as he exited his vehicle and walked up the steps to greet Michael. "No entry there. Come with Basil."

Basil guided him around the side of the building, down another stairway, and into the cellar. The door was unlocked, and they entered. Basil had come prepared with a bright fuel cell lantern, another of his many tech-toys.

"One of Basil's pals left the door open for us. The building is abandoned, but it's being maintained for possible future renovation and occupation. They still pay their utility bills - a corporate oversight. We need to walk towards the front of the building. That's where we'll find the box."

By box, Basil meant the communications junction box. When they arrived, Michael surmised that either Basil had been here before, or that it was a shared secret among some hacker brethren. There was a small table and several chairs. One chair was near a window - a lookout's perch? An optical fiber had been pulled out of the box and fitted with a small box. Basil proceeded to unpack a portable computer and plug it into a utility outlet on the fuel cell. He ran another cable from the computer to the improvised interface box. When it was all connected, Basil gave a running tutorial.

"Physical Layer," he said, pointing to the interface box. Then he pointed to the portable computer. "Transport Layer - at least after Basil breaks into the network and gets the proper software running. The first step is to log onto a major computer, in this case Mother Wode's"

Michael was confused. "If we're on Mother Wode's computer, why do we need to be out here?"

"Michael and Basil are in this place, and not at the university, since this link is much harder to trace. It's slow speed out here, with antiquated hardware. No automatic traces are possible. Also, when Basil says log-on, he doesn't mean the usual log-on. We are going to spoof some data and get Mother Wode to think she's logging onto herself. An unusual protocol, but one that was accidentally allowed by the system administrator. Actually, he uses it for some important functions, just not what we're doing."

After a few more keystrokes, "Basil is in! That was the easy part. Now Basil gets onto the global network with the proper permissions - somewhat harder, but not for Basil!" There was a flurry of keystrokes. A frown. Some chin rubbing. A few more keystrokes. Then a big smile.

"Give Basil a letter of the alphabet."

"X."

"No. No state names start with X. Give Basil another."

"G."

"OK. Guam... Georgia... Georgia must have a lot of hub routers."

A list appeared on the display. There were about forty names.

"OK. Basil finds one about two-thirds down the list... Ah, Athens_01. Sounds as likely as any."

Basil pecked away at the keyboard for a few more seconds then sat back.

"Basil will have the binary in a few seconds. Then we disconnect as fast as possible and do some analysis."

There was a beep.

"Very short download. As Basil said, very small, very fast code."

Basil did a few more keystrokes and unplugged from the interface box.

"Now Basil does some analysis. First Basil disassembles the binary into something Michael and Basil can read. Basil has incorporated the published network protocol commands into a shell script to make the disassembled codes much more readable."

Basil punched a few more keys, and a progress bar appeared on the screen. When it reached a 100 percent, it went back to zero and started ramping again.

"It's a two-pass process - first pass for tokens, last pass for the labels."

Michael knew in an abstract sense what was happening. He had learned about assemblers as an undergraduate. He and other Computerati wrote only in high level languages that were quite removed from the actual machine code. Sometimes, they were using languages that were written in other languages, and most of the time they didn't even know the type of machine that they were using - everything just worked. What Basil was doing wasn't magic, but as far as Michael was concerned, it was close to it. Another beep, and the display filled with columns of numbers and letters.

"OK. Here we have it, the magic code of the global network. It's actually pretty boring stuff. Most of it hasn't changed in about twenty years." Basil pointed to the display. "Here they do some preliminary memory mapping, just so they don't step out of bounds. Then they get the data packet, save it in memory, find the header - the part with the addresses and command - then strip out the command." Basil scrolled down a little. "Here they do a very long case statement to find out what command was sent. Obviously, the frequent commands are first, things like just send this data directly to the destination address without error checking. At the end of the list..." Basil scrolled much further "... are the last two statements, which are the administrator request for control - very password protected by a hardware key - and a jump to *DAD*."

"What's *DAD*?"

"That's the *case else* condition where you should fall off the face of the earth because the command wasn't recognized. This jumps to an instruction that sends a message back to the sender - actually just a number - which is politely stated, Sorry, I didn't understand you. In actuality, the programmers call it *DAD*, for *Dumb As Dirt*. It's an exhortation from one programmer to another to learn how to write code. As you can imagine, these assembler guys think they're alpha dog. So, the *DAD* code is here, at 3C4A1." Basil pointed to a statement that read JMP #03C4A1. He then highlighted the leftmost column and executed a find for 03C4A1. "So, here's Dear Old *DAD*."

The display flashed, and 03C4A1 was highlighted in the leftmost column. Basil paused, tapped his fingers on the table, and made a frown.

"Basil must have typed the wrong number. Let's do that again."

Basil typed a few more keystrokes and found himself at the same place in the code.

"OK, that's the place, but that's not *DAD*!"

Basil continued to scroll. He pointed to the display.

"Here's the routine that sends *DAD*. Basil doesn't quite understand what the rest of this code is for. *DAD* should send *DAD*, nothing more, nothing less. Someone's twiddled with this code."

"What does the code do?"

"That's going to take a little thought..." Basil looked around "... and a space more conductive to thought. Basil said everything we do stays here - no evidence - but this code is too deep for an instant analysis. Basil is happy he brought this along."

Basil reached into his pocket - God! Do they still sell pocket protectors? - and pulled out a pencil.

"You're going to take notes?" Michael said incredulously.

"Looks like a pencil, and writes like a pencil, but watch this!"

He unscrewed the eraser end to reveal a fiberoptic connector.

"Basil bought this last year. In fact Basil bought two, but the other one is presently non-functional. It's an encrypted memory device, with a twist. If you mistype your pass-phrase three times, it destroys itself with a high voltage pulse. Basil wasn't taking the manufacturer's word for it, so Basil did a test on the second unit. Still works as a pencil, though."

Basil plugged the pencil into a port on the portable computer, and typed a few more lines.

"Basil is done for now. Everything was done in volatile memory, and it's been erased. Only the pencil knows."

Basil screwed back the eraser and pushed the pencil into his overstuffed pocket protector.

"Basil will get back to you in a few days."

Michael and Basil left the room as they found it and went their separate ways. It was after 3:00 AM when Michael arrived at his apartment. Although 3:00 AM was well past his usual bed time, Michael's mind was racing. He was too stimulated by his hackfest with Basil to go directly to bed, so he switched on the entertainment display in his living room. His entertainment display was quite primitive compared to Sandra's, but he didn't mind. It was used mostly to view the occasional news summary, and it was good enough for that purpose. He was curious to see what was on at this late hour.

When Michael was a child, it seemed as if on demand would be the terminal trend for home entertainment. The studios loved the idea, since they had dollar signs in their eyes from projected profits on all those demanding eyeballs. The one thing they didn't consider was that people can be very selective about their demands, and there wouldn't be any demand for something completely unknown, no matter how much it was advertised. In the end, on demand became only a niche player, and the traditional deluge of thousands of random shows remained on the entertainment networks. The increased bandwidth of the networks allowed a greater number of specialty channels. The now global audience and instantaneous aural translation made even the most obscure hobby channel viable.

The problem for Michael, and for everyone else, was how to select a channel to watch. Artificial intelligence, in the form of computer programs built into entertainment displays, were able to sort the wheat from the chaff for any particular viewer by keying off his past viewing habits. In Michael's case, this now worked to his disadvantage, since his display started its session by bringing him the London Morning News and offering him choices of other news programs from most of Europe. After paging through a plethora of these news options, Michael retreated to the random button to see what surprises might await him. And random it was! First, there was crocheting, followed by the life-cycle of some unrecognizable insect, a replay of a soccer game, and an old movie about some little girl making all the adults around her behave foolishly. If he had to choose from among these, he would side with the little girl. Instead, Michael shut down the display and headed to bed.

8 CRACKING THE CODE

Since the Haematite project was essentially on hold until Basil got back to him with his analysis of the mysterious router code, Michael spent the majority of his time at Mother Wode. He reminded Sandra that he was still in transition to Haematite, and his contract allowed him "reasonable time" away from work to complete his Ph.D. Of course, the unreasonable demands of Sterba expanded the definition of "reasonable time," but Sandra seemed to understand. She was busy working on other things, so it didn't matter at the moment, but management might come knocking in a few weeks for an interim report. Their project would not continue without an upbeat prognosis, and since it was good work, neither of them wanted the project canceled.

Sterba was away again on one of his many trips, this time to some government agency with another plea for funding. Perhaps he was using some of Michael's research as leverage. Whatever the case, Michael was left undisturbed as he finished the drafts of the few remaining manuscripts that Sterba required.

It was two days before Basil called him down to his office. When Michael arrived, Basil grabbed his portable computer and led him down the hall to another room. It was ostensibly a storeroom, but there was a desk and two chairs in one corner. The door locked behind them.

"This is Basil's private space. The added fireproofing has a side benefit of shielding us from electromagnetic eavesdropping. No network connection in here!"

Basil plopped the portable computer on the desk, plugged-in his magic pencil, and in a moment the display filled with color-coded text that was presumably a more readable representation of the router code.

"The usual code is all junk, at least as far as you're concerned, so Basil stripped it out of the file. These assembly coders are sharp. Basil did get a few pointers while studying the code."

Basil smiled, but the joke, if any, went right over Michael's head.

"Anyways, the code does call *DAD* in the usual way for all undocumented protocol commands, except three. If it receives these three commands, in sequence, in a span of less than about a millisecond, the router goes into an overriding administrative mode, locked to the network address of the command sender. Neat trick."

"But, what is this mode used for?"

"That's proving a little harder to find. Does Basil bill by the hour? Ha! Have you ever heard of obfuscated code?"

"Do you mean the kind I typically write?"

"Ha! Michael knows a little about what Basil means, but not the full story! This is purposefully obfuscated code, not just code that's difficult to understand, but code that's designed to be difficult to understand. Some of it is like a treasure hunt. You get a slip of paper that sends you to a box with a key that unlocks another box with another slip of paper that divulges the location of the treasure. You can do this in code, too, to hide the values of variables and the locations of subroutines. Worse yet, the code can be self-modifying. Look at it again, and it's different from the last time you looked. The amazing thing is that the code still does something useful. But Basil likes puzzles, so there's no problem. It will just take a little time. Maybe a few more days."

"OK. Let me know as soon as you have an answer. I've been shielding you from my management, but I can't do it for too much longer."

"Basil has a Guardian Angel! Basil always needed one of those!"

As Michael worked his way up the stairs from the storage room to his office, he wondered whether he would be happier if Basil wasn't able to make sense out of the router code. Things were getting too complicated. Michael was comfortable with numbers and programs that make sense out of number ensembles, but they were now moving one step back from the numbers to whatever generated them in the first place. This was unknown territory for him, but Basil didn't have a problem with it. Things were still relatively under control, and control is what computing is all about. Suddenly, Sterba's tasks seemed a lot easier in comparison.

Michael had anticipated spending a few hours the next day at Haematite, if only to see Sandra. By coincident circumstance, he was being pulled in too many directions at the same time, by Sterba, the Haematite project, and Sandra. The Haematite project was on a back burner again until Basil worked his magic, he was handling his Sterba tasks fairly well, but it almost seemed that he was avoiding Sandra. That was the last thing he wanted to do, especially since their relationship had just started to blossom, and he decided to spend some time with her. Unfortunately, opening his messages that morning changed his plans. Sterba, although out of town, must have been bored sitting in his hotel room, so he had time to pick through Michael's manuscripts line by line. Most of his corrections and comments were minor, but there was a graph in one paper that Sterba didn't like. To Michael's chagrin, it wasn't just the graph that was the problem, it was the underlying data that was graphed. Michael needed to run a few more trials and reanalyze the data. He thought about protesting this additional work, but he didn't want to antagonize his professor, and he had to admit that Sterba was probably right.

The research area of the particular paper was a new type of neural network architecture they had devised. Sterba had led him onto the right topic area, since neural network theory was gaining renewed interest after a considerable hiatus. Most of the reason for this was the inordinate amount of computing power available compared with the limited software resources. It was a typical Malthusian problem in which computing power was increasing exponentially, but software code was still written in a linear fashion by human programmers. The lure of neural networks was that each node required just a small amount of code, and you could fill the hardware space with as many nodes as it could handle. Of course, the software had to be self evolving, or it could never take advantage of the nearly infinite hardware space available. All that even the brightest Compterati could do for such a complex system was write a reasonable starting program, and then stand back as his machine evolved.

Sterba's idea was this. Since the neural network was evolving, we needed to help the evolution proceed. Of course, all the Darwinian stuff had been done to death, so it was difficult to do anything new in this area. Sterba had stumbled across an ancient, but discredited, idea of biological evolution called a morphogenic field. In this strange view of evolution, organisms were affected by a mystical field that shaped their development. It was as if a city-dwelling moth's distant cousins in the forest were sending out signals about what it means to be a moth. A consensus would develop in the species as to what the quality of "mothness" was, and this would amplify the field by a resonance effect. Scientists were quite upset about the whole idea of such a mystical field effect, and the idea had died within a decade.

Although the morphic field likely doesn't exist in real life, that doesn't mean that the idea wouldn't be useful in a neural network. A typical neural network is partitioned into layers, and connections are only made between nodes in adjacent layers. Adding a morphic field in a neural network would be like adding connections between all the nodes in the network, something that would be too hard to do, and the computations would take forever. Michael added fixed, random connections between some nodes and hoped for the best. His results showed some improvement, nothing really to write home about, but something Sterba could use to get further funding.

Michael's neural network needed a purpose, so they decided that language translation would be as good a purpose as any. It had the benefit that many classic texts had translations into multiple languages, so the network training data were already in place. Since the computing power at their disposal at Mother Wode was enormous by most standards, their network could actually be trained using entire chapters of books at any one time. The only problem was how to measure how fast the neural network was learning how to translate from one language to another. The simple solution was to do a double translation; namely, Language A to Language B, then back to Language A. A program would compare the final Language A translation with the input Language A data and find the differences.

Michael had found that doing a simple, word by word, comparison wasn't possible. Sometimes contractions were spelled out, and sometimes they weren't. The original text might contain "aren't," and the translated text would come back "are not." After examining the translations, he was able to build in tables to eliminate these errors. One other problem was word order, since a sentence can still have the same meaning if the sequence of words is just changed. That was an easy fix, since you could just look for the occurrence of the same words in a sentence. In the end there were still a few sentences that were marked as incorrect by his scoring program that could be judged to be correct translations. Michael had decided to intervene and manually mark these as also correct.

Sterba had no problem with the scoring program's automatic corrections, but he did have a problem with the human intervention for some of the sentences. Since these were just a small percentage of the total number, Sterba decided it would be best to just use the program's judgment and eliminate Michael's hand scoring of the rogue sentences. This meant that Michael had to plow through his records, delete his "biased" scoring, and redo the graph with just the computer scoring. This was not intellectually challenging, but it would take quite a bit of time.

It was another three days before Basil called Michael back to his office. When Michael arrived, Basil was in a jubilant mood.

"Michael, the code could be a problem for most, but not for Basil! Come, look!"

Basil had not taken the precaution of dragging them into the storage room. Perhaps the new accumulation of littered boxes in his office now contained lead sheets.

"Oh, you must wonder why we aren't in the other room. Basil decided to work in the comfort of his office. This took some time."

Basil reached into a top drawer of his desk and pulled out a metal box, about the same size and shape as a half-pint milk carton. It appeared to have a spiral pattern etched onto its surface, along with a solitary switch and status light.

"This is Basil's latest acquisition. It's called a broadband jammer. Any radio signals within this office are effectively scrambled. No television, no radio, no wireless network, and no stray emissions from Basil's computer. Of course, to be safe, Basil has unplugged the transceiver and the wired network connections. Communications-wise, Basil and Michael are in the dark. Oh, Basil was sure to check the light bulbs, too!"

Michael didn't quite understand the last part, but knowing Basil's paranoia, he was sure that all the appropriate measures had been taken. He gazed at Basil's display screen.

"Basil, I was wondering, why did they choose to obfuscate the code, rather than encrypt it? If they didn't want it to be seen, encryption would be the best way."

"Well, there are two problems there. The first is that that code would need to be decrypted, which means it would need to be put into a writable memory space. The routers only have enough memory for a small stack. That's because the memory must be really fast, so there's not enough room. The other reason is that encrypted code would stand out like a pregnant mule."

Michael winced. He had never seen a mule, nor was he likely ever to see a mule, but Basil seemed to know his way around mules, so he took his word for this.

"If no one suspects anything, the obfuscated code just blends in, but Basil had reason to be curious."

Basil pointed to some code on the display screen.

"As Basil found before, when the hub router receives three sequential commands in a very short time, it goes into an administrative mode controlled by the network address that sent the command. By unraveling the code, Basil found that this super-administrator can modify some look-up tables in hardware. What these tables do is a rapid routing of some addresses to others. There is no code, since it's all done in hardware, and it's really fast. In the old days, these were links to what were called Domain Name Servers, but now they're usually links to a super network - government and emergency stuff. These tables are updated regularly, but a normal administrator needs to physically access the router to do that. This is a security measure. Have you ever seen a hub location?"

Michael confessed, "No."

"Well, there are concrete and steel doors; and guards with guns. Basil saw one once, during construction. No armed guards around then."

Basil winked. Another insight into his past. He must have downloaded code right from a router when no one was around. Michael had made the right choice of a consultant.

"Very secure, at least on paper, but it seems that all that security has been bypassed. And another thing..."

Basil pointed to some code, as cryptic as the rest. Michael didn't understand any of it, but he tried to act interested.

"When these routers are shutdown or pulled out of service, the code erases the modified portions of the tables on the next power-up. Maintenance people would never know something is amiss, since there are just two rogue code bytes left after all that. Of course, these maintenance guys don't access the code on the fly like Basil did a few nights ago."

"OK. Someone modified these tables. Where do we go from there?"

"Are you adventuresome, Michael?"

"What do you mean?"

"As Basil said, the tables are in a special cache in the router. The rogue code proves you can modify them remotely, although that really should have been prevented in the hardware. But as far as Basil can see, you can't use the code to read them remotely, an obvious security measure that still stands. If you want to see what's going on, you need to physically access the router."

"So, to paraphrase what you just said, we need to visit an active router; and not just visit, but take it apart and examine it, all without anyone noticing. I suppose we just buy the armed guards some donuts!"

"Michael, it's not as bad as that! Yes, you need physical access to the machine, but Basil just needs a few seconds alone at its back panel. There's a port I can plug into. Zip, zip, we're done."

As he left Basil's office, Michael started to wonder whether Haematite was paying him enough.

9 SKI MASKS OPTIONAL

Basil did not advocate a full frontal assault on a hub router, just a little time at the back of the equipment racks. The scenario still pointed towards some risky business, and it was contingent on their getting access. From Basil's description, access was closely guarded, and he couldn't think of any excuse that would get them into such a place, let alone do what Basil had suggested. It was time to get Sandra involved, at least for a second opinion. He and Sandra would be together for the weekend, but Michael decided not to fill her in on the latest development until working hours, sometime next week.

Michael and Sandra's weekend plan was to spend Friday night at her place, and then take a tour of some antique shops in the vicinity of East Wodenstumpf on Saturday, probably taking a quiet dinner at some country restaurant before returning to her apartment. Michael had no interest whatever in antiques, but love can lead a man down many untrodden paths. He enjoyed new items, the latest technical gadgets, and didn't understand how old junk could command such high prices. He had noticed some old utilitarian furniture at Sandra's place, dresser drawers and the like, but he thought they had been in her family for years. He now realized that she had bought those items herself - another side of Sandra that made her unique, but a side that took getting accustomed to. Friday night in bed with Sandra made the whole adventure palatable.

Fortunately, Sandra was not an early riser on weekends, so they lingered in bed until about 9:00 AM, ate a hasty breakfast, and were on the road by ten. Sandra had mapped out a search radius of about thirty miles around East Wodenstumpf, and she had plotted an efficient path through several small towns with small antique shops. It was a beautiful, sunny day, so the ride was enjoyable. Sandra did a lot of looking, found a few small jewelry items to purchase, but no bulky items. Michael figured that any large purchases would need to be shipped, since they weren't equipped to transport anything like that. Some of the other customers came with vans or trailers. These were probably dealers from larger cities who routinely acquire stock at country shops, auctions and house sales, hauled them to their shops, and marked them up for a large profit.

It was 5:00 PM, and they were politely edged to the doorway at the fourth shop on Sandra's list. The shopkeeper wanted to close for the day, which was fine by Michael, whose mind had numbed to this whole antiquing concept midway into their visit to the second shop. Sandra was starting to look a little fatigued herself.

A few miles down the road, they found a modest little restaurant and decided to stop there for dinner. The restaurant was so small that it had a fixed dinner menu of traditional New England fare centered on the single entrée of pot roast and potatoes. The food choice appealed to both of them, quite possibly because they hadn't stopped for lunch and were famished, so they slumped into their chairs and ordered. Both were exhausted, and neither of them was up to much conversation until the biscuits and butter arrived and they had a chance to fuel their stomachs. Michael started.

"How is it that you're into antiques? It seems like a strange hobby for a girl from California."

"Actually, it all started in California. My mother, Helen, came from a family that traced its beginnings back to the Forty-Niners, or at least that's what she was told. There were a few memento items from what may have been that period in the house, an old chest and some items in it, that interested me when I was young. Mom would take us to flea markets - of course, there were rarely any genuine articles there, just reproductions - but I enjoyed the excitement of the quest. When I had a good income and found myself in New England, a place where real antiques passed frequently into the market from house sales of the last of the family line, the lure was irresistible. Unfortunately, I need to temper my ambitions because of lack of space at my place. Come to think of it, you've been occupying as much space as a good-sized armoire. Oh, the difficult choices I have to make!"

The meal spanned almost two hours, mostly because of the carefree demeanor of the restaurant, which was quite unlike the hurried service they were accustomed to, but it was an enjoyable time. They were back at Sandra's place around midnight, but this wasn't a night for romance. They were both exhausted when they plopped into bed.

Sometime Sunday, Michael made it back to his office at Mother Wode. There were no new messages from Sterba, and the automated data analysis he had started to handle Sterba's last request had completed. With an additional half-hour's work, he revised the graph, but he didn't send it to Sterba. He decided to do that on Monday. A message from him to Sterba might only invite more work, and he needed a day's rest.

Michael spent most of Monday at Haematite. He wasn't purposely avoiding Sandra, but he wasn't actively hoping to run into her. He had to tell her about Basil's findings, which would mean he would need to tell her about Basil. Basil would be an acquired taste. Michael decided for the moment to shield her from Basil and talk only in general terms until he got a sense of Sandra's position. Maybe Sandra would enjoy wearing a black ski mask and raiding a hub router.

It was Tuesday morning before he got the courage to bring Sandra up to speed on the hub router problem. As usual, she wasn't in her office, but he found her in the lab. Michael paused in the doorway a moment to savor the gentle glow of the display light on her face. Direct lighting seemed to age most women - every little wrinkle and crease are exaggerated - but Sandra's face seemed to glow in a most beautiful way.

Finally, he knocked gently on the door, and Sandra looked up.

"Sandra, I've done a little more digging in the Black Swan problem, and I have a possible next step to resolve it."

"Wonderful! Details! Details!"

"With some help from a capable fellow at East Wodenstumpf, we did some investigating. It looks like the hub routers are sending packets off into deep space, and they are somehow retrieved a while later."

"So, we call the hub manufacturers and clue them in?"

"It's not as simple as that. This doesn't seem to be the fault of the hub manufacturer. There appears to be some outside agency responsible. We may need to tread lightly."

"The government? Oh! Maybe a foreign government!"

"Could be. I just don't know."

He paused, and Sandra interjected.

"You said you had a possible next step. What is it?"

Did Sandra see his face grow the slightest shade paler?

"Well, to discover who's responsible for the lost packets, which I think are our Black Swans, we need physical access to an active hub. It would just take a few seconds at the rear panel."

Michael decided not to mention that he didn't know anything about accessing the router information himself. He would need to bring Basil with them.

"My consultant at East Wodenstumpf says that that's the only way, so we're stuck. We can't just storm a hub with guns blazing. I guess the project's dead."

"Well, can't we just give the hub people our information, and let them sort it out? If they fix the dropped packet problem, that will fix our Black Swan problem, and I'm certain they would do this with utmost haste!"

An obvious point. Now Michael needed to put his cards on the table.

"The trouble is... they would wonder how we got our information. What my consultant did wasn't exactly legal. And if the government is in cahoots with the manufacturer, then it's high level government trouble, and not something I would care to be mixed up in."

He had expected Sandra to look shocked. Her response was unexpected.

"Those government SOBs! I wouldn't be surprised if some government functionary was somehow lining his own pockets this way! Maybe he's redirecting financial transactions to work the market, or stealing industrial secrets, or blackmailing his government's own citizens! Things like this used to happen in the early century. Illegal government wiretaps, and all that. Tighter controls were put into place to stop such shenanigans, but that was a simpler time."

Sandra's face had turned an intense, but appealing shade of pink. She paused for a moment, collecting her thoughts.

"Perhaps the time was ripe for a second wave of such nonsense. Whatever, or whoever, it is, they should be stopped. I think we're obligated to look more deeply into this, as long as we can handle it discretely and anonymously. Access to an active hub might not be too much of a problem. Haematite is a big company. We must do business with router manufacturers on a regular basis. Our shadow network didn't just materialize out of thin air. I'm sure I could get a well placed introduction. If we're potential buyers, you'll be amazed a what some guys will do to make a sale." Sandra laughed. "Maybe I can keep the salesman busy while you do your dirty work behind the racks!"

10 THREESOME

Michael knew that he wouldn't find Basil in his office anytime the next morning, so he spent some time at Haematite. He didn't really have much to do, so he did some deep dives into the network looking for tutorials on the types and mechanisms of securities trading. Most of the information he found presupposed some sort of financial background, and the texts were filled with all sorts of jargon. He imagined it was similar to what would happen if a finance student tried to figure out what Michael was doing for his Ph.D. He did find that computers mostly ran the show. In the rare instances when a human made a transaction, the human was playing a hunch, but he was relying on a display screen full of data from computer models.

Michael arrived at Mother Wode around noon, but Basil had still not arrived. He left a note on Basil's door that he would try again at about 1:00 PM, and he walked to Wode's End, the closest of the small campus eateries, for lunch. He tried not to eat there too often, since the greasy food was designed for younger stomachs than his; but he hadn't treated himself to a Wodeburger in quite a while, and he remembered that they tasted quite good when layered with a thick spread of sweet relish from the fixings bar. Since he was on a roll, he ordered the accompanying fries but promised himself he would eat only half the portion. Promises are too easily broken.

When Michael returned to Basil's office, he found him there.

"Michael! Basil got your message. Sorry about my lateness, but Basil had a very full night."

"You mean a full-figured woman?"

"Ha! Just some code, but Basil does prefer women!"

Michael informed Basil of Sandra's idea to pose as a potential customer to gain access to a hub router. Basil said he only needed about thirty seconds at a particular rear-mounted connector. The trick, said Basil, was that the optical connector was non-standard - another precaution to prevent accidental data leaks.

"Not to worry, Michael, Basil has a connector! Zip, zip - it is done!"

"OK, Basil, I'll take your word for it, but it's time for us to get together for a strategy session; and by "us," I mean you, me and Sandra. Sandra knows I'm working with someone at Mother Wode, but I haven't told her anything about you. She's probably expecting my associate to be some academic type, like me, so we'll need to ease her into things."

"Michael, don't worry! Basil cleans up nicely! Basil knows how to charm the women, too!"

"Clean is good, but forget the charm. She barely tolerates me. I'll set up a meeting."

Once again, the difficulties of his Sterba tasks paled in comparison with his real world problems. Michael needed to introduce Basil to Sandra and then get her comfortable with the idea of bringing Basil with them to a hub. It had surprised him that Sandra was so agreeable to Basil's idea of compromising hub security. He still had much to learn about her, or perhaps about all women in general.

Sandra had been playing transceiver tag with a few people, trying to line up a visit to an active hub. She found someone at Haematite who had bought a hub router - actually, almost a dozen - for the electrical futures shadow network. Dropping his name got an invitation to visit an active hub. A minor inconvenience was that the hub was near Hartford. Although they could rent a car in Hartford, public transportation to Hartford was not that convenient. They decided to drive the entire distance, and an appointment was set for early the next week. It was imperative that Sandra and Basil meet, and soon.

Basil's waking hours did not make this easy. Michael suggested to Basil that he would buy him a late breakfast - at 6:00 PM - and he would bring Sandra with him. For Basil, breakfast was two burritos at Miguel's. Sandra had agreed to dinner that same night, and Mexican sounded good to her.

"I've invited my colleague from Mother Wode. Is it OK if he joins us? It would be good if you finally met, especially since you're paying the bills."

Since Sandra thought the only real romantic dinners were in the privacy of her home, Michael was fairly certain she would agree, and she did. Basil was never on time, so their arriving promptly at six meant they would precede him. Then he would have time to soften her up. A cocktail would help, if only for his own nerves, but when they arrived at the restaurant, Basil was already ensconced in a chair at the entrance, waiting for his table number to be called.

"Basil, you're right on time!"

Michael glanced sideways to see Sandra's reaction to this nearly spherically shaped human with whom she was to dine.

"Michael, you are a paying customer! Basil is always punctual in such cases! This charming young lady is the colleague Michael mentioned to Basil?"

"Sandra, this is Basil. He's the East Wodenstumpf consultant I brought onto the project."

Well, all the cats were out of the bag, now. Sandra's lips tensed as she turned to Michael.

"He signed all the proper non-disclosure agreements?"

"Don't worry, young lady. Basil discloses to no one! Too dangerous! In fact, Basil's mother doesn't even know Basil's birthday! But, let us eat and talk."

They were seated quickly and ordered. To Basil's credit, he didn't seem to imbibe at breakfast, although it was cocktail time in the real world. Michael ordered a Dos Equis and Sandra ordered a Corona. When the drinks arrived, Michael didn't know how to start the conversation. Fortunately, Sandra took the lead.

"So, Basil, you're our mystery consultant. Michael was keeping you a secret until now, but you've uncovered some interesting information that may advance our project. Did Michael outline what we're doing?"

Michael realized that Sandra was testing to see how much Basil really knew.

"Michael didn't say anything at all, except for the fact that Michael suspected a problem with the hub routers. That must be why Michael didn't think Basil needed to sign any non-disclosure forms. Michael didn't disclose any business information. Basil prefers things that way, so keep Basil in the dark as much as possible. Basil prefers computers to the harsh realities of the business world. Computers are much more predictable, at least for Basil!"

Sandra relaxed noticeably.

"OK, I'll accept that. What's your background? Are you a student like Michael? A post-doc, perhaps?"

Basil outlined his earlier funding problems, confessed he was a staff employee, and gave a resume of some interesting things he was doing at Mother Wode. He purposely refrained from divulging details of his supposed dark side, the side that made him a valued consultant. He refrained from this, possibly because Sandra had not yet won his trust. Basil continued.

"Sandra, do you code?"

Sandra looked a little surprised by the question.

"Yes, I'm a Computerati. I code a lot. Why do you ask?"

"In Basil's experience, there are two types of Computerati, those who know how to code, and those who produce elaborate schemes for others to code. As far as Basil is concerned, the non-coders are just philosophers who don't deserve to be called Computerati. Michael, here, codes a lot, and that's why Basil decided to help him. Michael understands the nature of the machine - sometimes you fight it, and sometimes it is your friend."

"I keep my machines friendly."

Their meals arrived. Basil turned the plate around, carefully examining his breakfast, somewhat like a dog does with his bone.

"If you want to solve the hub router mystery, Basil is your man. As Michael must have told you, Basil would need physical access to a machine for about thirty seconds."

Sanda turned pale.

"You're going to get the data, not Michael?"

"Basil knows his way around hub routers. Michael is a fast learner, but it's too tricky to try to teach someone else, especially when there is no router for practice."

Sandra paused for a moment.

"I've been able to arrange a visit to an active hub near Hartford. I could add you to the guest list. What you plan to do is not quite illegal, is it?"

Michael choked on his beer.

"Basil will be discreet, and you have a good cover story. Besides, how important could a few bytes of information bo?"

Michael could tell that Sandra was getting more and more uncomfortable with the hub venture. She was conflicted. On the one hand, she was curious and wanted to know what was happening. Also, as he had found, she had an anti-establishment bent that was somewhat exciting to him. But there was the added element of risk. He decided that the best way to manage her attitude towards the risk was by giving her more data.

Hoping that Basil would understand the purpose of his phrasing of the question this way, Michael said, "Basil, as I remember in our conversations, you mentioned that you had once helped in the construction of a hub router. Perhaps you could reassure Sandra that there would be no real danger of our being detected."

"Ah, yes. Basil has direct, hands-on experience in this area. The first thing to understand is that all the security is at the perimeter, the front door, so to speak. If you are welcomed through the front door, no one is worried at all about you."

Sandra interrupted.

"But there must some safeguards inside. The routers must be inside some cabinets. Won't the cabinets be locked?"

Yes, there are cabinets, but if they have locks, they are left unlocked. Technicians can't be bothered with locks. When they need access, they want it right away. Perhaps on days when some manager makes a call, they'll sweep the floors and lock the cabinets, but that's a rarity, not the norm. Besides, we're there to examine the routers, so the cabinet will be unlocked for us."

Sandra started to look a little more relaxed, but she had another question.

"What about security cameras?"

Basil smiled.

"Yes, there will be security cameras, but they will be pointed at the doorways, just to see who enters and exits. Technicians are people, too, and everyone values his privacy. Remember, anyone inside has been authorized to be inside. Basil, Michael and Sandra will be authorized to be inside. No one will worry about us. Besides, if Michael acts as a shield, no one will see what Basil does in those thirty seconds."

Sandra had no more questions, so she concentrated on her meal, as did Basil. For his part, Michael did more sipping of beer than eating, and he tried to fuel chit-chat so that Sandra would get to know Basil.

"Sandra, you'll be amazed at the number of programming languages that Basil knows. Most of them are only a name to me. Basil, why did you ever learn so many? Is it like a hobby?"

"Basil likes to code, but he doesn't like to work! There's always a best language for a particular application. If you write in that language, the application flows from your keyboard like a symphony. If you know only one or just a few languages, the whole venture is a chore. Sandra, have you heard of Fortran?"

Sandra paused to wipe her lips and then answered.

"Yes, it was a popular mathematical language last century. A lot of physical scientists wrote code in it, but it wasn't very user friendly and it's not used much except for some legacy applications. I think the *For* part of the name derived from the word formula."

"Right. It was the programming language of choice among physicists. In fact, it was usually the only language they learned, although most were quite proficient in it. Well, there was a joke among the Computerati in those days that physicists would write a database in Fortran. Sure, you could do it, but it's the wrong language to use."

"I guess it's like using the right screwdriver for a screw," said Sandra.

Once the conversation got started, things mellowed a lot. They were a group of Computerati talking shop, with so many possible topics. Knowing that Sandra was driving, Michael ordered another beer.

11 HUBBUB

Sandra requisitioned a company car for the trip. Michael had spent the night at Sandra's, ostensibly for efficiency's sake, but the subtext was wonderful. They arrived at Basil's at about 8:00 AM. Michael was worried about Basil's physical state at that hour, but Basil sprung from the door as they pulled up, neatly dressed in a suit, looking for all the world as a genuine businessman. He was too cheerful and too awake for that hour, and Michael suspected a greater chemical augmentation than a strong cup of coffee.

Sandra decided that she would travel the secondary roads, rather than linking onto an interstate convoy. It was a beautiful day, and she argued that the scenery would be worth it. It had been so many years since the Intelligent Highway Vehicle System had been implemented on the interstates that there was rarely news of spectacular pile-ups that were common in the early days. All of them, of course, were attributed to computer error, but everyone knew it was an error on the part of a human who programmed the computer. Finally, there was a vast influx of government funding into methods of proving a program's correctness. Unfortunately, this money was channeled to mathematicians, keeping the Computerati away from the funding trough for a decade. In the end, it took a generation of Computerati to try to decode the mathematics into useful applications. The time lag was fortunate, since it allowed an advancement in hardware that added only 5% to vehicle cost, making the system universally affordable, then finally mandated.

Basil was in a talkative mood for the entire trip - another indication that he had medicated himself to get through the day. Basil's girth took about half the rear seat, but he never complained about lack of food. This was a rare opportunity for Michael to learn more about this complex person.

"Basil, any girlfriends in the wings?"

"Michael, we need to turn back! Basil forgot the stick he uses to beat them away! No, no girls now, but when Basil was younger, it was a different story. In the homeland, women admire men of intelligence much more than here. Here they want athletes. Basil is no athlete!"

"How did you get started in computers?"

"My older brother was an electrician - you know, light switches, that sort of stuff - but he repaired display screens and small electronic items part time. In such repairs, it's usually a switch that's bad, or a broken wire, so no complex knowledge is required. He would let Basil watch him, and when Basil was older, he would let Basil experiment with the pile of dead circuits in the back room. Basil would scan the components and run them though the global net to see what they did. Then Basil would wire them together to make gadgets. When Basil was introduced to coding in school, everything came together. It was what Basil was born to do! Basil was forced to do the math stuff to get ahead in school, didn't like it, but did it to get ahead. Then there was East Wodenstumpf, and here is where Basil is."

"Do you think you will ever pick up where you left off - I mean, continue with your Ph.D. and become a real Computerati?"

"A real Computerati! No disrespect to those present, but Basil is what a real Computerati should be! Basil is happy enough in his little office. That's all Basil needs."

Michael moved to sooth any rift. They needed Basil for this caper.

"Basil, no disrespect intended here either. After all, we're Computerati who need your help. You're one-up on us here."

"Sorry for the outburst, Michael, but Basil gets a lot of that sort of talk at Mother Wode. Sometimes Basil gets upset. Now Basil asks his own question. Are you two, how should I say, intermingled?"

Sandra laughed.

"Now that's a euphemism I hadn't heard before! Yes, we're intermingled, but it's a state secret. Haematite should never hear about it."

"Not to worry, Sandra. Basil is very good with secrets."

Sandra used the satellite system to navigate to their destination. It was good that she did, since the term, remote, did not do this place justice. Those who think the world is overly populated should travel a few tens of miles beyond their city limits to see how sparsely populated the world really is. The hub router building was situated atop a small hill accessible by a narrow road. The location was originally used as a repeater station for a cross-country microwave transmission system. The microwave systems were eventually replaced by fiber optic cables, but they were used as a backup to fiber for many years as a consequence of government paranoia. Then they were abandoned. In this case, this was a convenient piece of real estate with obvious security advantages that was interposed between some major population areas, so it became the home of a hub router for the global network.

Since they traveled the secondary roads, it was hard to estimate the travel time, and they arrived about fifteen minutes early. As Basil predicted, the location was fortified by a razor wire fence. The parking lot held six vehicles, so the estimated staff was indeed small. At least two of the staff were likely to be security guards, and the rest were technicians. One vehicle could have been that of the sales representative who was to meet them. They parked and walked towards the reception area, if that's what it could be called. It was actually a holding pen between a locked outer gate and the front door. A display flashed the image of a security guard somewhere inside the building. Sandra acted as spokesperson. She stated their business and introduced everyone. Basil got a combat promotion to "Doctor," so it was the three doctors making a house call. Sandra fed the coded invitation into the appropriate scanner slot. The guard confessed that the scanner was out of repair. He had requested to have it fixed weeks ago, but since it still acted as a deterrent in its present state, he wasn't too concerned. Also, the team looked like what he expected.

They were buzzed-in and escorted to folding chairs in a makeshift lounge that was half filled with electronic equipment. Basil's eyes widened as he surveyed some of the electronic antiques.

"Michael, I can't believe it! Have you ever seen a traveling wave tube? I thought these were only found in museums! Most of these contained a special platinum-cobalt magnet, so they were recycled when they went out of service. I wish my pockets were larger!"

Sandra frowned.

"Best behavior, both of you!" I don't want any trouble."

That is, any more trouble than what they had planned. The sales representative had yet to arrive, and the collection of magazines left much to be desired. These were likely left by previous visitors, most of whom must have been engineers, judging from the titles. One issue did catch Michael's interest - a popular computing magazine from his childhood. It was nostalgic scanning the ads and seeing some of the equipment that had littered his childhood bedroom.

After about fifteen minutes, someone entered the room, and they rose to greet him. The man apologized that he wasn't the person they were expecting. He was one of the technicians, and he was there because the makeshift lounge area served also as a coffee station. There was a rack of single-serving beverages and an ancient machine that mixed hot water with the package contents to produce a simulacrum of coffee, or tea if one preferred. He offered to make them some, but the aroma was not what they associated with good coffee, so they declined. Basil, seeing a chance to get some information, introduced himself and started a conversation. Much to Sandra's relief, the technician excused himself because of a pressing matter.

"We need to swap-out a flaky unit, or a sizable fraction of the little old ladies in the Eastern Locale might miss out on their mid-morning soap operas."

They all laughed, but Michael started to realize how essential these hubs were. In his university classes, they were just points in a diagram connected by lines, all very abstract and mathematical. In the real world, they shuttled messages from grandmas to grandkids and a plethora of video signals from one distant place to another. Only specialists knew how all these connections were made, but he had heard once that a message sent to the guy in the next office might go around the world to get to him. The network speed was so fast that it didn't matter.

Eventually, a man in a suit entered the room and introduced himself.

"You must be the team from Haematite! I'm Bob Smith. Sorry about my lateness. It's been a while since I was here last, and even with my automobile direction finder, one country road looks just like another.

Sandra, as usual, was their spokesperson.

"I'm Sandra Webb. No problem. We didn't wait that long, and we enjoyed catching up on our reading. This is Michael, and this is Basil. We're all Computerati, so forgive us if we ask too many questions and we can't keep our hands off the equipment. Especially Basil. He's our hardware guru. We'd be lost without him!"

Michael didn't know whether she had rehearsed this speech, but it was a perfect lead-in to their activities. Smith, eager for a sale, was all smiles.

"Let me show you our routers. This hub, as most, has a mix of models spanning quite a few years. Fortunately, our latest and fastest model has just been installed. You'll be impressed!"

Sandra replied.

"Yes, we've seen the specifications. I guess the specifications tell the real story, but there's nothing like seeing the real item, especially when it's priced about the same as a small condominium. It's a touchy-feely sort of thing."

Smith laughed.

"We give good discounts on quantity purchases. Judging from our experiences with Haematite in the past, you're not thinking of buying just a single router. We'll even give you credit for prior purchases of the same model made by any of your subsidiaries."

"We're just technical people. We can specify and recommend, we don't do any actual purchases, but I'm certain that a purchase agreement with mutual benefits would be easy to achieve by the proper parties."

Smith, who seemed to know his way around the hub, led them through a few short corridors and into a very large room. The room itself was very large, but the concentration of equipment was enormous. About 20% of the floor space off to one side was completely barren, except for a basketball hoop. Sandra was beginning to understand what Basil was telling her about the technicians' desire for privacy. She surmised that this area had been planned for future expansion, but the pace of router efficiency had been so great that the existing equipment space was adequate, as long as the newer models kept replacing the older ones. The room was very clean, but not well lighted.

"Sorry about the lighting. To save energy, they illuminate only the areas in which work is being done. They tried motion detection sensors to illuminate the working areas, but they didn't work as planned. Most of the work here involves sitting in back of a rack for very long periods of time, and the lights would turn themselves off. The technicians got tired of doing a little dance every five minutes to keep the lights on, so the motion sensors were deactivated. Wait here and I'll have one of the guys light up a few sections."

Smith went in search of one of the technicians, which gave the group some time to assess the situation. Sandra took the lead.

"Well, Basil, how does it look?"

"Wonderful! It's been a few years since Basil was in a hub, in his homeland, but that hub was quite primitive compared to this."

Sandra stopped him.

"Forget the hardware! I meant, will our mission play-out as planned!"

"Basil says not to worry. The space between racks is very narrow. One person at any one place at a time." He patted his stomach. "Basil may need to take a deep breath before he enters!"

Naturally, Basil was the least worried of the group, but now that they were finally inside, Michael was not as brave as he was in the planning stage. For Sandra's benefit he tried not to show it. Suddenly, the lights came on in one area of the room and Smith came walking back to them. Michael wondered whether Smith's face ached at night from all the obligatory smiling.

"I had them light a representative section with our newest model, and a few of the older ones. In this case, I trust that your interest in the older ones would be only for comparison purposes. Haematite generally orders the newest items. It doesn't pay to economize on routers when you're building a high speed network."

Smith led them through one of the wider corridors, and they stopped in front of a gleaming panel studded with a few flashing lights. At one corner was a small display with green characters on a black background with some alphanumeric information. The information was changing at a slow rate, but it probably indicated the state of some super fast processes happening behind the panel. Above the panel, at the top of its hosting rack, was a five digit code engraved into a plaque. The plaque seemed out of place. The other racks were also numbered, but typically with just a marker on a wide tape, or with marker alone. This particular rack must be special.

Smith proceeded with his sales pitch.

"What you see here is our newest router. It's so new, it's still on loan here for testing before final batch acceptance. There are hundreds of identical units being built as we speak, and they'll be shipped to this, and other hub locations, when we get final authorization. Of course, this acceptance testing is a mere formality. They'll find nothing wrong with the hardware, although they may require a few software tweaks. We're projecting tens of thousands of sales for this model alone."

This gave Michael an entrée into the conversation.

"Who, exactly, owns the hubs?"

"A lot of people assume it's a government operation, but it isn't - The hubs are too efficient for that!" Smith laughed.

"Then, there have always been some groups that are suspicious of too much government interference in communications - unlawful wiretapping, stuff like that. The hubs and the interconnections are owned by a private corporation, a consortium of users. The users are the large local network provides, but there are a few content providers in the mix just so they have a voice in decision-making."

"Since you mention it," said Sandra, "Have there been any recent stories about illegal wiretapping? I haven't heard of any, myself, but that's always a temptation for some over zealous government bureaucrats."

"Can't say I have. Sure, there are a lot of fringe groups out there who post accusations on the network, but my experience is that things like this hub router are completely secure. If there were any problems, it would need to be an inside job, and that's unlikely."

Yeah, thought Sandra, if only you knew why we're here! It was Michael's turn to fuel the conversation with Smith.

"About the software. We can modify the software to suit our needs? Would we have access to the source code, or would all changes need to be done through you?"

Smith wasn't at all disturbed by the question.

"What you ask is a very common question. As you know, the router code is not that large. It must be small to be fast. The size of the code is what troubles people. They think that something that small must be easy to write, but it's an uncommon skill to write such compact and fast code."

Basil made a muffled snorting sound, and Sandra gave him a sharp but stealthy nudge. Smith continued.

"Furthermore, and I'm sure you will understand this, there are security reasons why we don't let the code out of our hands. We can preload some translation tables for you, but if you need the code modified for a special purpose, we would need to do that for you."

Much to Sandra's consternation, Basil decided to speak.

"What about a blank box, just the hardware, with a hardware specification, so we could write the entire code ourselves."

"With suitable non-disclosure agreements - and with Haematite this would be no problem at all - it's possible to get a blank box. I don't need to tell you that it would be a major undertaking, starting from scratch, to devise a router code. It isn't recommended."

Before Basil could reply to this, Michael interjected.

"Can we see the rear panel connections?"

"Sure."

Smith led them down the long row of racks, around the corner, and to the rear of the rack they were just viewing. The corridor was cluttered with some miscellaneous pieces of equipment, some on wheeled carts, some on the floor, and one unit atop an adjacent rack. There were cables everywhere.

Basil peered inside and quickly stepped away. "Michael, I need to ask you something about our planned interface."

Michael excused himself and met Basil a few racks down. Seeing how they were alone together, Sandra started making small talk with Smith. In whispered speech, Michael asked, "Basil, what's up?"

"Michael, they're doing diagnostics on the new router."

"So?"

"They're using the same port Basil needs to use to access the code. It's a multi-purpose port. Basil can't unplug their cable to insert ours. They would know."

Michael felt weak in his knees.

"What do we do?"

"Basil needs to see an older router. This may be for the best. Perhaps this new router is too new to have had its code patched. An older router is sure to have the code changes we're looking for."

"Do you have some believable excuse? Smith has too many dollar signs in his eye for us to rebuff his newest baby that easily."

Basil thought for a moment, comparing in his mind's eye the external appearance of this newer router with some older units he had seen. Quite possibly, he had taken them apart and rebuilt them during a changing of the guard somewhere.

"We can zero in on the cooling. All these units are Peltier cooled on the inside with a heat pipe sticking out of the back to remove the heat. Users need to mate the heat pipe with a cold finger. It's their option how to cool the finger, but they still need to plumb to the finger. The new router seems to have an odd heat pipe location near the center of the rear panel. The older routers all had the pipe towards an edge. I think it's harder to plumb to the new router. Let's go with that."

Michael left Basil and walked towards Smith and Sandra, who were still engaged in polite conversation. Sandra saw him from the corner of her eye, but she couldn't read his face to see what may be happening. Michael joined them and waited for a break in the conversation to speak.

"Bob, Basil is impressed by your router, but he asked if we could view one of the older units. Basil's the hardware expert, so I don't quite understand what he's interested in, but he basically wants to see the different ways the hub people route their cooling lines, or something like that. He says that there's a big difference between the new router and the older ones."

Smith continued to smile.

"I can see I'm dealing with knowledgeable people! Yes, there is a difference, as he's noticed. Our engineers tried to pack as much performance as they could into a standard-sized box, and one compromise was how the cooling was implemented. As I was told, they needed to make the heat path to the panel as short as possible. As a consequence, the heat pipe - I think that's what it's called - goes directly to the rear panel without making any turns. The hub people here didn't have much of a problem with this, so you shouldn't either. But a picture is worth a thousand words! Call your friend over and we'll bring him to view one of the older routers."

Michael waved Basil over and Smith preceded them down the corridor, peering into the racks and finally selecting one about fifty feet down the line.

"I found one without too much clutter. These technicians can be pretty careless when stringing their connections. If it wasn't for the number bands on the cables, they would have no idea which line goes where."

Basil finally caught up with them, peered inside the rack, and gave Michael a quick smile. That was Michael's cue to distract Smith.

"Bob, while Basil is getting an eyeful here, do you have any glossy photos or simplified diagrams you could share with us? We need to sell this idea to our management, and they need to see more visuals than just columns of numbers on a display."

"Yes," said Sandra. "Perhaps we could move into a wider and better lighted corridor, so we can see what we're doing!"

"An excellent idea," said Smith, as he led the way. Sandra breathed a short sigh of relief. The game is afoot!

12 MAN DUC CORP.

The trip back was uneventful. Basil had no problem accessing the hub data. As he had promised, the entire interface took just a half a minute, aided by both his skill and the compact nature of the code. The busy day had depleted Basil's supposed chemical booster, and he was starting to fade. Michael expected that a little nervous exhaustion was there also, but a tough guy like Basil would never admit it.

When Sandra and Michael dropped Basil at his apartment, Basil first made certain that his magic pencil was still in his pocket, and then he told them that he would call when he had something to report. Michael's guess was that Basil would stay in bed for the next twenty four hours to get his schedule back into synchronization. Sandra, too, was tired, and she dropped Michael at his apartment rather than suggesting he spend the night at her place. It was just as well, since there was a message from Sterba asking for a progress report in the morning. This meant that Michael had to first make progress, then write a report, by the morning. It was going to be a long night.

Michael decided that it would be best if he gave his progress report to Sterba in person, to get immediate feedback, so he pulled himself out of bed fairly early in the morning and drove to Mother Wode. If Sterba wasn't around, he planned to just slide the report under his door to indicate he had been there. When he arrived, Sterba was in his office and he was surprisingly cheerful. Sterba had just heard that his next grant had come through, so his near term goal was to boost Michael out the door, Ph.D. in hand, to make room for the next apprentice.

Sterba had organized an examination committee, and Michael's dissertation defense was penciled in for a Thursday at the end of the next month. Things were moving fast, but as Michael continued to get involved at Haematite, and also with Sandra, he was looking forward to this culmination of his years of research. Sterba would never admit it, but the defense was a mere formality. Michael did owe a debt to Sterba for pushing and polishing him to the point at which his Ph.D. was nearly anticlimactic.

Since he hadn't had any breakfast, Michael decided to get an early lunch. The lure of Wode's End and a Wodeburger was too much for him to resist. After all, there seemed to be cause for celebration. In a number of weeks less than he could count on his fingers, he would have his Ph.D. If you counted just the years of his formal schooling, this event was at least twenty years in the making, although Michael was certain that if educators employed just a little more optimization, an equivalent preparation could be reduced to about sixteen. Historically, there had been a few child prodigies with Ph.D. in hand in their early teen years.

Most people ascribed these feats to exceptional intellectual prowess, but Michael thought that these prepared minds accelerated their education by merely bypassing formal instruction with independent study. You don't learn much munching cookies in kindergarten.

On his way to Wode's End, Michael ran into Robin, another Ph.D. candidate, who had started at the same time as Michael. Michael and Robin had dated a few times, but nothing much came from that, so they remained just friends throughout their years at Mother Wode. It was likely that a romance didn't blossom because they were so young when they first met, and they each had their own professional ambitions. In retrospect, she was probably the female version of Michael, and that should have been enough to end the deal right there.

Robin didn't seem to be in a hurry to get anywhere. Like Michael, her schedule was set by her own deadlines and not by any classes she needed to attend. She was fiercely independent, and at one time she dropped a course in which she excelled just a week before its end because of some remark her professor had made. Robin and Michael didn't part under a similar circumstance, but perhaps it would have been just a matter of time before something like that happened. Michael was happy that it didn't, since he valued Robin's friendship.

"Robin, I'm on my way to Wode's End, and I have some news. It's a little early, but can I offer you some lunch, or some coffee?"

"The news must be good for you to offer a free lunch! Then again, you're a working Computerati, now. Haematite, isn't it?"

"Yeah, Haematite. Of course, that was locked in stone from my first day here. I've been there part time for a few weeks now. Interesting work, although not exactly what I expected. It's fairly unstructured, not at all like at Mother Wode, where Sterba tells me what to do."

"What did you expect? To be chained to a chair in front of a display eight or ten hours a day with a task list taped to your forehead? Computerati are professionals. We set our own goals and directions. We're still scientists, after all. When I've graduated, I'll demand no less from my employer!"

Ah, Robin. Always the activist. In an earlier day she would have been occupying the student center or doing pickets in front of the administration building. But all that is what made Robin, Robin.

"You're right, we are professionals, at least as professional as the lawyers. They're treating me really well, and I enjoy the companionship of my coworkers."

Michael pluralized coworker as a defense mechanism. Perhaps he had associated with Basil too long.

"OK. I'll accept your invitation, but the joke's on you. Not just coffee for me. I'm famished! Expect a big bill, at least as far as "big" goes at the End."

Michael ordered the Wodeburger and fries. For Robin, famished just meant a large salad. She was thin and exquisitely formed, which is what attracted Michael to her so many years ago. They were older now, but the years had been very kind to her. She might even pass as an undergraduate.

Robin tossed her salad about in the bowl for a few seconds and then asked, "So, Michael, what's the good news? Getting married now that you have a job?"

Michael laughed.

"No, nothing like that! After all, you spoiled me for all other women, didn't you?"

"I'm glad we can joke about it. I value your friendship. Honestly, I wasn't that good, and neither were you."

Michael laughed, again. One thing he liked about Robin is that she made him laugh, although sometimes it was at his own expense.

"OK. Here's the scoop. Sterba is finally pushing me out the door. My defense is scheduled for late next month."

She stood at her seat, bent across the narrow table, and kissed him on the cheek.

"Congratulations!"

"Thanks. It was a lot of work. In retrospect, the time seemed to fly."

"Sterba may have worked you hard, but it was all in your best interest. Often, I wish I had been apprenticed under Sterba. My research program is nearly stalled. Danforth isn't well organized. We'll latch onto some fringe topic, play with it for a while, and not even get a publishable paper. I'm sure if I stick with it, I'll get my degree by default, even without any spectacular results. Danforth still has a lot of clout in the department. I just hope he doesn't retire, or have a stroke, or something like that."

"Yeah. The old guy must have been something in his day, but things move so fast in our field. Actually, they move too fast in general."

Robin sighed.

"I agree. Maybe I should have followed in my mother's footsteps and became a news presenter." Robin struck a pose that revealed her comely face and a profile of her bust, pushed out just a little for emphasis. "What do you think?"

"I would believe anything you said, and I speak for the entire male demographic."

They chit-chatted through lunch and went their separate ways. Every time he saw Robin he always wondered what might have been. It was always hard to put those thoughts out of his mind.

Michael didn't make it to Haematite until well after lunch, but he had e-mailed Sandra the night before about his Sterba meeting, so she didn't expect him for lunch or any other time of day. When Michael finally arrived, he found her in her office, editing a manuscript before publication. He certainly wasn't going to mention anything about Robin.

"Michael, you're finally here. Banker's Hours, but you aren't a banker. What a life."

"It'll get worse, but then much better."

Michael filled her in about the meeting with Sterba, and the scheduled defense.

"That's great! Now we have a genuine excuse for a party! Let me show you what I've been doing while you were away."

Sandra led Michael into her laboratory and popped some items onto the display screen. He noticed that the white boards were filled with diagrams and equations in her handwriting, but they were interspersed with some comments in another person's hand.

"I dragged Lanczos in here for a critiquing session this morning."

"Who's Lanczos?"

"Oh yeah, you don't know about Lanczos. He was a long time Haematite Computerati who retired a few years ago. He still enjoys coming to work now and again to keep his mind sharp. They even issued him a special ID badge that still gives him unfettered access after his retirement. It's either an honor, or a way for Haematite to extract some free work. I found him in the hallway and dragged him here. A really sharp guy. I didn't tell him about the hub router, but we went over the network architecture, and he showed..." pointing to the white boards "...that we can get away with fewer routers if we use a combined star-ring architecture. It works because the network is relatively small. I'm running some simulations, now."

They discussed some improved simulations, and Michael went to work on the code. He was amazed that even as developed as computing was, it was still difficult to transcribe something that took just a few minutes to outline on a white board into useful code. He was in his usual coder trance-like state when Basil rang him on the transceiver.

"Michael, this is Basil. Basil has some information on our problem."

"OK. Shoot."

"Hasn't Michael learned anything from Basil in the past few days! You come here to Mother Wode. Basil will discuss things only in private."

"Can I bring Sandra?"

"Basil enjoys her company. Yes, and bring a check! Ha, joking! That can wait."

Michael located Sandra, who was ready to quit for the day as well, and she was as curious about the results as Michael. She volunteered to drive, and within a half hour they were standing at the entrance to Basil's office. This was Sandra's first experience with Basil's office, so she stood there silently for a few seconds, building the courage to enter.

"Michael, Sandra, enter, enter! Basil would offer a chair and refreshments, but you can see that no chairs are available. Let's find an empty classroom. Basil will disable all the vid links, just in case. Basil is always careful."

Basil led the two up a fire stairway to a small classroom on the second floor. With a few careful pulls, he disconnected the video link equipment and microphones. He was so facile at this task, it seemed that he had done this before, possibly for monthly meetings of some secret society of hackers. He arranged three chairs in a circle, pulled a wad of papers from his shirt pocket, and motioned for them to sit.

"Basil wrote some routines to help in the analysis of the hub router table. The object here was to filter the proper links from any improvised links in the destination field. The links are obviously just numbers in the table with no clue to what they are. You read 130.132.51.8 from the table and wonder what that is. You need to do a reverse look-up. Basil coded the look-up into his analysis routines, so you see that that 130.132.51.8 is really Mother Wode. The table links should always point to important government destinations and other hub routers. When you find some that don't, these are the ones you need to question."

"First, there are a lot of links! Even Basil was surprised. Too many to search by eye. Once again, analysis code to the rescue. Basil programmed a Bayesian Filter to sort the probably valid addresses from the suspect ones. Here's what you have."

Basil showed them a page with two columns. The first was labeled source, and the second, destination. The source column was an apparently random collection of corporations, banks and other financial institutions. The destination addresses were all to the same. Basil pointed for emphasis.

"Man_Duc_Corp. Sounds Chinese, doesn't it? Wrong! The Man_Duc_Corp address resolves to a region served by a hub router in Pennsylvania. Basil did a fine traceroute that puts it in Ardmore, Pennsylvania, near Philadelphia."

Sandra wrinkled her face. "OK. So... we search for information about Man_Duc_Corp - Dunn & Bradstreet, government records, that sort of stuff. Did you do a Whois and a general directory search."

"The Whois record is locked, but that's a common measure for small companies nowadays. Hijacks are common - Basil knows! A directory search gives nothing. But here's the real surprise. Basil did a general search on the network, and he got no results. There is no information about Man_Duc_Corp anywhere on the network. A search for Basil - at least this Basil - gives no results, but Basil needed to do a little creative erasure here and there to make that possible. Basil doesn't like to be traced!"

"Do you think that this Man_Duc_Corp has purposely hidden itself," said Michael.

"That's what Basil thinks. Even a two year old child has multiple hits on a search."

"OK," said Sandra, "I'll have Haematite do a D&B on the name. If it's a corporation, there must be a physical record. It's just a few hundred dollars."

Michael had his own theory.

"It might be a government front. You know, the spies in the back room of the tailor shop."

"If that's the case, they would front with a perfectly legitimate business, so this doesn't make sense. Hiding themselves just makes them more suspicious."

"Yes, if you knew they existed in the first place. As Basil said, they're invisible."

"Let's see what the D&B shows."

Michael didn't see how this would help.

"What will we do when we locate this Man_Duc_Corp? Knock on their door and ask them to stop? This seems like pretty serious business. How could they keep such a thing from the government? It must be a government front."

"We'll decide when we have more information," said Sandra. "If it is the government, it might not be prudent to blow the whistle on this. We may need to fabricate some excuse for Haematite to discontinue the project."

Basil reconnected the optical links. It may have been Michael's imagination, but it looked as if he was wiping his fingerprints from the connections. They exited the classroom and went their separate ways, Basil back to his dungeon, Sandra and Michael to her condominium.

It was simple enough for a large corporation like Haematite to obtain a Dunn & Bradstreet report, but Sandra needed to go through the proper corporate channels. Not surprisingly, all such requests went to the sales department, and when Sandra approached them, she was deluged with questions about the reason for her request. Sandra's cover story was that she had heard that Man_Duc_Corp had purchased the type of router Haematite was considering for its phantom network, and she needed the information before approaching them with technical questions. About a hour later, a secretary in sales rung her up to tell her that she must have misspelled the name, since the search came up blank. A wildcard search for similar names gave a few hits, but none of those looked remotely like the target. Sandra thanked her for her efforts and said she would recheck her source of the information. She looked at Michael and said, "Where do we go from here?"

"To Basil, of course."

Sandra's face dropped. Apparently, another round with Basil didn't catch her immediate fancy.

"I think we should cool down for a few days. This cloak and dagger stuff is taking too much time, and I'm starting to feel drained. Let's get away, together, for a few days. I have some vacation time, and you - you're still on a student's perpetual vacation!"

"Well, Sterba's been in a good mood. I'll tell him that something came up at work and I needed to travel."

Sandra rubbed her body against his for a few seconds.

"Now you won't even need to lie to Sterba. From what I can tell, something has come up at work."

13 THE CAPE

Sandra knew of a quiet group of seaside cottages in Dennisport, Cape Cod. Many of these cottages were available on a moment's notice, since most couples and families gravitated to the air conditioned hotel complexes in the same area. Roughing it was a nice concept, but modern people must have their air conditioning and wide screen video panels! Michael, an habitual office-dweller, had grown accustomed to air conditioned comfort in the summer, but Sandra told Michael not to worry - the sea was nature's air conditioning. They eschewed public transport and drove the 2-1/2 hour trip in Sandra's car so they would have a vehicle for the many excursions she had planned while they were there.

The ride was pleasant enough. They were locked into the interstate IHVS for about eighty percent of the trip and dropped out into manual navigation only when they entered the Cape. The absence of automobile autopilot on the Cape was not because the Cape was a technological backwater. It was mainly because most traffic on the Cape was local. Aside from the high-rise hotel complexes and the highways required to populate these with tourists, there had been a valiant effort to preserve the rustic splendor of the entire region. Venturing off one of the main arteries by only a quarter mile put you onto narrow roadways with broad, sandy shoulders, speckled only occasionally with hardy grasses.

After they had registered and dumped their luggage inside their room, it was time for lunch. Michael had noticed a small diner a short distance from their motel as they were driving, so they decided to walk the sandy shoulder of the roadway to their meal. The restaurant, it was claimed, was started by a retired fishing boat captain who enjoyed eating fish as much as catching them. There was an oil painting of this character, in full maritime regalia, positioned at the inner entrance to welcome his guests from beyond the grave - as stipulated in his will that passed the establishment to other family members.

Sandra, always the light eater, ordered a small seafood salad with dressing on the side. She never used the dressing, but she found that this type of order ensured that she got what she wanted more often than when she ordered a salad without dressing. Michael ordered fried clams in a basket and a bowl of Quahog clam chowder.

The Quahog clam had been driven almost to extinction by the combination of over-harvesting and the nearly imperceptible changes in ocean chemistry that had progressed for decades. The occasional brown tide of toxic algae didn't help. The environmental movement had brought the Quahog and many other species back from the brink in just a decade, although the warmer oceans still limited their numbers.

They were waiting for their orders, and this gave Michael a chance to ask a question that bothered him for most of their journey to the Cape.

"You were at the Cape before. Were you alone, or with someone?"

"Michael, I must confess that in my youth I was not as chaste as I led you to believe. In fact, it was a different man nearly every weekend. I think it was two college men at the same time in the same cottage we've just rented."

"No, seriously."

"Oh, but I am serious." Sandra struck a pose. "Men can't resist me. It's a curse, but I've grown to live with it."

She laughed, and so did Michael.

"When I first started work at Haematite, it was quite a shock. I enjoyed the California lifestyle while working at Tressor, and suddenly I was deposited in a backwater rural village."

Michael objected, "East Wodenstumpf is not a backwater rural village. It's one of the largest cities in the state. Not only is it home to Mother Wode, but it's home to many corporate headquarters, Haematite included."

"So, I exaggerate a little. Well, it was a shock, and I was alone. Surprisingly, one of the things I missed the most was the ocean. I never really thought about it while I was in California, but the ocean defines the California lifestyle. Surfer boys, bikini chicks, the whole works. I saw ads for the Cape, decided that one ocean is as good as any other, and I came to Dennisport for a long weekend. I enjoyed it so much, I've come here at least once each summer while at

Haematite. You haven't seen much of the place, yet, but I'm sure you'll enjoy it as much as I."

Michael smiled.

"Probably much more, since I'm with you."

He was prepared for a cynical reprise from Sandra, but their waitress interrupted by placing their lunch on the table. The clam chowder was buttery, full of huge clam pieces and evenly cooked potato cubes. It was excellent. Michael wondered whether he could ever eat Manhattan-style clam chowder again. The fried clams were tender, quite unlike the item by the same name at Wode's End. Michael gave the waitress a good tip, and he gave the Captain a thumbs-up as they left the restaurant.

After an few hour's rest in their room, the pair decided to take to the roads and act like tourists. Their first stop was at a roadside salt water taffy stall. Michael knew from reading the Sunday Supplement as a child that there was no salt water in salt water taffy. He supplemented his meager education about taffy by reading the descriptive cards stacked on the counter top. He learned that salt water taffy had originated in New Jersey in resorts along the Atlantic sea coast, but most of it was manufactured and sold in Cape Cod, perhaps because the Cape had blossomed into a more popular tourist destination. The recent hurricanes and persistent pollution had taken its toll on the seacoast of the Garden State. Michael had never encountered so many flavors in a single type of candy, including the venerable jelly bean; and when it came time to weigh his goody bag, his enthusiasm was quite apparent.

Other roadside attractions were the variously named Christmas stores. Whoever first thought that people would enjoy buying Christmas merchandise in the heat of summer must have been laughed out of his business class reunion. His revenge, of course, had been the piles of money his unique venture had made. This type of business had been aided by the rampant secularization of the holiday into a year-end festival extending from Halloween through to New Year's Day. The origin of the holiday was lost amid the snowmen, Santas, reindeer, and the beeping cash registers.

After viewing various specialty stores, mostly looking and never buying, it was time for dinner. Sandra suggested that they look for a restaurant built onto a pier extending into the ocean. There they could dine outside, literally on the ocean. They found some candidates on the display in Sandra's car, and Michael suggested the expensive one with the prettiest photos. This went against Sandra's skeptical nature. Her gaze gravitated to the middle price range, and she located a small restaurant that had an outside dining area on the water very close to where they were.

"We don't want just to be on the water. We want a cozy place without too many people."

The restaurant was as Sandra had pictured it in her mind's eye. There was no bar, which definitely reduced the number of customers. Neither Sandra nor Michael were big drinkers, so this didn't bother them at all. The server staff, who all looked as if they were college students doing their summer jobs, were quite cheerful. These young kids liked the money; and unlike professional staff, they had higher ambitions away from the restaurant after their three months of working were finished.

After dinner, Sandra and Michael lingered over coffee on the deck overlooking the ocean, but as the sun went down, the temperature started to plummet and the sea breeze picked up. It was time to call it a night.

They had left the patio doors open slightly as they went to bed, but the chill overcame Michael sometime in the middle of the night, and he closed them. He remembered Sandra's comment about "nature's air conditioning," and he was now a firm believer. As he closed the doors, he looked out at the ocean, still visible because of moonlight, and he knew why people were attracted here, year after year. The only sound was the gentle pounding of the waves. Absent were the distant vibrations of heavy traffic on the motorways and the occasional noise from local vehicles. Although the moon offered sufficient light to walk about at night, there was no one to be seen. It was an oasis of peace in a busy world.

Sandra awoke as first light was breaking through the windows. She showered and dressed, and then prodded Michael to do the same. The incentive of a pancake breakfast finally drove him to action. After breakfast, at Sandra's request, they drove to Hyannis Port for a boat ride. Unlike its similarly named neighbors, Hyannis Port was an actual port that serviced a wide variety of small water craft, fishing boats, a few touring boats, and ferries to the nearby Nantucket and Martha's Vineyard islands.

Sandra wanted them to take a one hour tour boat ride. Michael confessed that, although he wasn't afraid of the water, he had been in a boat only a few times before, canoes and row boats at a youth camp lake. He had never been out on the ocean.

"It's just a bus without wheels! The shoreline is always visible, and you can tell by all the electronic gizmos on the roof that it's perfectly safe. You'll be fine."

Aside from a refreshing ride along the coast, the tour didn't involve much more than viewing the Kennedy

Compound, which contained the summer White House of John Kennedy and the residence of his brother, former Massachusetts Senator Edward Kennedy. They didn't go too near to the shore, either because of the need to stay within a deep water channel, or for privacy and security reasons. They were told that "Ted" Kennedy enjoyed the sea, and his boat, a fifty-foot schooner called The Mya, now sat in a nearby maritime museum. Michael enjoyed the tour, and he was happy that Sandra convinced him to go.

Since the day was still young, Sandra suggested a trip all the way to the tip of the Cape, to Provincetown. There would be an opportunity for them to stop for lunch somewhere along the way. At Orleans, the mid-Cape Highway terminated in a roundabout before transforming into a more narrow road. The narrow road was an indication that they were leaving the majority of the commerce areas behind. Sandra, who was at the wheel, decided they would bail out there for lunch, and she went full circle around the roundabout and doubled back onto the main road.

There was no mistaking which direction they should take, since there was a raft of signs for various restaurants pointing in a single direction. Sandra, quite out of character, turned into the parking lot of a rather stately inn which was established, if the sign could be believed, in 1875. This was apparently not her first visit here, since her comment as they exited the car was, "Pricey, but wonderful!" She was right on both counts. After lunch, they continued to Provincetown. There was not much scenery - just sand and scrub grass - for the longest time, until they reached their destination.

Provincetown had been an Art Colony during the last century. Art Colony was apparently a code word for a gay commune in those days, and as time went on the artists came fully out of the closet. Provincetown became a gay tourist resort, and its isolated location kept the inhabitants safely away from anyone who might object to their lifestyle. When the tip of the Cape was nearly destroyed by a hurricane that vastly reshaped its boundaries, religious extremists said it was a judgment of God upon them, much like AIDS had been many decades ago. But Provincetown survived and thrived, and it was still the main art center in the region.

Sandra enjoyed browsing the various small art shops. Michael noticed, not surprisingly, that most of the items were paintings and photographs of beaches, the sea, ships at sea, and lighthouses. Lighthouses had outlived their usefulness, but many were still maintained as tourist Meccas. Satellite positioning systems had rendered them redundant quite a few years ago. Perhaps in another hundred years, space-faring tourists would visit the still-orbiting global positioning satellites much as earth-bound tourists visited these lighthouses. Michael tried not to act too bored as Sandra waded through such "art." What a man won't do out of love!

It had grown quite late, and Sandra and Michael were both tired. They decided to forgo a heavy restaurant meal and dine, instead, at the old captain's diner they had enjoyed on their first day. The captain didn't disappoint. Michael decided that the Quahog clam chowder would be too heavy for that time of day, so he and Sandra both ordered the iceberg lettuce and seafood salad, dressing on the side.

They arose early the next morning to take a sunrise stroll on the beach. It was low tide, the beach extended far into the ocean, and it was littered with a wide variety of sea shells. As the sun rose, they could see a few large ships near the horizon, a safe distance away from the just barely visible wind turbines that supplied the majority of electrical power to the Cape. Unseen, but supplying most of the Cape's remaining power, were the vast underwater turbines generating electricity from the tides.

Michael, pointed to the wind turbines and said, "I guess that technology is so well integrated into life that we hardly notice it anymore. Zoning laws, at least, protect us from the worst visual offenses, and environmental laws have protected the other senses. Walking here, on the beach, makes you feel quite independent of artificial enhancements of our lifestyle, like we don't need any of it."

"Sort of like Rousseau's Natural Man."

"Sandra, I must confess I'm not as well read as you."

"Michael, don't worry. Rousseau's a little distant from computing, but you did study the history of computing in school, didn't you?"

"Just a few chapters in the usual introductory course, many years ago. Whirlwind, Eniac... stuff like that."

"Computer history is one of my hobbies. Have you ever heard of Vannevar Bush?"

"The name sounds familiar. Then again, who could forget a name like that! I don't remember why he's famous."

"He pioneered analog computers. Not the electronic analog computers, but the mechanical ones with motors, shafts and gears. They filled entire rooms! All that stuff was forgotten when electronic integrated circuits took over, but it was a big deal at the time."

"He would be surprised to hear that our best computers now are once again analog and mechanical, although they don't really move all that much, and they're too small to see. Why do you mention him?"

"He used to vacation at the Cape, not far from where we are, at South Dennis. His wife's family owned some land there. His family was originally from Provincetown. Maybe he got some of his best ideas looking out at the ocean, like we're doing now. There's nothing more analog than a bunch of water."

"So, why do you know so much about this guy? Was he an inspiration in your student days?"

"No. During one of my earlier visits to the Cape, I stumbled upon a plaque. It was a *George Washington Slept Here* type of plaque, but it said *Computer Pioneer, Vannevar Bush*, so I looked him up. Interesting guy."

They spent most of that last day in love-making in their room, capped by a sunset walk along that same beach. The next day, it was a quick pancake breakfast, followed by the several hour's drive back to "civilization." Michael thought that the Cape lifestyle was more civilized than what they were returning to, but he hadn't been at the Cape in the winter, and he still needed to work.

14 NEXT STEP

Michael was refreshed from his Cape Cod interlude with Sandra, and he was relieved when he found that there wasn't a flood of messages from Sterba. It was time again to settle down to business as usual, and that meant another trip to Basil.

Basil was hunched over his display screen in his typical pose. He greeted Michael as he entered.

"Hello, Michael! Any news about Daffy-Corp?"

"If Daffy-Corp is our code word for Man_Duc_Corp, then nothing. Dun and Bradstreet came up nil, which is very unusual, unless it's a really small operation. Sandra reasons that a government front would operate as a legitimate business and there would be a D&B entry. All this stealth stuff is confusing. I'm here to entertain suggestions."

"Ah, Basil is always entertaining - and easily entertained. Basil has given this some thought, and what Basil proposes to do will be fun. Michael, Sandra and Basil will do some cloak and dagger stuff - less the dagger part."

The hub router exploit was stressful enough, and Michael had reached his limit on what he would do in the name of science, or for Haematite's mighty dollar.

"Basil, neither Sandra nor I will break into any building! Sure, I have a scientist's curiosity about all this, and I'll bend the law a little, like we did at the hub router, but I won't break the law, if only for the threat that Sandra would break my neck."

Basil laughed.

"Sandra's too gentle a woman for any of that - she would probably hire someone to do it for her! But not to worry, Basil has a plan..."

They met that evening at Miguel's so Basil could brief Sandra on his proposed next step. Since this was Basil, most of his dinner was eaten before he started to talk.

"Sandra, did Michael outline Basil's plan for you?"

"No, Basil, he didn't. He was certain I would strangle him, but he wasn't that concerned if I strangled you, instead."

"Ha! Sandra, Basil always enjoys your company at dinner!"

"So, what's your plan?"

Basil chewed the remainder of his mouthful, wiped his face with a napkin, and began.

"I suggest a reconnaissance of Daffy Duck."

Sandra blanched.

"As if the hub thing wasn't stressful enough, you want us to ring their front door bell? At least with the hub router we had a plausible cover story. There's no such cover for any reconnaissance of Man_Duc_Corp. We aren't even supposed to know it exists!"

"Perhaps reconnaissance was a poor choice of words. Basil is not a native speaker. Basil would like to do some electronic eavesdropping on their location, all done at a distance. No chance of detection."

"This isn't wiretapping, is it?" asked Sandra. "I seem to remember that wiretapping is illegal."

Basil grinned.

"Not to worry. No wires involved! This is more like listening to music on your radio. Of course, it would be Basil's radio. No one would need to leave the car."

It was time for Michael to mediate.

"OK. Here's how I see it. We're at a dead end with Daffy Corp, or whatever we're calling it, and Basil has a way to move forward. He assures us that there is very little risk, less risk than at the hub router. There are no charades. In fact, we stay inside a car at all times. If questioned, we're respected professionals who got lost during a sightseeing trip. I'm sure Basil is skilled enough to make certain that there will be no physical evidence. Right, Basil?"

"Basil, as you know, is always careful. There will be no problems."

Sandra stared into her water glass for a long moment.

"So, less risk than our hub router exploit?"

"Yes," said Basil.

"Well, I signed on for that adventure, so why not this one? My scientific curiosity has gotten the better of me. We'll do it, mostly because I trust Michael's judgment. You say that the Man_Duc_Corp server's location is in a suburb of Philadelphia? I'll think of some cover story for a trip."

The next day, Sandra sent a message to Lanczos asking him to recommend a network expert in the Philadelphia area. She explained that she would be there on an errand,

and she wanted to make good use of her time. Lanczos responded almost immediately that an acquaintance of his, a Professor Shatinski was at the University of Pennsylania, not to be confused with Penn State, and he would send him a message of introduction. He didn't think that Shatinski would require any payment for a casual visit. Professors are always glad to harangue corporate visitors, since it might lead to future work.

The next day, Sandra received a message from Shatinski with an outline of his schedule for the next few weeks, and inviting her to make an appointment. He hoped that one of his free days would overlap with her planned visit to Philadelphia.

Sandra booked Shatinski for early Monday morning, four days hence, and simultaneously submitted a travel plan for a trip to Philadelphia for Michael and her. She didn't reference the fact that Basil would tag along. Three could travel as cheaply as two, especially since Michael and she would share one hotel room, leaving the other open for Basil. She entered a reasonable excuse for the trip, although whatever happened during the visit with Shatinski would be inconsequential. They would travel to Philadelphia on Sunday by public transport and stay two nights in the hotel. The cost of the trip was minimal, so no red flags would be raised at Haematite. They would meet with Shatynski on Monday morning, leaving the afternoon and evening free for their Man_Duc_Corp reconnaissance.

Sandra found Michael in his office, and she outlined the travel plans. She reminded him that Basil needed to be ready at their planned departure time, which was 1:00 PM Sunday. He would need to synchronize his sleeping schedule a little, but he would have about two hours to sleep on the train if he wanted.

"There's one other problem."

"What's that?"

"We need to think of something to discuss with Shatinski. Our cover story"

Michael thought for a second.

"What about that star-ring topology that Lanczos described. Are we really sure that's optimum?"

"Hmmm... Our simulations show that it's better than our original architecture, but maybe it's not the best. That sounds like a good talking point. I'm sure Shatinski's eyes will light up, since it's the type of topic that might lead to some consulting money for him. Let's go armed with a ream of simulation data to make it appear that's our intent."

Sandra left, and Michael spent the better part of the next few hours organizing some graphics that described network topologies and summarizing the simulations. It was time for lunch. Sandra had a business luncheon with another colleague, so Michael decided to travel to Mother Wode for lunch at Wode's End. After lunch, he hoped to find Basil in his office. He would advise Basil of the particulars of the Philadelphia trip, and make certain he had whatever electronic equipment he needed.

Michael also needed to learn the physical location of the Man_Duc_Corp server. He decided it would be best to commit it to memory, possibly with reference to some landmarks and major streets, so there wouldn't be any physical evidence. Some of Basil's caution was beginning to rub off on him, and he realized that things would get more dangerous as they proceeded. Was it a government operation? Some organized crime thing? Either way, he was worried they were letting their curiosity get the better of them, but it did seem far less risky than the hub router adventure. They were becoming veterans at this.

The campus was quiet. It was between semesters, most students were away, and many faculty and staff were taking summer vacation. Michael was able to linger for a time at Wode's End after taking his recently regular, unhealthy luncheon fare, to draw up a rough schedule of activities leading to his Ph.D. defense. Not only did he need to make certain that all the necessary paper work was completed on time, but he had to sandwich-in his Haematite work and these extracurricular adventures that centered on solving the Man_Duc_Corp mystery. There were extracurriculars involving Sandra, but those were not to be scheduled. They were rather to be accepted as often as the opportunity presented itself.

He took his time walking to the computer building. He wasn't certain that Basil would have arrived even at this late hour, so there was no need for speed. He even stopped to read some of the notices posted on the central bulletin board. Network posting had made some inroads in campus communications, but it was always hard to separate the wheat from the chaff. Search, even with intelligent agents such as those Michael programmed, was all too easily gamed by complementary computer countermeasures. A colored sheet of paper, often illustrated with a cartoon figure, still grabbed attention. Perhaps students were overloaded with the electronic buzz of daily life and sought refuge in these little oases of manual communication.

Most of the posted notices were for rides, either wanting or offering. The public transport system in the Eastern Locale was excellent as a result of the government-sponsored build-out of the past few decades. The problem was that it connected only major population centers. Most cities smaller than East Wodenstumpf were still quite a way off route. For most students, East Wodenstumpf was the largest city they had visited, and their hometowns were well off the beaten track.

Tutoring services were the next most advertised item. The proliferation of online tutorials had not diminished the effectiveness of one-on-one communication. Michael had never required a tutor, but he had made some money tutoring other students in some of the more abstruse computing topics. He found that teaching a subject increased his own understanding of it, and that was probably the reason why professors seemed to be so smart. Facts repeated year after year would likely be remembered.

He arrived at Wode's End ahead of most of the luncheon crowd. The few students who were on campus had likely just had breakfast. Some of them were keeping Basil's hours. After having the great seafood fare at the Cape, Michael found it hard to order his usual Wodeburger and fries. Scanning the posted menu, he decided that a tuna salad sandwich might be worth a try. It was served with a half-sour pickle, and it wasn't half bad. He lingered over his sandwich and coffee, since he knew there was no need to rush to see Basil so early in the day. After lunch, he decided to make a stop at his university office to check his messages and organize a few things.

As he reached the lobby area, he was surprised to see Basil there, pondering some selections at the vending machines. Breakfast?

"Basil, I'm here to make final arrangements for our Philadelphia trip and see if there's anything you need."

"Michael, Basil is prepared. But let's go to Basil's office to talk." Basil looked around. There was no one else in the lobby, since the university was fairly deserted at this time of year. Still, Basil moved towards his office, and Michael followed.

When they arrived, Michael was surprised to see that his papers were somewhat more organized than usual. Michael waved his hands around the office.

"Basil, trying to impress some girl? This place looks halfway decent."

"Two things, Michael. First, there was a fire marshal who inspected the building last week and pointed out that papers can't be stacked within two feet of the ceiling."

"Two feet? Even when the ceiling is concrete, like yours? Talk about the letter, but not the spirit of the law. So that's why you cleaned up?"

"Well, no sense in antagonizing a government man. Basil doesn't want too many follow-up questions. But this was not the only reason, Michael. Basil needed to find some technical information for our trip. This is stuff you won't find on a network server. Basil's private archives. It took a little while to find it. Basil is not that good with the filing systems."

"OK. So, you're all set with your electronic gizmos, whatever they are, but I still need to know the physical location of the Man_Duc_Corp server. How close do you have that?"

"Very close. Fortunately, the high speed network links are sparse in that area. Basil has it located to within a city block. That's all Basil needs."

Michael frowned.

"A city block? Are you sure that's good enough?"

"Basil studied the satellite images. Not too many buildings there. Should not be a problem."

"Basil, can you get us there without any maps? I don't want to have any evidence laying around if we're stopped."

"Not to worry, Michael, Basil can get us there." Basil tapped his head. "Basil keeps many secrets here, and this is just another. And Basil has a special memory technique. Basil uses restaurants as landmarks!"

"Yeah, turn left at the Thai food. OK. Sounds like something that would work."

Michael walked from Basil's office up to his own, fully intending to execute his original plan of checking status and getting a little work done. After five minutes in his office, his heart wasn't into it, so he left. Slowly, his mind was migrating from a Mother Wode mindset to one consumed by Haematite. It's good that Haematite paid him well, since his mind was twenty-four hours on their clock.

15 PHILADELPHIA

Once again, they were traveling by bullet train, always the best option for travel between major population centers in the Eastern Locale. This time, they were accompanied by Basil, who spent the entire trip staring at the scenery. It seemed as if Basil didn't get out much, and Michael imagined if the window were open, Basil would have his head hanging out. The windows didn't open, since 200 miles per hour would not be quite safe.

They arrived at the Philadelphia station, and took a short walk across the platform for the Main Line shuttles. Sandra had called earlier to reserve a car with Haematite's designated rental agency. They needed the flexibility of their own vehicle for the reconnaissance operation; that, and Basil had advised them that he needed to make a stop at an undisclosed location upon their arrival. Sandra drove, and Basil directed her through a tunnel under the Delaware River into Camden, New Jersey, through most of Camden, and into a marginalized suburb. They arrived at a nondescript single family house, and Basil asked them to stay in the vehicle. There were two reasons for this - first, Basil's friends weren't expecting company; and second, they needed to ensure that the vehicle would still be there when he returned.

Basil returned after about ten minutes, clutching a brown paper bag.

"Some necessary equipment. Basil needs to return this before leaving. Basil's Camden friend always took a liking to Basil's pencil. Haematite needs to buy Basil another. If anyone asks about the contents of the bag, Basil is an amateur radio operator just returning from a flea market sale."

Sandra was not privy to the uniqueness of Basil's pencil, and Michael decided to keep silent. How much is a Basil pencil? Michael would rather not guess, but it was probably more expensive than the gold pens some executives flash around.

Tunnel traffic was a little heavier on their return back to Philadelphia, so Basil took the opportunity to nap. Although it was only a little after 3:00 PM, it was way past Basil's bedtime. While Sandra was intent on the traffic, Michael took the opportunity to assay Sandra's face. Short, dark hair framed her narrow face and spilled out upon a high forehead and middle-sized ears. Her face was punctuated by thick manicured eyebrows, slightly upwards-slanting eyes and a short, chiseled nose. The nose ended in a full pouty upper lip above a narrow mouth. Her chin was slightly rounded with a shallow dimple. Her high cheek bones finished the sculpture that was Sandra's face. Her unique combination of features was especially attractive to Michael. You would think that many women would have a similar combination, but Michael had never seen a face like hers. After meeting her, he made it a pastime to compare Sandra's face to those of other women. So far, he found only one woman with a slight resemblance - a worker behind the counter at a fast food restaurant.

They had reserved rooms in an upscale hotel in Bryn Mawr, close to Ardmore. The hotel was a converted apartment building. The local universities had become so huge that hotel room occupancy from parents and sports enthusiasts approached a hundred percent, and a hotel room generated far more monthly revenue than an apartment. Fortunately, they were visiting at a rare time between parent weekends and basketball games. If they were getting an off-season discount, it didn't show in the room rate, but Haematite was again paying the bills.

On the register it looked as if Michael and Sandra were in separate rooms - a convenience for expense reporting. In actually, he and Sandra would share one room, and Basil would occupy the second. They had decided to meet in the hotel lobby after unpacking and settling-in. When Michael and Sandra arrived at the lobby, they saw Basil chatting-up one of the female desk clerks. He motioned for them to come to the desk.

"Sandra! Michael! This is Louise, a lifelong resident of the area. She was kind enough to recommend a real place to eat - not one of those expensive places where you wait a half hour just to get your salad. Basil has directions. It's a short walk. Basil will lead, you follow."

Sandra grimaced, wondering what she was getting into, but Michael was game for an adventure.

Their hotel was about a block off a major city street. This street was just four lanes, punctuated by a stop signal at each cross street, but it ranked as major for the area they were in. The volume of automobile traffic attested to that. The street was lined with businesses on each side, most of which had closed for the day, since they catered to a business clientèle. There were a few casually dressed youngsters walking, probably students from the nearby colleges venturing out for an evening meal.

It was a good strip to wander in search of food, since there was a small restaurant every few hundred feet, and there was a wide variety of food types from which to choose. Basil passed quite a few of these, including a regional simulacrum of Miguel's, without stopping.

Sandra and Michael were about to protest at the length of their walk, but Basil finally stopped at a small storefront. In the window of what looked like someone's parlor was a small sign advertising an Afghan restaurant. Sandra seemed a little dismayed.

"Sandra, Michael, this is the place. This food will be much like what Basil would eat when Basil was a young boy, in the old country. You won't be disappointed."

Michael turned to Sandra and said, "If Basil was willing to walk this far, then it must be good."

"The problem is," replied Sandra, "if the food is too good, Basil won't be in any shape to walk back to the hotel."

Basil laughed, stroking the sides of his stout figure.

"Not to worry. The hotel is downhill from here; and, as you can see, Basil's body resembles a ball. No? You can roll Basil home!"

As they entered the restaurant, Basil exchanged a few words in a foreign language with the hostess, who somewhat understood, and excused herself to fetch the owner.

"Just testing," said Basil, "to ensure the authenticity."

"You're from the region once known as Afghanistan?" asked Sandra.

"No, but near there. The languages are similar. Just a few different coughs and squeaks. Not too hard for Basil to improvise. Basil speaks other languages besides the computer ones!"

An old man appeared before them. Although he looked ancient and frail, he walked steadily and with great authority. A short conversation followed, over the course of which the old man's face seemed to brighten, as if remembering old times and old friends. They were led to a nicely decorated table, not far from the window, but far enough so that the rays of the setting sun wouldn't disturb them. After they were seated for a while, Sandra noticed there were no menus.

"I don't see any menus, Basil."

"Basil has arranged everything. It will be, as Americans say, the Chef's Special. Sandra will make certain that Haematite leaves a large tip!"

Almost immediately, they were served hot tea, a heaping plate of appetizers, and a basket of flat bread. Basil gave a running commentary as they chomped away.

"These turnovers are filled with potato and onion. They can be dipped into the yogurt sauce, but Basil prefers them plain. In this bowl we have cucumbers and onion, and a little mint. Spoon the mixture onto the flat bread to eat. But Basil's favorite is this - Kadu Buranee - steamed pumpkin slices topped with a meat sauce. These others are meat dumplings, steamed, served with a similar meat sauce."

Shortly thereafter, their table was piled with plates of various delicacies. There was rice mixed with raisins, nuts, and carrots, spiced with saffron, cardamom, and coriander. One plate had chicken breasts in a tomato sauce, and another had lamb with raisins. Michael started to think that sweet was an underlying principle of most Afghan food.

"The lamb dish is called Qabili Palao, another of Basil's favorites."

And then there were the kebabs of beef, lamb, chicken and assorted vegetables. From the tenderness of the meat, it was apparent that they had been marinated.

When they had eaten their fill of these wonderful dishes, their plates were cleared and were replaced by an assortment of desserts. There was the expected Baklava of walnuts and honey, but unlike Greek Baklava, it was flavored with saffron and cardamom; and there was also a custard with pistachio pieces. The custard was flavored with cardamom and rosewater, as was an ice cream that was also topped with pistachios.

As instructed, Sandra authorized a sizable tip on her corporate card, realizing she would need to hide it, somehow, in her expense report. The meal was worth it. It was a pleasant night for their casual walk back to the hotel. Sandra and Michael were so stuffed with food that by mutual agreement it was right to bed without any sex.

Michael gave Basil a wakeup call the next morning. He answered immediately, which made Michael believe that Basil had not slept that night. After meeting in the lobby for a continental breakfast, the three drove to the university for their 10:00 AM appointment with Shatinsky.

Shatinsky's office was in Rittenhouse Laboratory. Rittenhouse was a somewhat ancient building, although frequent remodeling had kept it serviceable and energy-efficient. There was no ivy, most likely because the building was surrounded by very little green. It seemed likely also that the maintenance crew was given instructions to remove any tendrils, since they might damage the old brick. These were mass produced, cast bricks, not very thoroughly baked, the typical impermanent building material of the period. Since Rittenhouse was a technology building of the old style, it was conceived by its architects as a bastion of thrift and efficiency, not as a showpiece. This was a building that was bypassed on parent-student tours, lest the prospective students be scared away, or the parents wonder why the tuition was so high.

After consulting the lobby directory, they found Shatinsky's office, door open, on the second floor. The scene was quite unlike Sandra and Michael's visit to Flory in Princeton. There was no outer office for a secretary, and the office was small and crowded with books and papers. The office occupant, whom they presumed to be Shatinsky, was reading a document on a display screen. He was a mustached middle aged man, slightly thin in stature, puffing a pipe. Actually, mouthing a pipe would be a better term, since all university building were smoke-free. Quite possibly, he never lighted the pipe at all, but kept it as a memento of his youth. He noticed them immediately, since his chair faced the doorway.

"Ah, you must be the Haematite people. I'm glad you came to Philadelphia, and you didn't end up in the middle of Pennsylvania at that other university often mistaken for our own. They're the football people. We're more like the soccer people. Oh, looks like we need another chair."

Shatinsky stepped around to the office next door, spoke a few words to the occupant, and returned with a chair. Sandra made the introductions, and they all settled into their chairs. Shatinsky started the small talk.

"It's a nice little university we have here. We've had quite a few Nobel Laureates in our history, a lot of those back in the time when the prize was worth a lot of money. Now, everyone works for some corporation or another, and before the Foundation went bust, everyone's contract had a Nobel Prize clause ceding the money to their employer. The clause was flattering at first, but if you had finally won it, you would feel like you had been suckered. You would end up with a nice certificate, and a gold medal that's property of your employer. You'd be lucky if you broke even on the trip to Stockholm."

Michael didn't remember a Nobel Prize clause in his contract. It would have been a moot clause now, but it was likely still there in the event the prize was somehow resurrected. He didn't read the sixty page document, which he was told was "standard." In any event, it was either the standard, or starve. Young people can't be too fussy. Shatinsky continued.

"Don't think I'm bitter. Our field wasn't even around when Alfred established his prizes. Even if you consider computer science to be a field of mathematics, Alfred disliked mathematicians, and there was no Math Prize. Then again, what would you expect from a chemist!

Sandra was compelled to enter the conversation, if only to get onto topic. This professor was obviously in some midlife crisis, and she wondered what Lanczos had gotten her into.

"Fortunately, many of us hung onto the coat tails of the physicists and got the Prize that way... Ziebart, for example."

"Yes, one of the few examples. But, we're well paid, the Nobel Foundation no longer exists, so it's just an academic question. Academic question, ha! Anyway, I'm certain at this point that I wouldn't have been Prize material, notwithstanding, so not to fuss. Lanczos says you're building a network, a big network, and you'd like some advice."

As they left the building, Michael said what was on everyone's mind.

"Well, that was a waste of time. I think I saw Basil taking a nap about mid-point."

"Remember, it was just our cover story," replied Sandra. "Shatinsky could have put on a puppet show, and it wouldn't have mattered. What matters is what we have planned for tonight. Basil, are we ready?"

"Basil is ready. Perhaps a light dinner tonight. Basil would have a hard time working on a full stomach. Perhaps Sandra, Michael and Basil can stop for a late night snack on the way back from our excursion?"

"Let's not do this too late," said Sandra. "It should be after dark, but before midnight. Anyone out after midnight is all the more suspicious. Unfortunately, at this time of year, sunset comes quite late. Basil, how long would this take?"

"Once there, much less than an hour."

"Good. A small timestamp keeps us all the more anonymous. A police patrol might make several tours of an area each night, maybe at two hour intervals. They can't be everywhere at all times. If we're lucky, we won't be seen.

Even if we are, we have our cover story. Let's leave the hotel just after dark, say 10:00 PM. We'll be there in less than half an hour, Basil will do his thing, and then we're gone. A good plan?"

Michael thought for a moment, and replied.

"Yes, it sounds OK, but if we're questioned, we would need to leave immediately. That would compromise our data acquisition. Basil, is it possible to make some preparation during the trip there, to shave some time?"

"Only five minutes. Basil does not need much lead time."

"Well, do it anyways. Every minute might count. And you still haven't told us exactly what you're going to do."

"Basil will be able to log all traffic into and out of the Daffy Duck server for whatever period we're there. We'll get more server addresses, and maybe see how big the Daffy network is."

"Wow, I don't know how you can do this without physical access to the server," said Sandra, "but that's exactly the data we need. Remind me to give you a raise if this thing works."

"Sandra, more money is always good, but your kindness is what Basil craves."

"Sure, sure. But remember, it's Michael and I who are intermingled."

16 ARDMORE

They decided to take their meals in their rooms that evening. Basil was allowed to charge food service to his room, which was actually on the books as Michael's room, but he was given a limit on spending. The limit was generous, proportioned to Basil's ample appetite, but it was a limit nonetheless. Sandra didn't want any problems with expense reports. As planned, they met in the hotel lobby at 10:00 PM. With Sandra at the wheel, they drove east along the nearby thoroughfare for about ten minutes. Basil consulted his list of restaurant landmarks, and motioned them onto the side streets. As they drove, the area began looking less commercial and more industrial - in a word, bleak.

They finally reached a small industrial park that was situated near train tracks for none other than historical reasons. In the past, no one wanted to live near a noise source like a railroad line, but electric trains and continuous tracks eliminated almost all the noise. High speed trains demanded nearly perfect wheels, tracks and road beds, and such perfection led to a quiet train. Sandra didn't enter the industrial park. It was sure to have video monitors, and a strange vehicle entering at that time of day would be suspicious. Instead, she made a U-turn at the entrance, something that lost drivers must do about a dozen time a day, and found a secluded parking space on the road along the perimeter fence.

Sandra flashed some papers. "I have a map here. If anyone comes around, I'll flash the map and ask for directions to the Afghan restaurant we were at yesterday. Basil, is this close enough?"

"Hard to say, just yet. Basil needs to get a signal."

Michael turned to Basil in the back seat and said, "What sort of signal? Do you think Man Duc has a local wireless network we can tap into? That sounds like a long shot, and it would be encrypted - although that might not be a problem for Basil, right?"

Basil was wrestling with a few wires in the back seat, but he seemed flattered by the compliment.

"Not even Basil could decode that stuff! But not to worry, Basil will use a different approach. Basil relies on the fact that computers are leaky."

Sandra made a nervous laugh.

"I'm sure you don't mean the liquid cooling system, right?"

"Right. Many things in computers are done with light, but that's mostly at the chip level. To communicate easily with other circuitry, some of that light must be converted to electricity at very high radio frequencies. Computers are supposed to be shielded, to keep all these radio frequencies inside, but every box has some slots, and people are known to leave access doors open, etc., so some of these radio signals will leak out. This causes a lot of radio frequency interference, and this interference could compromise important things like fireman's communicators, so it was decided that these electrical signals would only be at certain frequencies."

"Nowadays, most computers use 24.125 gigahertz, but the fastest ones, usually servers, use 61.25 gigahertz. Basil's helical antennas - these pencil things - are tuned for those frequencies. What Basil hopes to do is first locate the server, then record data leaked from the server. It's called van Eck phreaking. It's named after some guy who demonstrated it in the 1980s. The government is so careful about preventing this that there is a standard - Tempest - for building and using secure computers. Fortunately for Basil, commercial servers don't use this. In fact, normal people can't buy Tempest computers, because the government wants to keep this covert information channel open."

Sandra's face went pale.

"So, what we're doing is not just illegal, it's state's secrets illegal!"

"Not to worry," Basil replied. "First, everything Basil has here is nicely concealed. The local police are - how do you say - dipshits. The antenna is a pencil. Everything else is just a music player. Plus, Basil is in the company of two respected scientists. Who would suspect anything?"

There was a moment of silence. Basil looked expectantly at Sandra, but it was Michael who spoke.

"He's right. We have our cover story, the visit to Shatinsky, lost on the way to the restaurant. We were doing some sight-seeing before a late dinner, we got lost, and we ended up here. We can even ask the cops for directions. All very innocent."

"OK," said Sandra. "I agree. I don't know whether it's my scientific instinct to solve a problem, or my love for you. Let's do it."

Basil laughed. "Sandra, you never before spoke of your love for Basil!"

That broke the tension, and Basil continued to fiddle with his apparatus. Finally, he pointed the pencil at the window and did a slow, methodical sweep of the buildings while glancing at the display.

"Well, there's more than one computer down there, but only one operating at the highest frequency. That must be it. There's no reason for anyone else to have a high performance system down there. Basil checks."

Basil pulled out his mobile telephone. Michael was confused.

"Who are you calling?"

"Basil is checking for new messages or that's what it looks like. When Basil logs onto the answering machine in Basil's office with a certain code, it will activate a program. The program looks like a student experiment gone haywire. It pings random servers, but one of the random servers is our target. Since the network routing from the university to here is imprecise, Basil can't just wait for a signal at a certain time, but that's not a problem. Since Basil knows all the bits in the ping package exactly, he can run a cross-correlation of those with the server signal. If it's there, that's our server."

Michael started to think Basil should count as one of the respected scientists in the car.

"That's it, the Daffy server," said Basil, as he fiddled with some controls. "It looks like the signal is strongest from that corner of that building. Michael, would you keep this pencil thing pointed there while Basil does his thing."

Michael complied, but after a few minutes his arm started to ache. Reaching backwards, and also pointing the pencil precisely at the target was taking its toll.

"How long will this take? My arm is getting tired."

"Basil will take over, now. The data logging is on automatic. At this rate, Basil's memory chip will be full in about twenty minutes. Plenty there for analysis later."

Basil grabbed the pencil, and eye-balled it directly at his target. Sandra, who had been on the lookout for other vehicles, turned towards Basil in the rear seat.

"Basil, how long will your analysis take? It seems to me that the signals you're recording are rather abstruse. I don't understand what you'll do with them"

"Basil doesn't know the word, abstruse, but if you're asking him how hard it will be to decipher the signals, Basil will tell you. Basil is not making a digital recording. Basil is making an analog recording he can convert to digital at his leisure. Basil will use adaptive filters and some neural network algorithms for this. Sounds complicated, but all the code is canned. Analog takes much more space than digital in memory, so our recording can be half an hour, only."

"Well, I haven't seen another vehicle since we've been here. That's both good and bad. We aren't bothered, but we stick out like a sore thumb. I'll be happy when the half hour is done."

Michael checked his watch.

"We're about half way there."

The words were barely out of his mouth when a police cruiser turned the corner.

"Keep it going," said Sandra, as she exited the car, papers in hand, and flagged down the police car.

"What's she doing?"

"Basil knows. She's running interference. Keeping the cops busy while Basil finishes the dirty work. Women in distress are a great distraction."

Michael could see Sandra talking to one of two police officers in the vehicle through the passenger side window. After a minute, the officer opened the door and studied the map Sandra held before her. The other remained in the car. With a little extra light from a flashlight, the officer with Sandra traced his finger along the paper, and pointed to a nearby roadway, gesturing as he spoke. After a little head nodding, Sandra walked back to the car.

"I told him that the rental car GPS wasn't working. He offered to lead us out of here. As you can imagine, I couldn't refuse. We'll need to follow him. Basil, I hope we've got enough, because we're through. Get that stuff out of sight, quick!"

Basil had finished stowing his equipment by the time the police cruiser passed them. It was likely too dark to even see Basil in the back seat, let alone get suspicious about anything he might have. Sandra started the engine and followed the police cruiser to the main road. Once on the main road, the cruiser pulled over to the side, right under an unmistakable road sign, so even the densest driver would know where she was. Sandra waved as they passed the cruiser and headed back west.

Once they were safely past the police cruiser, Sandra asked Basil, "Did we get enough?"

"There's a lot. Basil won't know whether a lot is enough until after Basil's analysis. This was always at the mercy of the traffic into the server. No traffic means no data."

"Well, we can't go back there again, whether on this trip, or another," said Michael. These cops must keep to the same neighborhood beats. We'd run into those guys again, and then they would be suspicious."

"Michael," said Basil, "don't underestimate Sandra's charms. She would have them forgetting all about police work."

"That's part of the problem. Sandra has a face a man doesn't easily forget!"

Sandra huffed.

"Michael, I trust you mean that in a good way!"

Their laughter broke the tension for the moment, and they were back at the hotel in a few minutes. Sandra reminded Basil about the early hour of their return train trip the next day and his need to return his stealth equipment back to Camden. They agreed that the Camden excursion would require about an hour and a half's additional time, maybe less, and this set the required time of their departure from the hotel. If there was a traffic problem they could catch the train at Camden, but this was unfamiliar territory. Sandra made the hotel's continental breakfast sound so enticing that Basil's stomach would become a reliable alarm clock, but she said she would give him a wake-up call in the morning.

Michael arrived early for the continental breakfast in the lobby. As a man, a quick shave and shower had him set for the day in about half an hour. Women, on the other hand, are required to devote at least twice that time to their toilet chores to bring themselves to the state of beauty men have grown to expect. The video heroine, tossed overboard and adrift at sea for days, still has perfect hair and is wearing eye shadow when she's rescued. Sandra, as Michael discovered their first night together, shaves more than her legs and underarms. Women are more attractive after they're depilated.

Basil appeared about ten minutes later and made a beeline to the pastry bar. Juggling a plateful of exquisite danish and a tumbler of orange juice in one hand, and his shopping bag of electronic goodies in the other, he waddled over to Michael.

"Basil, why the bag?"

"Basil is cautious, as usual. Basil's suitcase and clothing are expendable - especially Basil's clothing! - but these devices and our data are not replaceable."

"Good point. I saved a place for you."

Michael grabbed the newspapers from the space alongside on the lobby divan and deposited them on a table. The papers continued their relentless visual chatter as they received updates from the hotel wireless network, strategically placing news between static ads for local restaurants and taxi services. The joke expression, "All the News that Fits," had taken on this new meaning since it was coined nearly a century ago.

"Basil, I was impressed by the depth of your knowledge last night. Neural networks, digital filters... all that's fairly advanced stuff. Why do you still do the mundane tasks you're assigned at the university and don't look for a better job? You could make a lot more money."

Basil paused for a few seconds to swallow his last bite of danish and take a swig of orange juice.

"Basil has several reasons. The first is freedom. Basil does the university tasks quickly, and that leaves Basil much time to follow his own interests. Mother Wode supplies the office and a fast network connection. This for Basil is heaven. Basil doesn't work! Basil plays!"

Another bite, another swig.

"Also, you may have noticed that Basil's technical circles are not the same as Michael's. Basil's friends are at the fringes of society, some farther afield than Basil himself. There would be security and background checks. Basil could not pass such scrutiny."

At that point, Sandra arrived at the lobby. True to her thin figure, she eschewed the pastry and grabbed a cup of coffee only.

"Sorry for the delay," Sandra said while fluffing her hair. "The hotel hair dryer is not as capable as my own. The design decision must have been to build it for ruggedness, rather than efficacy."

Sandra glanced at Basil's plate, still over laden after being lightened to half its original load.

"If you two are nearly finished with breakfast, let's grab our suitcases. You can munch in the car. I'll drive."

When they met at the elevator after clearing their rooms, Basil had transferred two remaining danish to an oversize napkin that he held in one hand as he carried his travel bag in the other. Since Sandra had signed them all onto her corporate card, they just dropped the key cards at the front desk as they headed to the parking garage. Sandra had to navigate out of the slender parking slip before Basil could open the door wide enough to enter the car.

In a few seconds they were onto the main thoroughfare, and a few minutes after that they were on the interstate highway headed to the Camden tunnel. The traffic was heavy, but moving. The interstate autopilot systems were shown not to work near urban centers, since there were too many exits and the traffic patterns were too changeable, so Sandra drove manually. The autopilot kicked in at the tunnel to improve travel through this bottleneck, and a few minutes after that they were in the Camden suburbs.

Basil left Sandra and Michael in the car, climbed the few front steps of the small suburban house they had visited at the start of their trip, and rang the bell. It was more than a minute before someone answered the door. Michael attributed the lag to someone scrutinizing a video display to see whether Basil and his accompanying car checked out. When the door opened, the occupant urged Basil to enter. Basil gestured towards the car, probably explaining their haste to arrive at the train station. Basil handed over his shopping bag of electronics, said a few more words, and then headed for the car. As he was walking, Sandra noticed another face peering at them through a window.

"They wanted to invite us to breakfast," said Basil. "As you know, it's hard for Basil to turn down a breakfast, but Sandra, Michael and Basil need to reach the train station."

Sandra turned to face Basil.

"Basil, who exactly are these people? How do you know them?"

"One of them is Basil's cousin. Basil has many cousins, some as skilled as Basil, but in things other than computers. The family is complementary. They sometimes ask for Basil's help on computers, just as Basil asked for use of the apparatus Basil used last night. Gregor works as an electrical engineer. He designs toys. They're kids' toys, not the Basil kind of toys. Basil must pay Gregor a genuine visit one day when there's no work involved."

Sandra easily backtracked to the Camden tunnel, and in a short time they were comfortably seated on the bullet train back to East Wodenstumpf.

17 MUGGED!

They arrived back at East Wodenstumpf just after noon. Basil had slept somewhat on the train, but he still looked tired. It was way past Basil's normal bed time, but noting the hour, Sandra offered to buy him lunch. Basil's face perked at the sound of food, but he asked if it could be a takeout lunch they could buy on the way back to his apartment. It was only 1:00 PM when they dropped Basil off.

Sandra and Michael decided not to go to Haematite, but rather have a relaxing time at Sandra's place. After their late hour excursion the night before, they thought they deserved it. The hotel would have posted their charges at their noon checkout time, so Sandra would be able to reconcile her expenses and submit her travel report without distractions. Michael pulled up a movie classic on the display and half-heartedly attempted to watch it. Most of the time he was admiring Sandra's profile as she sat at her desk.

"Michael, we didn't watch any videos in our room, did we?"

"No. We were too tired the first night after the big meal, and you were entertainment enough the second night."

"Thanks! It looks like Basil enjoys his videos. Thankfully, there are no titles listed here, but I can guess the content. We can't expense all of these, and I don't want to rile Basil unnecessarily. He's come through for us time and time again. I'll pay for these myself."

"Nice girl. You can't blame the guy. The night is his wakeful period. He couldn't sleep, and you can eat just so much, even Basil. Just be thankful you weren't the one changing his sheets!"

Michael had resisted the urge to check his messages upon their return, but he did when he arrived at his Haematite office the next morning. There was one stray message from Sterba "encouraging" him to complete a particular paper by week's end so Sterba could personally deliver it to the journal editor, along with a sales pitch, when Sterba saw him at a particular conference. This would be a little work for Michael, but he saw the advantage in this maneuverer. He replied to Sterba that the manuscript would be ready for him.

Sandra and Michael had a simple dinner at Sandra's place, and Michael retreated to his own apartment for the night to work on the manuscript for Sterba. At about 10:00 PM, the door bell rang. Switching to the front camera revealed Basil's unique outline, shadowed by the courtyard lights. Although the time was within Basil's waking hours, Basil wasn't one for a casual drop-in visit, and he had never visited Michael before. When Michael opened the door,

Basil said, "Hello, Michael. Basil was involved in a small altercation this evening," and collapsed at the door.

Michael pulled Basil through the door - no mean feat - assured himself he was still breathing, and called Sandra. Sandra had taken an early bedtime, and was a little annoyed at Michael's call until she understood the reason for the call.

"How bad does he look? Should you call for the emergency medical service?"

"Well, he got here under his own steam, and he's still breathing, so I think he's been roughed-up but otherwise not seriously hurt. But he is unconscious." Michael laughed, "All the padding must have protected him."

"Michael!"

"Sorry. I guess that wisecrack is another reason for you to believe me when I say he's OK. Basil certainly wouldn't want me to call for outside help. Would you come over - motherly touch and all that? I'll get him mostly cleaned up by the time you arrive. Bring some medical stuff - you know, antiseptic, bandages, that sort of stuff."

"I'll stop at an all night pharmacy on the way." Sandra paused. "Do you think we're responsible for this?"

"We'll ask Basil when he's awake. With his shady past, it might not be related."

Sandra arrived about a half hour later with a large bag full of emergency medical supplies.

"I looked pretty suspicious at the pharmacy. Nearly midnight, buying a bag full of this stuff. I dropped in a few female items so it would look more like a routine purchase. Where is he?"

"I somehow got him into my bed. I rolled him onto a sheet, and then used the sheet to roll him up onto the bed. He groaned a little, and I took that as a good sign."

Sandra entered the bedroom and wordlessly examined Basil.

"You're right. He looks worse that he probably is. Get me a pan with some warm water, and bring the bag with the meds."

Michael retreated to the living room, and let Sandra's motherly instincts take over. Basil was, in some respects, still a child. Sandra returned about fifteen minutes later.

"I've got him in pretty good shape. The spray-on bandages work well. The bruises will need to tend to themselves. He regained some consciousness while I was working on him. I think he tried to invite me into bed with him, but some of the words weren't English. I need to get back home for a little sleep before morning. What's your schedule?"

"I can stay with him tomorrow. I can do a few things remotely; and there's the manuscript for Sterba that can be done as well here as any other place. If he can walk by evening, we can get him back to his apartment."

"He doesn't have a fever now, which is a good sign that he doesn't have a concussion. Check his temperature in the morning. If he starts to hallucinate during the night, you need to call the emergency medical services."

Michael let Sandra out, and arranged the living room couch for his bed. Obviously, he wasn't going to get much sleep.

Michael slept a little later than usual in the morning, since he had been awake long after his usual bedtime the night before. He was so tired, the fact that he was sleeping on the couch didn't bother him at all.

When Michael was awake, the first thing he did was to check on Basil. Basil was still breathing, which was a relief, and he was still asleep. Michael placed his hand gently on Basil's forehead to check his temperature. He was slightly warm, but there didn't seem to be any fever. Michael finished his toilet chores. He didn't shower or shave on non-working days, except when he was with Sandra, so he eschewed breakfast and went right to work on Sterba's manuscript.

After a couple of hours at the keyboard, Michael ambled into the kitchen for some breakfast. The first order of business was to see what food he had in the house. Since he was spending most of his time at Sandra's place, he hadn't been stocking his pantry. He was happy to find some frozen bagels in the freezer. Although he wasn't able to find any cream cheese in the refrigerator, there was butter and some marmalade.

The kitchen noises must have awakened Basil, since Michael saw him first staggering to the bathroom, and then holding himself up at the kitchen doorway.

"Michael, is there enough for Basil's breakfast, too?"

Michael pulled out the chair from the kitchen table closest to the doorway and motioned Basil to sit.

"Basil, sit right here and I'll toast you a bagel. Maybe two bagels. You've got some explaining to do!"

"Yes, Michael is right. Basil must explain. But first, Basil must eat to maintain his strength!"

Michael fixed the first bagel, and he noticed that Basil was having a hard time chewing. He must have taken a hit to the jaw.

"Michael, Basil needs only a single bagel, but some juice would be good."

Michael rummaged around the cupboards and found a few boxes of "juice." They were a little past their expiration date, but he was sure they were still good, since they had been kept at an even room temperature. He would look for Basil's reaction at the first sip.

"Michael, Basil remembers Sandra. Is she here?"

"She came here last night to tend to your wounds. From the looks of it, I think she was successful."

"Does Basil need to apologize to her for anything Basil may have said. Basil can't remember."

"As far as she knows, you were a perfect gentlemen, but she doesn't understand your language. I suspect apologies might be in order if she did."

"Good. Basil remembers saying a few things, but Basil is happy Sandra did not understand."

Michael angled his chair towards Basil.

"Now, about last night... Did it have anything to do with Man Duc?"

"No, no. These were some past associates of Basil, once friendly; now, not so friendly. Basil and these associates parted ways many years ago, but they believed the parting was not on even terms. They held a grudge towards Basil."

"They could have killed you!"

"Roughed-up, yes. Killed, no. They know that Basil would not involve the police for a simple beating. They tried to make sure Basil wasn't injured enough for even a hospital visit, but they went a little too far. They, like Basil, would not want the police involved. If Basil were killed or in hospital, the police would definitely be involved. What irony The dipshit cops avenging Basil!"

"Well, it's good we have Sandra. I wouldn't know the first thing about tending to you, but it came naturally to her. That girl has talents I have yet to plumb. I should ask Sandra how she knows so much of this medical stuff.

Maybe one of her parents was a physician, or maybe I don't want to know."

"Sandra is an angel. You're lucky to have her, Michael. Her plumbing, as you say, is an extra advantage."

Michael thought for a moment and started to get what Basil was talking about.

"Basil, you still need a little help with this English idiom thing, but we'll work on it. What troubles me, is why did it happen so closely after our Man Duc adventure? If it's been that many years since your last contact with those people, why did they accost you now, right after our reconnaissance of the Man Duc server?"

"Basil knows about "reconnaissance," but Basil doesn't know what means "accost." Basil still gets the idea. Basil met these people before coming to Mother Wode. When Basil left, they didn't know where Basil had gone. Basil keeps everything very private, but he thinks his cousin Gregor must have told someone about the visit. Basil may have mentioned Mother Wode to Gregor, and Gregor doesn't know about Basil's problems."

"So, they tracked you to Mother Wode. Is that where you were attacked?"

"Yes. It was obvious that Basil would work in the computer building, because of what Basil does, and that Basil would keep Basil's usual hours. They saw Basil arriving for his nightly work routine. Basil was on the ground for a while until Basil had the strength to drive to your apartment. It's good there were very few people on campus, or there might have been questions for Basil."

"Most people would have wished the opposite, but I understand. Let me call Sandra and fill her in."

Michael rang up Sandra to advise her of Basil's health and the lack of Man Duc association.

"Michael, I'm relieved that we didn't get Basil almost killed, but how much do you know about him? He's useful, but his shady past seems to be a nagging problem."

"Sandra, he couldn't get a job at Mother Wode and hold it for that long unless there were no significant criminal complaints."

"Or he's adept at erasing them from the record."

"Well, either way, he's clean. And he doesn't hesitate to travel. There are still a few security precautions for traveling, although not as bad as they were in the past, and they let him ride the trains."

"Once again, Basil's magic fingers at work. He may have even gotten into the country by manipulating some database or other."

Sandra's analytical mind uncovered scenarios that Michael had never entertained.

"Then there's the best possible reason."

"What's that?"

I know Basil, and you're starting to know him. He's just an overgrown teddy bear. I can't believe that he's malicious in any way."

"OK. You've got me there. I agree. Since Basil's at your place, let's make it a threesome for dinner. I'm sure Basil wouldn't refuse. Oh, and how's that Sterba thing coming? Can you spend the night with me?"

"With that incentive, I'll work at double speed! Basil will likely sleep most of the day, so he won't distract me, but I'll need to get him back to his place for a shower and a change of clothes. After that, we'll meet you at your place ."

"Good plan."

18 DATA ANALYSIS

Michael had never seen the inside of Basil's apartment. This was the first time, and he wasn't surprised by what he saw. There were heaps of things on chairs, tables, and the floor, but there appeared to be an organizing principle - Books in one pile, random papers in another, and heaps of electronic gadgets in one corner of the living room. Michael was surprised by one thing. The walls were covered with art prints, mostly abstract, but all museum quality. One print that Michael recognized was Klee's Twittering Machine, still beautiful in its simplicity after more than a hundred years.

While Basil showered and dressed, Michael took the liberty to rummage through some of the piles. The books were an eclectic mix of applied mathematics and software manuals in several languages. English, the lingua franca of the modern world, predominated. Most other titles were in German, and there was one volume in Russian, or possibly Bulgarian. Michael could read neither language, but he knew that the character set was the same. Technical manuals in foreign languages are not hard to decipher if you know a few key words in their language. Knowing how to transliterate their character sets into English is another big aid. Even Michael knew that **нм** in Russian symbolized nanometer.

Michael and Basil appeared at Sandra's place about half an hour after she had arrived. This was good timing on Michael's part, since it allowed Sandra sufficient time to wind down from her work day, change her clothes and spruce her makeup. In Michael's estimation, Sandra needed very little makeup, but she had a inviolate makeup routine she practiced since her teens, and it would be difficult to get her to change. She pecked Michael on the cheek as he entered, and she greeted Basil.

"Basil, you look almost normal, although I don't know precisely what normal would be with you. At least you're walking under your own power, and your dark complexion seems to mask the bruising quite well. Michael updated me on your problems. Do you think they'll be back."

"No. Basil's infraction was not that great. Also, they would need to travel a great distance. Basil isn't worth it."

"Well, you're worth a lot to us."

"Thanks, Sandra, and thanks for ministering to Basil's medical needs last night."

"No problem. I volunteered as a hospital aide when I was in high school. Didn't know quite what I wanted to do for a living at that point."

So, that was it, thought Michael, as he pictured Sandra in a nurse's uniform with a much shorter than regulation skirt.

"Sandra, Basil and I were talking in the car on the way here about dinner. The Afghan food was great in Philadelphia, but there are no Afghan restaurants in East Wodenstumpf. Basil suggested Indian as a good substitute. About the same taste, but substituting hot for sweet in most cases."

"Sounds good to me. Have you ever dined at The Sultan's Palace?

Michael nodded in agreement, but Basil had his own commentary.

"Somewhat expensive. The food is good, but it's just an American version of Indian food. They even have a liquor bar, something a real Indian restaurant would never have. Can Basil make a suggestion?"

"Since your Afghan choice was right on the money," said Sandra, "You can choose the place."

"Basil will take you to a place where real Indians dine." Basil paused a moment and restated. "Basil should have said that Basil will *direct* you to a place where real Indians dine. You are paying for Basil, yes? Basil does not have funds to pay."

"Yes, we're happy to pay, Basil, especially in light of all your problems. I'm hungry. Let's go."

The place Basil directed them to was past Mother Wode on the opposite side of the city. It was an area that Michael had never seen. This was the type of neighborhood so off the beaten track that you never drove through it. To see it, you actually had to want to go there; and without knowing what was there, there was absolutely no reason to go. The locale reminded him a little of the area around Basil's apartment. The area was tidy, but these were definitely economy digs. This was how the other half lived. The streets were paved with older model cars, all kept in excellent condition by their proud owners. He saw children of many ethnic backgrounds playing together in the street, some quite literally in the street - they had to interrupt their ball game to let Sandra's car pass.

The restaurant was located between residential buildings. Michael tried to find its name, but the sole sign contained what appeared to be Hindi script with the English phrase "Indian Food" added as an afterthought. There was no parking lot, but Sandra managed to park on the street a short distance away. The entrance door, originally rectangular, had been roughly modified by the addition of a half circle at the top. This attempt at creation of an Indian palace entranceway was crude, but the door was ornately patterned in gold paint. The dining room was dark, but it was neat, and it had the pleasant scent of exotic spices.

A sari-clad young woman led them to one of about a dozen tables in the dining room and handed them menus as they seated themselves. They had apparently arrived earlier than the usual dinner crowd, since they were alone in the restaurant.

"Basil, are you certain this is a popular place," asked Sandra. "We seem to be alone."

"Another reason Basil likes this place. Not crowded, at least at the times Basil chooses to eat. Not to worry, Sandra, more will arrive. This is a popular place. Basil knows from experience."

"Speaking of experience," said Michael, "Perhaps you could suggest some of the better dinner items. I once ordered chicken in a real Chinese restaurant and got a plate of chicken feet. Not very appetizing to my western tastes."

"Ah, Basil knows exactly what to order! Sandra, Michael and Basil will eat family style, sharing a little of several dishes."

Basil studied the menu intently, as if plotting a best return on investment strategy. After a few minutes, the same sari-clad woman came for their order. Basil explained he would order for the group, and he quickly rattled off a list of foods in what sounded like their proper pronunciation. Either Basil's home country bordered on India, or he had spent some time there.

"Basil, were you ever in India," asked Michael.

"Yes. Basil worked for about a year there doing some computer odd jobs when he was young. The food was good, but the pay not that good, so Basil left. Basil came to America right after."

"About America, and forgive me for asking," said Sandra, "But why did they let you in?"

"Ha! Sandra makes a little joke! By America, Basil means Canada. There's a pipeline, so to speak, between India and Canada. Easy access. A little time spent in the North, and Basil was certified to work at Mother Wode. Another pipeline, Canada to the US. Things are easy when you know the pipelines."

Their food started to arrive. They were each served a large tumbler of mango lassi, and their table was filled with huge baskets of the breads, naan and roti, followed quickly by plates of paratha, vegetable pakoras and samosa. Basil lavished considerable attention on the pakoras, which he dipped in a red onion chutney before devouring whole. Soon the entrées arrived. According to Basil's tastes, these were mostly chicken, but they were chicken prepared in very different ways. There was Jalfrezi chicken, chicken vindaloo, and chicken tikka masala. Included for variety were lamb korma, whose sweetness reminded Sandra of the Afghan food they had during their Philadelphia trip; and a vegetarian specialty of the house, cauliflower and potatoes cooked with ginger and mild spices. When the entrée plates were cleared, Michael was stuffed. Basil still had room for dessert, and he persuaded Sandra to try an iced cream called kulfi, spiced with cardamom.

As they lingered over dessert, Sandra asked Basil for an update on the analysis of the data they had obtained at the Man Duc server.

"Basil had just a little time to work on this. Basil is still polishing the signal processing algorithms. Perhaps another couple of days."

There seemed to be a definite correlation. A dinner with Basil leads to overeating, but the food was always so good! Michael and Sandra dropped Basil at his apartment and spent the night at Sandra's condominium.

True to his word, Basil called Michael in two days with a report on their Man Duc surveillance. Since he had telephoned, he spoke in generalities, only.

"Michael, it looks as if our data are useless. Except for Basil's pings and some typical system chores, the server didn't appear to be doing anything."

"You're sure?"

"Yes, Basil is sure."

"Of course, of course... What was I thinking." Michael hesitated. "Yes, I know what I was thinking. I was thinking that Sandra is paying the bills, and she would want to see the data. You know, get an explanation. Also, with the effort we all expended on this escapade, she has more buy-in than just the money."

"Basil is good at explaining. But Michael, perhaps you can explain escapade? Basil is not familiar with the word, and it's probably not what Basil has in mind!"

Michael let the question pass.

"I'll try to get Sandra to your office this evening, say around nine o'clock?"

"Basil will be here. Where else is Basil to go?"

He figured Basil was angling for another dinner invitation, but Michael needed some quality time alone with Sandra. He let that question pass as well.

"OK. Nine it is. And prepare an invoice for your work, so you can present it while we visit. Without data, the project might be winding down, and I want you to get paid."

Michael was waiting for Sandra at her place when she arrived back from work and he gave her the bad news.

"I need to see that data."

"Exactly what I thought. We're scheduled to meet with Basil at his office at nine tonight."

"Do I need to bring gloves to hide my fingerprints?"

Michael laughed.

"Not a bad idea. And wear some sunglasses so the security cameras can't finger you."

"Good idea. I let only one person finger me!"

Michael recognized her cue to head to the bedroom before dinner.

They arrived at Basil's office promptly at nine. Basil, as expected, was hunched over his keyboard punching out code.

"Sandra, how good of you to visit Basil!"

"I'm here to visit my data, Basil, but it's nice that you're here, too."

Basil, who was accustomed to getting the cold shoulder from women, brushed off the sleight with no hesitation. He motioned them forwards.

"Come around the display screen, and Basil will demonstrate what's been done."

At the top of the screen were some waveforms, in the middle a raw data dump of ones and zeros, and at the bottom some human-readable script. Basil pointed as he spoke.

"At the top is the raw signal Basil sniffed from the Man Duc server. Nice amplitude and detail after some cleaning with a digital signal processor. One problem, not unexpected, is that there are concurrent signals from several processor cores, but the amplitudes are different, since they use different parts of the peripheral machine. Luckily, Basil's pings exercised the parts of the machine Basil wanted to see, the network access parts, so Basil could strip out these data from the server housekeeping chores. This is not a busy machine, so none of this was hard. Finally, knowing what the packet structure is, Basil could zero in on the message parts, here, on the lower part of the screen."

Sandra studied the display, but Michael could tell she needed to take Basil at his word. This real-word computing was far removed from either Michael or Sandra's expertise. Sandra responded.

"So, what did you see?"

"Aside from Basil's pings, the server didn't have a single network access in the 22 minutes we monitored. Perhaps the time interval we monitored was too short."

"Or perhaps Bankers hours differ from Basil hours," replied Sandra.

"You might have something there, Sandra," said Michael. "Financial transactions happen during business hours, not late at night. Sure, there might be some international stuff, but I'm certain that if it's important, the sender would transmit during a time when the recipient could verify receipt and act on it. Whatever this is, it involves finance - Big Finance. We aren't talking about a credit card scam. We're talking about hundreds of millions of dollars, and the occasional billions of dollars."

"Well, we aren't going back to the server to stake it out for several hours during daylight hours."

Sandra accepted Basil's invoice, and they left. When Michael checked his messages before bedtime, he was surprised to see he had been scheduled for an appointment with some guy named Robbins at the Haematite Human Resources office the next morning.

"I don't know the man, but it's probably just a formality," said Sandra. "Just to see how you're getting along. Now, come to bed."

19 PUSH-BACK

"Dr. Martelli, thanks for coming on such short notice. Please sit down."

"It's still Mister, but we're about ninety-nine percent to the Doctor part."

"A mere formality at this point, I'm sure. Have you enjoyed your work here?"

Michael was unsure how to respond. Was this polite conversation, or was he building up to something? Michael assumed this was just polite conversation, but it didn't hurt to clearly establish the fact that he enjoyed his work.

"Haematite Corporation is everything a Computerati would desire in a work environment. There are many interesting problems, sufficient resources to solve them, and talented colleagues."

"Yes, yes. Haematite is a research powerhouse, no doubt about it."

He paused for a long moment, and shuffled some papers at his desk.

"I see that you're assigned to Dr. Webb. How is that working out?"

Damn fine, but Michael couldn't admit to that. If there was a formal policy on employee fraternization, he still hadn't bothered to read it. He had just followed Sandra's lead, assuming that if she had no problem, neither should he. Sandra was technically his boss, but on paper they were just colleagues, both reporting to someone else. He definitely wouldn't admit anything about their intimate relationship, especially to an HR type.

"Dr. Webb and I have been collaborating on an interesting project. She's an excellent mentor, and she knows how to direct my work to achieve the best value to the corporation."

Michael said that with a straight face, but he was laughing inside at espousing such a company line. Mr. HR kept a straight face, also.

"Yes, Dr. Webb is one of our most respected employees, but sometimes we worry that she wanders too far from an appropriate path. It's not that her work is not up to standard. Her performance has always been rated excellent. We expect scientists to have a good measure of curiosity - we would never try to stop their curiosity. Curious and creative seem to go hand in hand. Quite a few psychological studies there. We allow reasonable time for professional development and an occasional wild goose chase, as it were."

Another pregnant pause.

"There are many psychological studies about creativity. Creative people sometimes tend to compulsive or abnormal behavior."

OK, thought Michael. That's mostly about artists, authors - that type of creativity. Scientists are too logical to go off the deep end - at least the successful ones.

Mr. HR continued.

"Recently Dr. Webb made an unusual information request about an apparently non-existent corporation. Also, she has been making an unusual number of business trips, and there's this consultant she's hired - a Doctor..."

He squinted through his reading glasses.

"I'm sorry, but the name seems unpronounceable."

Of course, it was Basil. This time, Michael wasn't going to make a correction about the doctor appellation.

"Ah, yes, I know the fellow. Very bright. As I understand it, his fees are very competitive."

"Yes, yes. No real problem with the expenses. We're just concerned that another wild goose chase may have consumed the passions of one of our most important scientists."

Michael decided to take a slightly offensive stance.

"Have you talked with Dr. Webb about any of this? I'm sure she would clear up any misconceptions."

"No, no. It's not important enough to bother her." He shuffled through a file folder. "We have her trip reports - all in order - and her expense reports are calculated to the penny. There's nothing really out of the ordinary. You're a fresh set of eyes, a new employee who works closely with her, so I thought you might have some insights into her current mental state."

Current mental state! Holy crap! Does this guy think Sandra has gone off her rocker! Sure, scientists are a little strange, but the Mad Scientist bit has been overworked!

"Mr..." Michael quickly glanced at the nameplate on the desk "... Robbins, I can assure you that I have found nothing Dr. Webb has done to be out of the ordinary. Research is like a flowing river. You follow the current where it leads, although you ultimately try to avoid the rapids."

"A very good analogy, Mr. Martelli. I think you've allayed any doubts I may have had about the conduct of Dr. Webb. If you would, please keep this conversation confidential. I wouldn't want her to think she's in any trouble."

"Of course, Mr. Robbins."

As Michael left Robbins and proceeded to his own office, he wrestled with the problem of how he should react. If he and Sandra weren't intimate, he would have no problem complying with Robbin's request for confidentiality. On the other hand, since he and Sandra were intimate, he didn't want to tell her about this interview since it would upset her. Imagine, your employer suspecting you may have gone bonkers! Sandra was high strung enough without that tidbit of information! It was an easy decision for Michael to keep silent and try to steer this Man Duc thing below everyone's radar.

Later that night, when Sandra inquired about his interview with Robbins, Michael told her that what she suspected was right. It was a perfunctory *How do you like the place?* interview. He shouldn't have been worried.

"See," said Sandra, "You can rely on the experience of someone who's been in the corporate environment for a few years. Everything is a pattern, driven by cause and effect, and scientists are good at recognizing patterns."

"OK, Miss Scientist," said Michael, "What do you divine from this pattern."

Michael unbuttoned the top few buttons of her blouse and started to kiss the back of her neck - Something that especially excited her.

"Well, you don't need to be a genius to figure that out," she replied, as they tumbled to the floor.

20 PROJECT REVIEW

Michael had just left Sandra at her office after they had arrived at work, so he was surprised when she beeped his transceiver.

"Have you opened your mail yet?"

"No, I was just thinking about some coffee. What's up."

Sandra paused for a second.

"Don't be alarmed, but we've been scheduled for a project review."

"I thought those were yearly things; and rarely more often for big projects. Why us, and why now?"

"Two people on a project might not qualify as a big project, but we have hired Basil as a consultant, and we've been doing some traveling. Oh, did I mention that they want you to be the presenter?"

Michael gulped. He was thinking of the detailed preparations he was making for his dissertation defense. That's stressful enough, but now to double this type of work, and to what end?

"Why me?"

"Well, if the usual rules apply, I can think of several reasons. First, you're a new employee, and they want to check you out. Second, they want to encourage you by giving you some face time with the upper management. Lastly, they want your unbiased opinion of the project. After all, since it's my project, they're likely to hear many more yeas than nays from me."

Michael's mind flashed back to his interview in the HR office with Robbins, the one in which he was asked whether Sandra had gone off her rocker. He never told Sandra about that. Maybe the idea that Sandra had somehow gone off the deep end still lingered somewhere in upper management. They just don't understand scientists, so they fear them. Fortunately for Sandra and him, it's the old adage - "Can't live with them, can't live without them." Without scientists, the managers' huge paychecks would vanish in a small number of years

"Sandra, you'll be in the room, won't you? How can they expect me to say anything bad about the project with you right there."

"Yes. I'll be in the room. But they know that if things are really bad, you wouldn't pull your punches, especially not during the question period. If things were really bad, you would want to distance yourself from me and the project as quickly as possible. They're giving you that opportunity."

"Fortunately, you've given me an even greater opportunity, and I'm not talking about work."

Sandra whispered into the transceiver, "Now, that's one thing we don't want them to know!"

"As if you needed to say. OK, what's expected of me?"

"There are some details in the mail message, but it's a lot easier than presenting a talk at a scientific meeting. You'll be able to recycle some slides from the presentation I gave last year that sold them on the initial project. Recycling is good. When they see some of the same things again and again, they start to get a warm, fuzzy feeling about the whole thing."

"How much detail should I give? We've got some results, but we've been working on this for just a few months."

Sandra laughed.

"That's the best part! Less detail is actually a good thing! Your audience is just marginally technical. Some of them may have gotten an undergraduate technical degree, but everything they know is stale. The best format is the one you'll glean from my slides. The upper part of each slide shows some graphs, tables, etc.. You talk about these in upbeat and general terms. All the while you're babbling, your audience is reading the single sentence in large type at the bottoms of the slide. This is the take-away. It's the summary of the slide is layman's terms. That's about all they'll remember when they start asking questions. Obviously, we won't mention any of our cloak and dagger work, but we will mention the Black Swans and how understanding them is critical to success."

"OK. Send me the prior presentation, and I'll work up an outline. How many slides will I need."

Sandra paused a minute to scan the mail message.

"Well, one good thing, we're lumped in with several other projects, so this might be just routine. It looks like twenty minutes for the formal presentation, and ten minutes for the Q&A session. These things always run over, but not by much."

"OK. I'll plan for ten slides. We can review my draft outline later."

Sandra closed the connection, leaving Michael in the utter silence of his office. It was dead silent, since it was too early to hear chatter from others in the area, and the building ventilation system was in a quiet part of its air-handling cycle. Nothing left to do but get his coffee and think.

Sandra's mind was still churning. There wasn't anything out of the ordinary about the requested project review, or was there? As Sandra scanned the mail message, she saw that the invitee list included the usual suspects, but there was one name she couldn't quite place. Searching the corporate directory, she found that one of the invitees was fairly high up on the food chain. Was this a courtesy invitation, or was he there for a purpose? Deployment of her project would be a huge capital expense, and perhaps somewhat of a gamble. There needed to be buy-in very close to the top, so perhaps this was expected. Still, this was something else to worry about, but she would keep the worries to herself and not spook Michael. After all, the presenter needed an air of confidence, and there was no point in eroding Michael's confidence unnecessarily.

The review was scheduled just three days hence. It wasn't that management was thoughtless, or enjoyed having its scientists scramble for data and work overtime to prepare slides. Their argument was that such reviews shouldn't detract from real project labor, and the project leaders shouldn't spend too much time in preparation. Furthermore, a well run project will have archived data available at a moment's notice, and a skilled project leader could give an impromptu progress report at any time. Fortunately, managers never ventured into the labs to hear such impromptu reports, and scientists still took great pains to craft their presentations. Scientists never leave anything to chance.

Michael's presentation was fourth and last on the list, the earlier three being given remotely via video link. The first presentation wasn't scheduled until 10:00 AM, supposedly in deference to the time zone difference of the first speaker, but Michael suspected that manager's hours were somewhat better even than bankers' hours. Since Sandra and Michael were at Haematite's headquarters and the obvious focal point of the meeting, their presentation would be live. There were always advantages to live presentation. Communications were clearer, the slides were crisper, and then there was body language. The presenter could adopt a confident persona, perhaps lifted from some mentor or role model, and he could read the audience, filling in detail in response to quizzical looks, and changing to the next slide when eyes began to glaze. Since Sandra and Michael would attend in person, they were invited to listen to all the talks. Sandra recommended against this, and they planned to arrive ten minutes before their scheduled time.

When they entered the meeting room, they found that the schedule was running late. In fact, the third talk was just starting, so it would be about a half hour before Michael's turn to speak. Michael took the opportunity to withdraw for a cup of coffee, and he brought this back with him to the room. Now, if he didn't spill his coffee and managed to drink it within a half hour, his voice would be well lubricated. Sitting back and watching the show allowed Michael to calibrate the mood of the audience.

Manager's were called Suits for a reason. Whereas Michael and Sandra maintained a casual business dress, all the managers wore business suits, and rather expensive ones at that. He reasoned that it was more for convenience than for any other reason. You really never need to decide what to buy or what to wear - It's always a slight variation of the same theme. This manager's dress code was liberating in a way, albeit expensive to maintain. From the talk around the table, the overall mood was informal, somewhat like the seminars at Mother Wode, which gave him a good feeling. This was something he had done before, and he just needed to do it again.

The previous presentation didn't generate many questions, and quickly it was Michael's turn in front of the big screen. Sandra was leaning slightly forward in anticipation of his first words, but he made a point to fixate on the center of the table and not make eye contact with her. He began as usual, introducing himself, then Sandra, and he pulled up the first slide which contained just the project title and date. Everything seemed to go smoothly as he cycled through the remaining slides, data on the top, a take-away at the bottom, but he noticed something strange. Everyone around the table had the same detached look they had during the previous talk, except for one, who seemed to grow more agitated as the talk progressed. His agitation was somewhat subdued to match the venue, but it was quite obvious. He shifted often in his chair, passed his pen from hand to hand, and stared at the tablet in front of him. This subtle spectacle was becoming unnerving, but Michael kept his composure and finished on schedule.

When Michael asked whether there were any questions, it was no surprise that the agitated man spoke.

"Yes, I have a question - Actually several. These Black Swans as you call them, you don't know what they are?"

Michael replied.

"They're the main object of our studies at this time. We hope to get a handle on them soon."

"As your slides show, and all of us here realize, they're a major risk. I think the fact that you've identified such a risk is reason enough to move on to more productive things."

Michael glanced towards Sandra, and he knew they were thinking along the same lines. That SOB wants to shut us down! Michael remained composed, and he was happy when someone else at the table interjected.

"Jack, give the guy a break! He's only been looking at this for a few weeks. And quite importantly, there's the Risk-Reward scenario, the one Haematite bought into when we authorized the project in the first place. You know, High Risk-High Reward. You can't build a business on penny-ante projects. Every once in a while you need to step up to the plate, point to the bleachers, and make your swing for a home run!"

The Suits seemed to be very fond of sports analogies. Michael had no idea who Jack was, and whether he was at equal or lower rank than his present champion, but he was wondering how this would play out.

"Sure, Hal, turning lead into gold is high-risk, high reward, but after spending just a little too much money on the attempt, you might decide to scrap the whole idea."

Hal turned to Sandra.

"Sandra, what's the spending been like?"

Sandra, prepared as always, pulled some papers out of her folder and scanned them.

"We're actually under-spent at this point, primarily because Michael joined us later than projected. We've been making progress, nonetheless, by adding a local consultant at a very reasonable rate and tapping into some regional academics. No one should have any problem with our spending rate, and we're still budgeted for a few more months."

Even with the double onslaught of Hal and Sandra, Jack wasn't going to back down. Perhaps their spending directly impacted his budget. Perhaps, because of Hal's intervention, Jack decided to proceed in a more reasoned manner.

"Any ideas about the cause of these Black Swans? Any guesses."

Sandra took this question, and Michael was happy she did.

"Well, what you call guesses, scientists call hypotheses. We have several that we're considering, but the front-runner at this point involves a problem with an unusual and random network latency. We might need more data to pin this down. At this point, we're running a simulation to see whether that's true."

Jack scowled.

"More data, equals more time, equals more money. What I would like to know is how soon you'll have this Black Swan thing under control and a draft deployment plan in place."

Jack's question seemed as much directed at Hal as Michael and Sandra. Hal turned to Sandra and Michael.

"I think that's a fair question."

Michael kept his mouth shut, hoping Sandra would have some response. The rest of the group had the same idea, since all eyes were fixed on Sandra, not Michael, and she replied.

"It's difficult to make any projections on this particular point. Unknowns are just that - Unknown. One thing I can tell you, if we don't have a handle on it in six weeks, I would be as eager to put this behind us as any of you."

Six weeks! Probably a little faster than Michael would have liked, but Sandra probably had a better handle on this crowd and knew to pitch a number in some middle range. Her phrasing of this indicated that they were directed to a goal and weren't just taking a free ride on corporate money. Hal, who seemed to be the putative leader of the group, spoke as if laying out the consensus.

"Six weeks. That sounds reasonable. Six weeks it is."

Jack didn't protest, although it seemed he would have rather shut them down immediately. The meeting broke up into small groups, and some headed out the door to lunch. Michael and Sandra were not the first to leave, but they made a fast second.

Back at Sandra's office, it was time to vent, and Michael took the lead.

"Who's Jack, and what was that all about?"

"Jack's some highly placed marketing type. For all I know, Jack shouldn't have even been in this meeting," said Sandra. "He isn't a stakeholder. He probably invited himself. He seems like the type."

"Well, he was sure trying his best to shut us down. Perhaps he's just a curmudgeon, a chronic naysayer. I hear corporations hire a few like that just to stir things up."

Sandra adopted a pensive stance.

“You know, it doesn't make sense. Any sense at all. Which makes me think - Is Jack a part of the Black Swan Conspiracy?”

“So, now we have a formal name for our imagined conspiracy?”

“Ever since we've started wrestling with the Swans and Man Duc Corp., things have gotten strange. This entire project review and Jack's attempt to shut us down is strange. We've been hitting this problem hard, perhaps harder than anyone else would have, considering our various adventures. Perhaps we're getting close to the truth, and someone is putting roadblocks in our way.”

“Adventures is a good term. It makes them seem desirable, like a theme park vacation. But we still haven't found a path forward through the armada of Black Swans. Philadelphia was a disappointment. You can't do any data analysis without data.”

“Anyways, we've got just six weeks. You should confer with Basil. Our spending rate doesn't matter at this point. Let's make the most of the money we have.”

21 TURNING UP THE HEAT

Michael left Sandra's office after their venting session, and when he arrived back at his office, there was a voice message for him to contact Basil. There were also several messages from Sterba. At this point, Sterba had priority. Michael was very close to his Ph.D. defense, and nothing was going to interfere with that - Sandra, maybe, but definitely not Basil. Since he needed to unwind from the project review, he left Haematite and traveled to Mother Wode. It was nearly a half hour before he could break free from Sterba and descend into Basil's dungeon.

Basil pounced on Michael at the door.

"Michael, it is good that Basil is cautious! Basil has discovered something sinister!"

He pulled Michael to a display screen and pulled-up some data. It was unintelligible to Michael, but it looked like some network addresses.

" Every hour Basil does a traceroute from my terminal to some major sites, just to to see where the data goes. Last night, someone added another node between the university and the global network."

Michael drew upon his graduate course in networking. It was first year stuff, learned long ago, but still remembered.

"The network is dynamically modified nearly every minute. Half the world sleeps while the other half becomes more active as the day wears on. The network understands things like that. It anticipates where the increased traffic will be, and it reconfigures to increase transfer efficiency. A change like that is not unexpected. There must have been some transient increase in data demand by the university, maybe from the radio telescope on the far side of the moon. The node will probably disappear in a few days. You worry too much, Basil"

"Basil survives because Basil worries! Basil checked the connectivity of the new node to other routers on the global network. This new node connects only from the university to the prior node. It's a tap."

"How can it be a tap. You said that it doesn't connect anywhere."

"It doesn't connect to any other router, but it does connect to another server. Basil did some sniffing, not from the university - too dangerous - but from the remote location Michael and Basil visited. This new node apparently sifts through the university data looking for something. If it finds what it looks for, it sends it to a remote server. Guess where the data goes."

"Man Duc Corp!"

"Yes, No one suspects Basil, but they know that someone at the university knows about their server. Man Duc Corp. never gets pinged. When it happens, they want to know who did it. Basil disguised our pings as a student program gone haywire. Any reasonable organization would take that at face value and not worry. Basil was able to mask the location of his terminal, but the university's numbers stick out like a red fig. Now they want to dig deeper and verify the source of the pings."

"A red fig?"

"Basil is not in touch with the local idiom."

"But how can they control the university to that extent? Perhaps the university doesn't know about this?"

"It can be done many ways, both inside and outside the university. In any case, all that would be needed is money in high places. Not bribes, per se, but some hefty research grants - that sort of thing. Perhaps the university doesn't know. Any good communications technician with proper access could have done it. Maybe his boss is on the take and he has no idea what he did."

Michael pulled Basil close. Basil's last meal, whether breakfast or lunch, had far too much garlic.

"We need to talk with Sandra. Maybe this Man Duc Corp. thing is getting out of hand. Maybe we should drop it. You say we can't be traced, at least to this point?"

"No, Michael, it is all still anonymous. Basil is surprised, but not afraid. Basil can give as well as Basil gets!"

"Basil, don't get all excited. First, we don't know who they are. They might just be a bunch of curious guys, just like us. Whatever they're doing is probably more justified than what we're doing. Second, these might be government types - very dangerous to deal with. I don't know about Sandra, but I'd like to call it quits."

"Michael, we've come so far, we shouldn't quit now!"

"That's up to Sandra."

When finally back at Haematite, Michael caught Sandra in the hallway. He shuttled her into her office.

"We need to talk."

He explained Basil's findings, and he was surprised at Sandra's response.

"Look, Michael, we have evidence of what may be criminal activity, but it's not enough to go to the authorities. On the other hand, what we may have found is some sort of government conspiracy that's illegal by any standard I'm familiar with. In either case, we should continue. If it's the later case, we must continue. We may be the only people standing between the common man and those who would manipulate him. I've been raised to resist oppression."

Once again, Sandra as activist. Michael frowned.

"Better dead than red, live free or die, or something like that? It all sounds so noble when you're ensconced in your safe little laboratory, but these people seem intent on protecting themselves. If they can wield such power over the global network and power over global financial markets, they must have the resources to do us serious harm. It might be as simple as having Haematite dismiss us, or it might be as bad as a rigged traffic accident - fatal, of course."

"Michael, you worry too much. Basil knows how to cover his tracks."

"So far, he has, but they seem to be closing in on his operation; that is, our operation. Have we done anything to arouse Haematite's suspicions? Do they have a mole at Haematite? After all, the things that Haematite are involved in are rather close to what they do. Hey, they could even be Haematite, for that matter!"

Sandra laughed.

"Yes, the true path to growth - the evil corporation strives to become more evil! I know how Haematite is managed. There is so much bureaucracy, they would never be able to pull something like this. Also, where does the money go? You could never launder such huge quantities of money."

"Maybe it's some rogue corporate executive, or group of executives. You don't need to report the money as income when it all goes to bribes soliciting legitimate business."

"OK. It is possible. But why Haematite? There is at least a handful of corporations that would be suspect."

"Let's not get sidetracked on who it is, exactly. Let's concentrate on what we should do, independently of who's doing what. Is it worth pursuing further? At what point should we quit?

"We need to get Basil involved in the discussion. First, his head is on the line as much as our own. Since we know very little about him, there's even a chance he could be deported to who knows where. Second, he can gauge what we're up against technologically, and estimate how far we can pursue this and still cover our tracks."

"Should we meet at Miguel's? Basil and food are an ideal combination."

"Yes, let's eat first. But no talking in the restaurant! We'll talk afterwards, in the car."

It wasn't hard to get Basil to accept a dinner invitation at Miguel's. They met at about 6:00 PM, possibly a typical breakfast time for Basil, and they made small talk, only, in the restaurant. Basil had purposely bummed a ride to the restaurant, so Sandra and Michael could drive him back home - home being Mother Wode at that time of day - and they could talk in the car. Basil interrupted at the start, pulling an electronic gizmo from his coat pocket.

"What's that."

"Basil's insurance policy. It's a broadband spectrum analyzer. It checks for bugs and any location device that may have been planted on the car. Looks clean."

Sandra was confused and worried at the same time. Her prior activist stance was starting to erode.

"What have we gotten into that we need to worry about things like that! I don't like it!"

Michael was too busy driving to offer any immediate consolation, so Basil filled the silence.

"Sandra, not to worry! Basil covers his tracks! Besides, if they want anyone, it's Basil, not our sweet Sandra!"

"OK, guys," said Michael, we're here together to discuss what to do next. At this point we've done the obvious. We tracked the problem to the hub routers, then to Man Duc Corp., and now we're lost. How do we get back on track? And remember, we've got only six weeks."

"Basil has an idea. A little risky, but the only thing left."

Sandra paled.

"Aren't we taking too many risks already? And don't tell me about covering your tracks!"

"Sandra, not to worry. At this point Sandra, Michael and Basil have just been observers, just like astronomers, much looking, but no touching. Sure, someone can get information that way, but the process is painfully slow. Basil suggests we do an experiment."

Michael laughed.

"An experiment? How can we do an experiment! Raise a billion dollars in funding, send out some financial transactions, and see what happens?"

"Basil needs to do some explaining. Actually, it's a confession. When Basil was at the hub router, Basil didn't just read the code. Basil replaced it with his own version."

Sandra was speechless for a moment, but when she spoke again it was at a significantly enhanced volume.

"You hacked the hub router!"

"Just a little hack, a few lines of code, and it's just one router, out of how many? Basil inserted a back door. You see, the original router code didn't allow remote updates, for obvious security reasons. Basil's version of the code does."

"Perhaps we were at the fringes of the law before, but that's clearly illegal!"

It was time for Michael to mediate.

"So what Man Duc does is legal, and what we're doing to expose them is illegal? What was that little speech you gave me a while ago how it's our duty to expose this activity? In an earlier age they called people like us the White Hats."

Basil turned to Michael.

"Michael, Basil is confused. In Basil's country it is only the old men who wear white hats. That's to match the old ladies' babushkas. What's this white hat?"

"In westerns, the videos - you know, with cowboys, stage coach robbers, those westerns - The bad guys always wore black hats, and the good guys always wore white hats. At one time there were hackers called White Hats who would hack to reveal security problems rather than exploit them. It's a lot like what we're doing now."

"Basil is proud to be in such company, but Basil confesses to wearing some black hats in his youth! It's not easy getting from the old country to America through good works alone!"

Sandra decided to tacitly approve Basil's path forward, at least for the moment, to see what the consequences might be.

"OK. That particular hub router is ours to command. Now what?"

"Basil suggests the following. For a short time Basil fixes things to relay all Daffy Corp. traffic to Basil for inspection before sending it on its way. And it's done at a time when the router should be most active."

Michael got the idea quickly.

"Just like at the Man Duc server, but more direct, and potentially less risky, at least less risky than a second daylight attempt at the industrial park. In fact, it's the only way we can get these data, now. Collecting Black Swans hasn't helped us at all. Now, if we can name the Swans, then we've got something!"

Sandra sighed.

"I never considered myself a submissive female, but confronted by you two, how can I refuse anything? Yes, knowing the details of some transactions would be valuable. It would tell us exactly what Man Duc is doing, whether it's crucial to the project, and whether it's a conspiracy. I confess that I'm curious about what's happening. Something is going on, right under everyone's noses, and we're now capable of unraveling this mystery. How can it be done without leaving tracks?"

"Basil has a place, a safe house, so to speak. Michael was there once with Basil. Michael, did you explain this to Sandra?"

"Well, no. I tried to shield her from our early cloak and dagger stuff. I guess all that became moot after the hub router visit."

Basil continued.

"Moot. That's a word Basil never heard in English! Basil doesn't know what it means, but it would be mother in the old language. To get on with the story, Basil and some friends maintain this house to do private links to the network. It's the best way to prevent a physical trace back to our homes and offices. Basil would never use the Mother Wode link for something like this, even before Basil discovered the tap. This safe house is where Basil would do this. A few hours, that's all. If anyone does trace the activity, it's just an empty building. And they would need to be smarter than Basil to do this - fat chance of that!"

Everyone seemed to be in agreement to proceed, so Michael decided it was time for the planning stage.

"Basil, is your client-side code already written for this?"

"Basil is always prepared. It's ready to go. The big unknown is how much traffic will appear. It's just one server of many. Perhaps there's a best time for the attempt? Basil wouldn't want to monitor too long - too dangerous! Four hours might be an upper limit. And there should be music, and maybe pizza!"

That's Basil, Sandra thought. Always thinking with his stomach.

"Basil, could you do this one on your own, or does Michael need to help you?"

"Basil can work alone - lower profile."

Low profile? Basil? He must be kidding. Sandra hashed out her version of a plan.

"First, Michael, get the temporal statistics on the Swans to pinpoint a good time. It's likely to be during business hours. Basil, is daylight OK with you?"

"Basil prefers night, but for Sandra, Basil will make an exception!"

"Thanks. I guess you can move as soon as Michael gives you a time window; and keep track of your hours. Remember that Haematite is paying for all this and our budget is - moot."

The car finally arrived at Mother Wode, and Basil exited to start his "day." Sandra and Michael adjourned to her place. Perhaps the excitement of the adventure was responsible for her mood, because the sex was exceptional that night.

22 EXPLOIT

It wasn't hard for Michael to pinpoint the most active times for Swan activity. As expected, there was a definite preference for daylight hours, but this was somewhat mitigated by the timezone differential across the country, and a few foreign transactions. It was unlikely their particular router would see much foreign traffic, so he filtered this out. Incoming traffic from the west coast to the east coast skewed a significant percentage of transactions towards late afternoon in the East.

There was a slight increase towards month's end, but they didn't have the luxury of sitting on their hands until then. They needed to act now! They might expect at least a single hit, maybe up to three if they monitored for an entire afternoon at this time of month. Michael was hoping for the higher end of his estimate. A single hit is anecdotal, and they really couldn't generalize from this single data point.

After vetting his numbers with Sandra, Michael called Basil and set things in motion. Of course, it was too early for Basil to be in his office - The sun was still shining. Perhaps Basil's real reason for leaving the Old Country was the persistent rumor that he was a vampire. Michael started to leave a message for Basil in very general terms, but then said he would see Basil later that day. As he hung up the transceiver, he wondered whether he was getting too paranoid or just cautious enough.

The rest of Michael's work day was like treading water. He admitted they were stuck without the new data they would obtain through Basil's hub router hack. When they got the data, what would they do? He reasoned that what they would get was whatever full transactions Man Duc decided to hijack. These would include the originator, destination, and full text. The text might not be strictly readable. It might be a list of numbers, the purpose of which would be known to the communicating parties, but perhaps not to the Haematite cabal. The messages might be encrypted, and would in principle be unreadable; but in that case, why would Man Duc be interested? Do they have everyone's password, or some sort of computer that cracks encrypted messages easily, based, perhaps, on a dictionary of likely passwords.

Man Duc's real purpose might be just to delay the receipt of messages by certain parties. The more Michael considered this hypothesis, the more it seemed ridiculous. What point was there to that. As far as he could tell, the Black Swans eventually all reached their proper homes, a little late, but intact and unchanged. Is increased latency important enough to justify the considerable expense involved in the hub router deployment and some necessary bribes? Eavesdropping, possibly for financial gain, seemed to be a more likely objective.

Michael caught up with Basil at his Mother Wode office after dinner. Basil volunteered to execute the hack the next day, and they arranged to meet in Miguel's parking lot to review the data at Sandra's place immediately after Basil got it.

The next day at work was as boring for Michael as the last. Anything he did was useless without Basil's data. He spent most of the time organizing his computer files. Sandra, however, was working on other things, among which was a proposal for their next project. Since her mind was occupied, she didn't feel the pressure as much as Michael. When Sandra and Michael met for lunch in the company cafeteria, there was not much to talk about except for Basil's concurrent exploit, something they couldn't talk about in public, so the meal went fast. If they were trying to give the impression to whomever might be watching that they were merely colleagues and nothing more, they couldn't have given a better performance. They decided to leave Haematite separately, meet at Sandra's place, and then proceed to Miguel's in a single car.

When they reached Miguel's at their arranged time, Basil was waiting for them. As usual, he had bummed a ride from someone at Mother Wode, and in deference to his friend's schedule he had been left waiting for nearly half an hour for Sandra and Michael. He smiled when he saw their car, and he hurriedly wedged himself through the door and into the back seat.

"Great news! There are five Swans! Basil had no time to examine them, but they are stored safely on Basil's pencil!"

Sandra was naturally confused, and Michael gave her a short tutorial on Basil's pencil, realizing that this must be a new pencil to replace the one he bartered away in Camden.

"Basil, this is a new pencil?"

"Yes, Michael. Look for a line on my next consulting invoice labeled protocol conversion hardware!"

Michael was still in the dark as to how much such a pencil would cost, but if Basil was able to front the money for it, it couldn't be that expensive.

Michael and Sandra were eager to examine the data, but dinner was the first item on the agenda. Basil must be fed, and Michael confessed to some hunger pangs himself. Sandra, however, was not as driven by food as her male companions, a fact that pleased Michael, since he enjoyed his women thin. He hoped the conventional wisdom that women grew in size as their relationships grew in time would not apply to Sandra. Dinner went quickly, since they had nothing to talk about except Basil's data, and that was something they couldn't discuss in public.

They traveled to Sandra's place after dinner. It was the first time that Basil had seen it, and he was noticeably in awe of the elegance in which his friends lived. Michael had always considered that Basil's bohemian lifestyle was by choice. He now began to consider that it might be from lack of money. Basil, capable as he was, was not a Ph.D., and his appearance and character probably doomed him to a lifestyle from which he could never transcend. He was useful enough to remain on the university payroll, but no one was tossing any raises in his direction. Michael was happy that Basil was getting some Haematite money for his "consultation."

The kitchen had the only suitable table area for their group of three, so Sandra set up her portable computer there. Basil ran his fingers rapidly around the keyboard, doing some checks.

"First, Basil checks for bugs. Then Basil disables network access to keep things private."

When his checks were finished, he plugged in his pencil and pulled some data onto the screen.

"Here's the first Swan. It's a raw dump, but Basil is sure you can identify the header and the message."

The message was extremely short. It was a buy order for a considerable number of shares of stock. As usual, it was phrased as a "bid"; that is, the purchaser would only buy at a particular price. It contained an electronic signature that verified its authenticity.

"That's something that might be time-sensitive," said Michael, remembering his earlier musings on what the messages might reveal to them.

"Yes," said Sandra. "If the stock price was particularly volatile, someone else might snatch the stock at the same bid price if they were first at the table and this bidder would lose some advantage. Is Man Duc cherry-picking some stock market action?"

"Well, there's a problem with that. Man Duc doesn't really exist, at least not in the sense that it can buy and sell stock. Maybe it's directing financial action to another party. Let's read the next Swan."

The next item was much shorter. In fact, aside from the header that specified the source and destination, it had no real content.

Sandra wondered aloud, " A test message? Something to make certain that a connection exists? Or did Man Duc delete the contents of the message entirely?"

"No, that's not it," said Basil. What's here is upstream from Man Duc, before it even gets to Man Duc's servers. Basil thinks it's just a test message. Maybe they're testing latency, too, but only Sandra, Michael and Basil know why some of their messages are late! Man Duc probably forwards messages like these pronto, so no latency exists. Everyone is in the dark!"

"Well, that would fit in with Michael's theory about planned latency. It's good Basil obtained five Swans. This one is a dud as far as our analysis goes."

Michael was starting to believe his latency theory, now that Sandra was on board with it. The third message was like the first. A bid on a huge quantity of stock. Things were starting to fall into place. The fourth message was a quirk. It was a love letter. Apparently someone in one large financial institution was having an affair with someone at another. Since the router was keyed off source and destination information, they were collecting the wheat and the chaff. Michael imagined an employee at Man Duc, on a lark, changing a few key words in the message before sending it along; but he didn't think the Man Duc brass, whoever they are, would find that at all funny.

That last thought got him thinking. Changing a message would be very evident in most cases. For the confused lover, the "I didn't write that!" would quickly transform to "How could that have happened?" Multiplied over many messages, there would be quite a few network people searching for a cause. Latency, on the other hand, is always expected. You throw up your hands and learn to live with it.

Sandra iterated, "Two duds out of five."

The last message was a summary of recent transactions. The monetary values were astounding, but they were in line with how much money was being electronically shifted around the world each day.

"I'll call that a dud," said Sandra. "That's three duds out of five, but I'm willing to put the blank message into the hit pile if it's a latency test and Michael's latency theory is correct."

Michael smiled.

"That reminds me of a quotation by some famous scientist about not believing an experimental result until it's been confirmed by theory. Your logic is a little shaky, but I'm starting to believe in the latency theory myself."

"We need more data. Basil, can we have another run at this?"

"Basil would say no, it's too risky - but it's actually impossible, now. Basil replaced the router code to hide any tracks. The network tap at Mother Wode, the extra attention we seem to be getting... All this has Basil spooked. Now, Basil is locked out."

Sandra was about to speak, but Michael was worried her reaction wouldn't land favorably on Basil, so he interjected.

"Well, I can't blame you, Basil. We were all freaked-out about this before it went down. I think we were getting too comfortable with our particular mode of breaking and entering. Sure, Man Duc does it numerous times each day, but two wrongs don't make a right, right? Erase your "pencil," and we'll go on from here."

"That's the problem," said Sandra. "Where do we go from here? We think we've pinpointed what Man Duc is doing, but what do we do with the information? Is Man

Duc's interference harmful to the project? Will they add Haematite to their router hit list. Do we tell somebody about Man Duc Corp.? If we do decide to tell, whom do we tell? Somebody at Haematite? The police? The police will ask some uncomfortable questions, and with three of us involved, we won't keep our story straight."

Basil interjected, "No police! That will expose other things about Basil!"

Michael responded.

"I agree with Basil. Maybe we should just characterize the Black Swan problem, don't mention Man Duc at all, work up a probability of project success, plop a report in front of Haematite's management, and let them decide what to do."

Sandra sighed.

"Yes, that would be the easy way out. Maybe we have reached a decision point, or the end of the line, or whatever. Let's give it some thought over the next few days. Michael, start producing a summary. Perhaps some Monte Carlo simulations of how the Swans - That is, system latency as characterized - might impact Haematite's planned network."

Michael drove Basil back to Mother Wode and returned to Sandra's for the night.

Arriving at work the next day, Michael did as Sandra suggested. He started to summarize his data on the Swans and started to play with some code for the Monte Carlo simulation. The simulation would be quite easy, since he could modify code from a university assignment he had done several years ago. The assignment was to model travel time for commuters going to work based on a number of variables, such as length of traffic signals. The traffic signals were the latency in that system, and generalizing to the Swan problem would be easy. In fact, the class assignment on vehicular traffic flow was conceptually harder than the Swan simulation. Code reuse is heaven when it happens!

Just at quitting time he got a call from Basil. Basil was noticeably upset. He didn't want to say anything on the transceiver, and he wanted Michael to see him at Mother Wode, immediately.

Quite a few scenarios sped through Michael's head as he sped along the local roads to Mother Wode. It couldn't be that bad, since Basil was calling from his office, and not from a police station requesting bail. He remembered Basil's paranoia at Man Duc's network tap at Mother Wode, and he was thankful that Basil was good at hiding his tracks. Basil's returning the hub router to its pristine state now seemed like a very good decision. They were all agreed about dumping the whole project, Man Duc and all, and getting on with their lives. A significant glitch at this point would be bad timing.

Michael had never seen Basil in such an agitated state before. When he arrived at Basil's office, Basil was standing. That would be unusual in itself, but he was pacing, also. When he saw Michael, he sprang to the door and closed it.

"Michael, the safe house was raided. Not by uniformed types, but by several men who kicked in the front door. They were inside for at least half an hour, so they must have found the cellar network connection."

"Basil, how do you know all that?"

"One of Basil's friends has a house nearby. That's how he identified that the safe house could be put to use without a problem. He keeps a camera pointed at the house, mostly as a security precaution. Basil and his friends don't want any squatters or drug addicts moving into that space. There is video of the whole thing!"

"Let me see it."

Basil shook his head.

"No, no, not here. Sandra's place."

"OK. Then Sandra can see it, too. Let me ring her up."

Michael grabbed his mobile and rang Sandra's place, hoping for an answer. When he didn't get one, he rang her mobile.

"Sandra, where are you?"

"Hi, Michael. I'm a few minutes from home. See you there."

"No, I'm not at home. I'm with Basil at Mother Wode. We'll see you at home in about fifteen minutes."

"Basil's coming, too? Michael, what's up?"

"Can't talk now. See you in fifteen."

Michael powered down and headed for the door with Basil in slow, but persistent, pursuit.

When they arrived at Sandra's place, she was waiting on the doorstep for them, obviously anxious about the reason for their visit. Basil's haste was a sure sign that something was up. She had never seen Basil move so quickly, and Basil was also the first to speak.

"Sandra, Basil requires your portable computer."

"It's still set up in the same place. It hasn't been network connected since your last visit."

"Basil checks again, just to be sure."

With all of Basil's security precautions, Sandra had felt secure that there was no trail of evidence leading back to them. Now, she wasn't so confident.

Basil plugged his pencil into the computer, fetched the video file, and explained to Sandra what they would be seeing.

"As Basil explained to Michael at Mother Wode, the safe house, where Basil did his Man Duc probe, has been raided."

"Raided!" exclaimed Sandra. "By the police?"

"No. No police as far as Basil can tell. These men didn't operate like police. There's video from a nearby house. Basil has selected only the scenes where there's something to see."

Basil started the video.

The camera angle was nearly a full frontal view of a house that Michael recognized as the place he had visited with Basil. From the time stamp on the image, it was about 4:00 AM.

"Nice neighborhood," said Sandra in obvious sarcasm.

A car stopped in front of the building, and there was no movement for a few minutes. Three men exited, walked up the steps of the house, tried the door, then smashed their way inside.

"Basil's right," said Michael. "I don't think police would make this type of entrance."

"There's a gap of about twenty minutes here that's been edited out, since there's nothing to see," said Basil. " That's enough time to search the house, which is empty, and find the network connection in the cellar. Basil and Basil's friends leave no evidence, so there's nothing to find."

"What about fingerprints, and things like that," asked Sandra.

"These are more like muscle men, maybe mob. These aren't police. Even so, not to worry. Basil does a wipe after each of his excursions."

The video continued with the men exiting the building, apparently empty handed, and leaving in their car. As the car sped off, the license plate was just barely visible, which gave Sandra an idea.

"Basil, can we zoom in to the plate number?"

"Too fuzzy on this frame. It's night, and there's not much contrast. But there might be hope."

Basil typed a few commands in the keyboard.

"Ah, we're in luck. The video is encoded as enhanced-8-4."

Sandra gave Michael her confused look, so Michael asked.

"What does that mean, Basil?"

"That means that every eighth frame has double the resolution, and every sixty-fourth frame has four times the resolution, etc., all the way up to sixteen times resolution. It's a way for, say, wedding photographers to get video and still images at the same time without thinking about it and not using too much memory. If Basil is lucky, one of the high resolution frames will fall into the desired time. Basil checks."

The video proceeded again, this time in a stop action mode. One of these images contained the plate number. Looking at an information box, Basil saw it was at eight times the usual resolution.

"Well, not the highest resolution, but maybe good enough."

Zooming in revealed a clear license plate number.

"OK, so we have the plate number," said Michael. "What do we do? Turn in an anonymous tip to the police?"

"Stop with this police talk," said Basil. "No police! Basil can get you the information. Plate numbers are easy."

"Then, what will that tell us?"

"First, whether the raid was directed at our operation," said Sandra, "or the operation of one of Basil's friends. It's nice to think that what we're doing is the most important thing in the world, but this raid might just be the result of some scam operation gone awry. Sometimes crooks target other crooks, since they know that the law won't be involved."

Michael had quite a few things to worry about as he ferried Basil back to Mother Wode. First on his mind before that night was his forthcoming dissertation defense. Those worries had suddenly taken a back seat to the current events. The university life, for all its faults, seemed preferable to the atypical corporate lifestyle he had entered.

23 TAILED

The next day, true to his word and by some unknown process, Basil had obtained information on the license plate. Since a lot of confidential information was being relayed, and it was difficult to keep meeting personally, Basil had given Michael an encryption key and the address of an anonymous posting web site mostly used by gamers to exchange hints and tips. Michael was to look for a posting by Code Turkey, Basil's screen name for this group. Michael grabbed the file, put it onto his mobile computer, ran a bit of code Basil had written to disconnect all wired and wireless network links, ran another program that checked for bugs that could capture information for later transmission on the network, and then finally the decryption program.

Perhaps not surprising was the owner of the license plate, MD International, a likely "subsidiary" of Man Duc Corporation. Basil did a search for the listed address of this company and found that it was a mail drop, a storefront that rents locked postal boxes. Aside from staking out the mail drop for perhaps a month, apprehending whomever fetches their mail, and grilling them for information, this was a dead end. But, as predicted, it did confirm that Man Duc was hot on their trail.

The question was, how?

"It was the blank message," said Sandra.

"What about the blank message?"

"Any operation as sophisticated as one that commands all the hub routers wouldn't stop just there. For quality control, they would send occasional test messages to verify the performance of their system. All they would need was a program planted on a computer to send the messages. They wouldn't need to worry about whomever would receive the message, since they would just not forward it."

"OK. That makes sense. But how could they track it back to the house."

"First, they knew the message had been intercepted, because of the added latency. System latency for these few messages is theirs to command, right? Anything else is suspicious. Then, the message was sent at a particular time, and it had a particular length. It was routed to the safe house anonymously, but there must be automated logs that track simple message details like those. An organization supposedly as powerful as Man Duc would have a way to read these logs and track the message to the house."

"Also," said Michael, "they knew about where to look. They would reason it would be near Mother Wode, since that's where they got pinged. Now that we say it, it looks all too easy. Easy, that is, for someone like Man Duc."

Their inquiries into Man Duc had reached a dead end, beyond which they dared go no further. Happily, though, it appeared that Man Duc's inquiries about them were also at a dead end. Man Duc wouldn't have raided the safe house unless they needed to discover who had penetrated their operation. Basil still insisted that there was no evidence in the house for them to find. Michael wanted to believe that, but Sandra and he were on edge after the remote outpost was raided, and they decided to take the low road; namely, forget any further follow-up with Man Duc, and just file the general report along the lines they had outlined. Man Duc Corp., whether a part of the mob or the cover for some government agency, fair or foul, was becoming too much of a threat. The adventure may have been fun at the start, but it had become too dangerous.

At their next dinner meeting, Sandra verbalized what was on everyone's mind.

"Michael and Basil, I've reached an executive decision to end this Man Duc business. Aside from the apparent risks, all this data collection hasn't led to a resolution of the Black Swan problem - At least not any resolution that advanced Haematite's objective."

There were no arguments about Sandra's decision. Sandra and Michael decided to rethink their strategy in the morning, and Michael ferried Basil back to his place.

The next morning, Michael joined Sandra at a white board in her laboratory, and Sandra started the discussion.

"Maybe we were being too specific in trying to pinpoint Man Duc as the culprit. Sure, it seems that Man Duc is the problem, but we might need to treat this only in a general sense, worst case analysis and all that. If we can assign some confidence level to what Haematite wants to do in the presence of the Black Swans, maybe that's all we need."

"Until Man Duc changes its tactics in response to Haematite's network," replied Michael. This isn't a static thing we're talking about."

"Let's just analyze one problem at a time. It might be that our analysis shows no confidence in Haematite's scheme - Game over, no more problems."

Sandra's plan to concentrate more on the general problem and less on Man Duc itself started to sound like a very good idea, so Michael headed back to his office to start the work. This called for a simulation. Modeling the general trend of the transactions would take just a few lines of code, since it was just a power law. He could add a little deviation from the beaten path to make it more realistic, perhaps using a neural network to play his simulation against the actual data to zero in on a best fit.

As for the Black Swans, they were few and far in between, but these were large transactions. Modeling both the time distribution and transaction values as separate distributions would probably work, but he would check for any cross-correlation. Obviously, really large transactions were rare, so there would be some correlation effects. This was turning into a bit of work, but not anything out of the ordinary.

Sandra let him handle the modeling on his own, since she was involved with several other things. It was good that she was separating herself from Man Duc for a while in light of Michael's interview with Robbins. Informal updates were exchanged at home in free periods. There was no evidence of Man Duc being hot on their tails, so Basil's many precautions seemed to have worked. Sandra didn't seem to have the same interest in Man Duc as before, possibly because the project was decaying in a dead end. Time to cut your losses and run.

After a few days it was apparent that the Man Duc Black Swans would have a significant effect on Haematite's arbitrage system, but only if Haematite played over the entire market. If it focused on smaller transactions, the Black Swans hardly impacted on Haematite's simulated returns. This was a potentially important result. Of course, more money could be made per transaction on the larger transactions, but many smaller transactions would give the same average return. Furthermore, Haematite would not need to maintain a large money account to start playing in the market, possibly another selling point for steering away from Black Swan territory.

By the end of the week, Michael's simulations were showing a good return on investment for the Haematite arbitrage scheme. Man Duc was effectively out of the picture, and Michael's decision to play where the Black Swans were absent allowed them to recover from near disaster. He was feeling rather smug, since all that was left of the work was the mere mechanics of the proposed process; and a simulation based on real time data, not their historical database. A few more weeks, and they should have enough for their final report. It seemed that a tremendous weight had been lifted after they had made the decision to ignore Man Duc and treat the Swans as a statistical object. Michael was able to devote more time to his dissertation and the various odd tasks that Sterba required of him.

About a week after they had put the Man Duc Conspiracy behind them, Michael noticed he was being followed. Since his normal state was utter distraction, this activity could have been happening since the time of the raid, or even before the raid. He noticed that in the evenings there was a car following at a distance even on roadways where there was usually very little traffic. At this point, he couldn't verify that they were staking out either his apartment or Sandra's condominium, since they weren't in sight whenever he parked his car.

Michael figured they could follow him as much as they liked. Since they were no longer on the trail of Man Duc, no suspicions could be raised. Sandra was considerably more worried, and she insisted that Michael should enlist Basil's aid. Basil's immediate fix was, as expected, technological. If "they" were going to monitor him, then he was going to monitor them. Armed with a sackful of wireless cameras, Basil installed them at the exterior of Michael's apartment and Sandra's condominium. These were the newer energy-harvesting models that needed no wiring and no batteries at all. They harvested their power from the sun in the daylight, temperature variations through the course of the day, and whatever wind was available high in the trees. They were sensitive to infrared, so night images were collected, also. All images were logged onto a local computer, and he could monitor the image history, or real-time images anywhere through network access. The image data, of course, were encrypted. The update rate on some cameras was slow when the environmental energy wasn't there, but they were assured of at least one image every few seconds.

Michael suggested a backwards-looking camera for his car, but Basil rejected the idea as being too expensive and likely ineffective. The shadow car kept too far back, and even if they were to read the license plate, he was sure it would be registered to Man Duc. Who else would follow him? No new information there. In fact, it was likely to be the same car that was used in the raid on the safe house. How many agents could Man Duc possibly have?

Sandra had a different take on the matter. Perhaps Michael was being tailed by an enemy of Man Duc, whoever that might be. Perhaps it was some police agency on the trail of Man Duc, and Michael had somehow gotten involved. Perhaps this wasn't related to Man Duc at all. It was all so confusing that they decided to stop theorizing and try to carry on with their lives. At least Sandra hadn't noticed anyone following her, perhaps a consequence of Man Duc's limited resources in the area, and Michael was the one with a connection to both Haematite and Mother Wode.

Michael spent most of his time while away from work looking over his shoulder and suspecting sinister intentions from each passerby. Work, however, was liberating, since it allowed him to take his mind off such things. His building was a presumed safe environment, a guard at the gate, access cards and all that, and he didn't think whatever he was doing would warrant the shenanigans of some spy movie - "Just here to replace a light, M'am. Yeah, that particular tool does resemble a gun, doesn't it? And this, a rocket-propelled grenade!"

Likewise, Mother Wode seemed safe. He was thankful that no car had ever followed him onto campus. The parking lots were quite distant from the main buildings, and he would be vulnerable on the long walk between. His area inside the campus computer center, since it contained sensitive computer and network systems, was secured by an access card system much like that at Haematite. He appeared to be as safe in his campus office as in his Haematite office, however safe that might be. Knowing Man Duc's capabilities, a simple access card system didn't seem that insurmountable. They could obtain an access card by just stalking and assailing some student.

Sterba wasn't traveling again for several weeks, so he interacted with Michael on a nearly daily basis. They had received some favorable reviews from the referees of their last submitted papers. Not to let the authors think they had a free ride, there were always a few "recommended" changes which the editors tended to consider mandatory. None of these involved any new experiments, but only some slight reanalysis, rewording, or different emphasis. The advantage of having Sterba as a coauthor is that the man had clout. No referee would cross swords with the Old Boy, lest his anonymity be compromised later. Sterba might in fact become editor of one of these respected journals, and an editor would have access to all files, no questions asked.

Most of these musing were moot, since Michael realized that these were quality publications that would pass muster in any case. Sterba worked him hard, but it showed in the results. At this point he was spending only half-time at Haematite, commuting between Mother Wode and his Haematite office daily. Most times he didn't sense anyone following him, but he would experiment by stopping at odd locations during his usual travels to see whether he would notice anyone.

He hadn't been to the local park in years. The last time he was there, he had a girl in hand for a romantic stroll on the walkway along a creek. At this time of year, the creek was unimpressive, being a mere trickle of its usual self, so he stayed only a few minutes and left. He was more conscious of the license plates of out-of-state automobiles and their occupants, but he confessed to himself that he hadn't crossed paths with anyone he considered sinister. He was more conscious of police patrol cars, and this was the first time in his life he actually welcomed the presence of the police.

24 BREAK-IN AT MOTHER WODE

After a few days, Michael was fairly certain he was no longer being followed. Despite the evidence, could it have been just an overly active imagination? He couldn't be sure about that, but he began to feel less paranoid and felt free to return to his usual schedule. After spending a late night at his Mother Wode office, he decided to descend into the basement and visit Basil. He had no contact with Basil since Sandra decided to end their pursuit of Man Duc, and Basil's subsequent help with the surveillance cameras, but Michael had grown attached to the overstuffed teddy bear, and he wanted to maintain a friendship. Not only that, but Basil could be useful for certain projects that might appear in the future.

As he rounded the corner and entered Basil's office, he was surprised to find two men there, and no Basil. These men were arrayed in standard business dress, quite unlike what any of Basil's associates might wear, and one of them was hunched over Basil's display. Michael was too shocked to speak, but one of the men spoke first.

"Can we help you?"

Michael decided to play dumb.

"Ah... I'm looking for a guy named Basil. They tell me he knows how to fix mobile computers. One of mine seems to have some problems."

"Basil stepped out for a bite to eat. You can find him in about an hour. Better yet, try him tomorrow. It's getting late."

Michael was sure now that these men didn't know Basil. Basil's business hours were just getting underway, and his food source was the vending machine near the lobby.

"Sure. I saw the light on, and I thought I'd take a chance that he was here. I'll try again tomorrow."

Michael recited those words sheepishly as he backed out the door. He headed towards the stairway, but ducked into an empty room where he could monitor what might be happening. He could hear murmurs of conversation between the men, but nothing understandable. What seemed like an eternity to Michael, but only ten minutes of actual time, the men left Basil's office and headed up the stairs. Michael could see that Basil was not in their company. He waited a few more minutes to ensure that they were really gone, and he headed back to Basil's office.

The lights were on, and the door was still open. Michael went inside and looked around. On the floor, in one corner, quite hidden by piles of papers and old equipment, was Basil. Michael feared the worst until he discovered that Basil was breathing. Basil would likely hate him for doing this, but Michael called campus security. This was serious business. They couldn't hide something like this.

While waiting for the campus police to arrive, Michael tried to revive Basil. There was no evidence of any injury, but Michael realized immediately what had happened. Basil's clothing smelled like chloroform. Basil must have been approached unawares as he was hunched over his display screen, knocked out with a chloroform-soaked rag, and then dumped in the corner. The *how* was easy to deduce, but the *why* was another matter. Michael was certain that Basil would be closed mouth with the police, perhaps feigning ignorance of why this would have happened to someone like him. It would be up to Michael to get to the real story and link this event to either Basil's past, or to Man Duc.

Basil was just regaining consciousness as two uniformed campus policemen arrived - Actually, one policeman and a policewoman. As if acting out their unconsciously learned roles, the woman went immediately to minister to Basil, and the man started to question Michael. Of course, it was not unusual for either Michael or Basil to be in the building at this late hour, so there was no problem there. Michael described the two unknown men and professed ignorance about why this would happen. As Basil became responsive, it became apparent to the police that he had seen nothing.

Basil refused any medical attention, and Michael said he would watch over him for the remainder of the night. Basil promised to inventory his office to see whether anything was missing, and check his computer logs to see if the intention was to break into the university network. Perhaps Basil was just a victim of opportunity, since his remote office location would have allowed unfettered access to the university network for an extended period. Basil assured the campus cops that he wasn't working on any classified government research projects, just routine tasks for some of the professors. After their interviews, Basil and Michael volunteered to appear at the campus security office the next day to review their formal statements and view feeds from some security cameras.

When the police finally left, Michael had his own questions for Basil.

"OK, Basil, what happened? I'm somewhat hoping these men were more of your past business associates, and not Man Duc, but I don't think so."

"Basil didn't see these men, but from what you described, it can't be anyone from Basil's past. It must be Man Duc. Basil checks his computer."

Basil walked to his chair. The lingering effect of the chloroform turned his stride into a comical waddle.

"Basil pulls up his system logs, and some things that aren't on other people's computers."

In a second, there was an image of a stranger hunched over Basil's keyboard. Noting the angle, Michael's eyes traced a path to what appeared to be an electrical outlet on the wall. Just like Basil's "pencil," this probably functioned as an electrical outlet, but also as a wireless camera. Michael was impressed.

"Basil, do you record continuous video in this room?"

"Basil is smarter than that. The computer knows how Basil types; the cadence, the time delay between letter keys. If the computer senses someone other than Basil, the recording starts."

"We need to give this image to security."

Basil scowled.

"No, Michael. There would be too many questions as to why Basil would want such a camera. Does Basil have something to hide? And, if Basil does give them the photograph, what use would it be? They will never find these guys, and these guys are not likely to come back. If Basil needs the photo in the future, it's saved, but Basil does not voluntarily give anything to the police."

"OK, Basil, I agree. What else do you have? Can you determine what they were doing?"

Basil labored for a few minutes over the keyboard.

"They were smart enough to try to hide their tracks, but not smarter than Basil! If it were any other computer, all their work would be hidden, but this is Basil's computer! Not only did they copy Basil's recent files, they installed a key logger to see what Basil does in the future. Guess where the data goes!"

Michael instantly recognized the sequence of numbers. It was the Man Duc server!

"Well, now we know for sure, but how did Man Duc track things specifically to you? I know how well you hide your tracks."

"Basil is perhaps too notorious. They knew it was someone at Mother Wode, because of the network access, and a simple search through the university records will have Basil appear as a red fig to the right people."

Once again with the red figs. Michael started to think.

"Basil, I'm sure there was no Man Duc content on your computer, but what about the invoice you prepared for Sandra? If those guys grabbed your recent files, the invoice would be there. It would point directly to Sandra."

"Michael, I'm afraid that you're right. Man Duc has a copy of Basil's invoice. Is Sandra in danger?"

"Not any more than before. Since I was being followed, it's likely they know about Sandra. We didn't go into details, but something happened at Haematite that makes us believe that Man Duc knows about our Haematite project and is trying to shut it down. They may even have an inside man at Haematite."

"But why were you followed, and not Sandra? It makes more sense to follow Sandra, since she's the project leader."

"Well, it could be these are gentlemen, and they don't rough up women. Someone like you, Basil, and perhaps me, are fair game."

Basil patted his stomach.

"Yes, Basil is often the punching bag. That's why Basil keeps the extra padding."

Michael continued, "Actually, I think there's a different reason they haven't bothered with Sandra. Project leaders are usually management types. They don't get involved with the real work. These Man Duc guys may believe that Sandra is out of the loop on this, so she would have no information. After all, you and I are linked by Mother Wode, and I just met Sandra a few weeks ago. If they put the strong arm on her, and she had never heard of Man Duc or the origin of the Black Swans, it would give them unwanted publicity. They might even know what type of woman Sandra is. She's not easily intimidated. I think tonight's adventure was a check to see whether your involvement was independent of Haematite. In that case, the invoice could actually keep you out of trouble. I need to tell Sandra what happened."

It was very late at night. Michael had planned to return to his own place, and not Sandra's, so it didn't make sense to rush over and disturb her. The bad news could wait until late the next morning. He and Basil had an appointment at the campus security office at 9:00 AM, which meant a short sleep for Michael, and a slightly longer working day for Basil. Michael still drove past Sandra's place to ensure himself that there were no strange men parked outside or looking through windows. Not a strictly logical action, but he was running on emotions.

Michael arrived at the campus security office at the prescribed time the next morning. He found Basil already sitting in a lobby chair. Basil must have a razor and some emergency clothing in a desk drawer, since he was nicely shaved and generally presentable. The policewoman who was in Basil's office the night before was there, also. Either she was on an extended or split shift, or she was there on appointment. The difference was that she was likely being paid, and Michael and Basil were acting as "good citizens." She approached the pair.

"I'm sorry to say that the security cameras came up negative. The outside ones don't show much, and the lobby camera in the computer building appears to be broken. My partner thinks your strangers blew out the camera chip with a high powered laser beam, or something like that, since it stopped working about the time of the break-in. I think he watches too many spy movies! Imagine, stuff like that happening at Mother Wode! It's just crazy to think that sort of thing would happen here. We get petty break-ins all the time, usually in the dormitories. Yours was one of the few that used force, but no weapons like some of the others. I'm having the Mother Wode Chemistry Department check for missing chloroform. Where else can you get something like that? Sounds like an inside job, maybe some relatives or acquaintances of a student or employee."

Michael and Basil thought differently, but neither of them said a word. Basil reported that the strangers had accessed some of his files, possibly looking for passwords, but they never got important access to any servers on Mother Wode's network. He didn't mention they were likely employed by an organization called Man Duc, they had copies of his recent files, and they had planted a bug in his machine. He didn't say he had a photograph of one of them. Michael and Basil read and signed their formal statements, which would be dutifully filed and forgotten. There was no mention of lasers disabling the security camera anywhere in the report. The possible motive was breaking into Mother Wode's network to steal money from student accounts. Nice and neat, and completely wrong.

The worst was not over for Michael. He still had to report to Sandra, and she might get hysterical at Man Duc's escalation of activities. For their part, Michael and Sandra had washed their hands of Man Duc, making no new investigations into the origin of the Black Swans, and Sandra had believed that was the end of it. Both Michael and Basil had insisted that there was no way Man Duc could track their activities and expose them. Now they were proved wrong. Whatever Man Duc was into, it must be serious business, since its expenditure of resources on tracking them down was impressive. At least they didn't kidnap Basil, or worse. Man Duc, like the Haematite team, wasn't adverse to some minor lawbreaking, but it seemed to avoid anything that would bring in any major police action. As Michael had said to Basil, these seemed to be gentlemen thieves.

After arriving at Haematite, Michael tracked Sandra to her laboratory and gave her a short summary of the previous night's incident. As he spoke, he could see her face pale and her eyes widen. Michael always enjoyed

Sandra's wide eyes, but he wasn't sexually aroused at seeing them this time. She was genuinely scared.

"Michael, what have we done! It seemed like a game at the start, us against the bad guys, but I never thought we would be in danger!"

"Sandra, sure it seems bad, but I've analyzed Man Duc's response, and I've concluded that they're gentlemen thieves. They'll only go so far, and then they'll stop. I think they just want to learn how much information we have and whether we're a danger to them. I think it's fairly obvious that they have a Haematite connection. Man Duc may have always had someone at Haematite; or, perhaps, this guy, Jack, the one who gave us all the trouble at the project review, was blackmailed just for the occasion. Either way, Man Duc seems to be as intent on closure as we are."

"Right, gentlemen thieves! They'll be sure to put on their cleanest white gloves before they strangle me!"

She began to cry, the first time Michael had ever seen her cry. Despite their being at Haematite, Michael embraced Sandra to comfort her.

"What are we going to do, Michael?"

"I've had a lot of time to think since last night's incident. The best tactic is to continue avoiding transgressions into Man Duc's territory, and work up a report along the lines we had planned; namely, characterize the Swans and infer their impact on Haematite's scheme without naming a source. If my guess is right, the project will be killed, and everyone lives happily ever after, including Man Duc Corp."

Sandra looked up at him with those wide eyes.

"Michael, I hope you're right. There's still about a month left before our final report is due."

The report could just as well be summaries of magazine articles. No matter what the content, Michael was sure that Jack would find a way to kill the project.

25 ACCIDENTALLY ON PURPOSE

As a precaution against any Man Duc intervention, Michael tried to spend as much of his time with Sandra as he was able. He slept at her place every night, and they even drove into Haematite together. They decided that they would tell anyone who asked that they were car pooling - Michael's car was unreliable, and they kept the same working hours. He planned his visits to Mother Wode during normal working hours, necessarily taking Sandra's car. He knew that Sandra would be safely ensconced at Haematite while he was away, and since she didn't have use of her car, she would stay there until Michael fetched her. This went on for more than a week, and they were relieved that there were no further Man Duc incursions. They checked Basil daily, and he had nothing to report. The three of them even went to Miguel's for dinner one night, and Man Duc did not enter into the conversation.

Mid-morning one day, while Michael and Sandra were at Haematite, the building evacuation alarm sounded. It was apparent that there was no accident in the laboratory area, or else the public address system would have made an announcement to avoid that part of the building upon egress. When they reached the designated assembly points outside the building, they could hear the sirens sounding in the distance at the nearby carbon sequestration plant. It was announced that there was "some problem" at the carbon sequestration plant, and they were advised to head home and listen to the news. Their supervisors would contact them if it was safe to return that day, or if it was unsafe to return the next. Michael thought about spending the day at Mother Wode, since it was well outside the evacuation area, but that would mean leaving Sandra alone. He decided to stay with Sandra when they arrived back at her place in her car.

The news reports were no help at all. Whatever the problem, it was not readily evident. There were videos of the outside of the plant, as huge and serene as ever, with no pillars of gas erupting and no fires. After a few hours, there was a press conference by the plant's management, who announced that a computer system had detected a failure in a critical system, and the alarm had been automatic. Since an inspection showed no indication that the system had actually malfunctioning, some "computer glitch" was suspected. However, as a safety precaution, the immediate area was still off limits to casual traffic. Haematite, in effect, was closed for the day.

For a moment, Sandra considered the idea that Man Duc was responsible for all this. Michael convinced her she was getting a little too paranoid, and they started acting like schoolchildren who got an unexpected snow day. Sandra immediately planned an elaborate, romantic dinner that she would cook herself. This required a careful study of her cookbooks, creation of a grocery list, and an impromptu shopping trip. Michael was not quite domesticated enough as yet to enjoy shopping, but his current task was to protect Sandra, so he tagged along without protest.

Sandra rarely cooked meals from scratch, but it wasn't because she wasn't a skilled chef. She was generally too busy. As she told Michael, cooking is just applied chemistry, and she had excelled in chemistry in college. Just measure carefully, watch the times and temperatures, and, except for the occasional equipment malfunction or spoiled starting materials, you can't go wrong. There was that one time she had used baking powder in place of baking soda in a cookie recipe. Although the cookies were ruined, she claimed that the experiment was a success, since it taught her what to check in the future.

Her creation that night was Beef Stroganoff on egg noodles with Harvard Beets, a hearty port wine, and Crème Brûlée for dessert. Sandra insisted that the port wine neutralized the fat in the Stroganoff, so it was a healthy meal despite its appearance. Michael's mouth was too full at the time for him to argue the point. It was then that he started to think seriously of Sandra as a possible life partner. Smart, beautiful, and she could cook! What more could a guy want?

Sandra checked the status of the emergency at the carbon sequestration plant before they went to bed. Everything was under control, which was not hard for them to do, since there wasn't a real emergency in the first place. It was just a glitch in the computer that monitored the plant's safety systems. No snow day tomorrow! School will be open!

When Michael arrived at his Haematite office the next morning, something was amiss. His tactile input tablet was moved from its usual place. Since no one should have been in the building during the evacuation, it couldn't have been moved by the cleaning crew. When he logged onto his computer, he discovered that all his files had been erased, including all his Black Swan data and analysis. He grabbed his transceiver and dialed Sandra.

"Michael, what's up?"

"Sandra, have you accessed your computer yet?

"Not yet. Is there some message this morning I should read?"

"No message, but do it now."

Michael could hear her tapping some keys and then pause.

"Michael, most of my files are missing!"

"Same here. I'm on my way to your laboratory so we can discuss what may have happened."

Michael must have raced to Sandra's laboratory on automatic pilot, since he couldn't remember the trip. His mind was racing through possible scenarios, both benign and malicious, of how their computers were wiped. The first thing to do was to check whether their experience was isolated, or whether these erasures were pandemic at the site. Sandra had the same idea, since she did some checking while Michael was traveling to her laboratory.

"Michael, I asked around, very generally, whether people were having computer problems this morning. It appears that our erasures were isolated."

"That's bad, very bad."

"I know what you're thinking - Man Duc. Do you think they caused the evacuation to get access to our computers? That's a pretty big escalation, even for Man Duc!"

"Yeah, it's somewhat suspicious, since it was a computer problem that shut down the carbon plant and caused the evacuation. Or maybe the evacuation was just an opportunity they couldn't resist. It's a lot easier to access a building when you're sure that there will be no one around, not even the cleaning crew or the security guards. We know there's an inside man at Haematite - Probably that guy, Jack. Jack held the flashlight while they hacked into our systems. I'm sure he isn't smart enough to do it himself."

"Michael, isn't all our data automatically backed-up by Haematite, somewhere? Should we ask?"

"I'm sure whoever did this also had access to Haematite's backup media. It isn't much, just a few weeks worth. All that media must be missing or somehow corrupted. I'm sure they wouldn't erase the backups. That would be too suspicious. They would render them mostly unreadable. Errors do happen. Also, we had better keep this to ourselves. It was just you and me, and our computers are in different parts of the building. The suspicion would center on us, not some unknown agent. Perhaps our project wasn't doing too well, so we arranged a convenient accident."

Sandra was silent. After a while, Michael continued.

"I have my own personal backups."

"Michael, how? No one ever does that anymore. The systems are too reliable, and there are the automated backups. Of course, the backup philosophy never considers the intentional destruction of data. There are also safeguards in place that prevent personal backups. Backups are considered to be potential data leaks, so they try to prevent them."

"Sandra, you've been away from a university environment too long. I always make backups. Trying to restore data through our administrative channels is a nightmare. It's not worth even trying. There's always the suspicion that they don't even make backups, although I know the process is automated enough that even the laziest computer administrator would still do it. As for safeguards, maybe they prevent most people from streaming their data, but that doesn't apply to me. I'm no Basil in that regard, but necessity has always been the Mother of Invention."

"OK. We still have our data. Now what?"

"I say, pretend like nothing has happened. Just go about our normal routine, complete the report, Black Swans included, but not mention their source. Then, sit back to wait for the project to be killed. I'm sure the project will be killed. Man Duc's finger is on the trigger. But Man Duc will need to act at the highest levels of Haematite. We're not going to make it easy on them by making it appear that we erased our own data to hide some incompetence."

"OK, Michael, let's do that, but let's keep a very low profile. We don't want Man Duc to suspect that their midnight raid accomplished nothing. They may try something else - Something worse."

Michael left Sandra's lab. As he sat in his own office, he found it hard to concentrate. Iterating in his head all of Man Duc's escalating actions against the Haematite team made him wonder how far they would go. Disabling a carbon sequestration plant for a day, if they were actually responsible for that, seemed drastic. Perhaps he needed to revise his "gentleman thief" concept.

26 BACK ON TRACK

Michael had streamed his data to Mother Wode in an encrypted format. He had redundantly streamed the data to two Mother Wode servers to make the data repository more secure. This was easy on the Mother Wode end, since he had authorized access to just about everything on the network, except for other users' personal files. The Haematite end was somewhat of a problem. Haematite, like all large corporations, wanted to keep their data private. As a consequence, methods for routine data streaming outside its local network were disabled. Michael merely disguised data packets as attachments to messages to his white-listed Mother Wode messaging address. A companion program at Mother Wode took all attachments, tagged them sequentially, and stored them on the servers. If a backup was needed, these individual files could be decrypted and reassembled to produce the original data.

It was a very easy matter for Michael to get the data back to Haematite. After a few hours of effort, it was as if

Man Duc's violation of his computer had never happened. Michael spent about the same amount of time replacing Sandra's files with versions he had stored in his backups. Sandra was very good at keeping Michael in the loop, and she was repaid for this by his recovery of nearly all of her files. Man Duc was careful not to destroy every file on her computer, since that action would likely lead to some sort of unwanted investigation. They deleted only recent files, knowing that this action conveniently erased all traces of the Black Swan project.

About a week after their data had been erased, Sandra received a "friendly" message from Jack asking whether the project was still on track for the deadline imposed at the project review meeting. Jack was obviously worried why he hadn't heard any news about their computer problems. Sandra thanked him for his interest (Sandra's verbal assessment, not translated into corporate-speak, was, "That bastard!"), and she cautiously replied that they had encountered some "computer problems." They were trying to resolve these, but she was still hopeful they would meet the deadline. All this was meant to lull Jack into thinking that they were trying to recover using the Haematite server's backup files. They hadn't bothered to ask for the backups, since Michael had convinced Sandra that they would be found to be unreadable.

"I think that will hold him for another week, but, after that, he will do some checking in earnest," said Michael. "Man Duc doesn't leave anything to chance."

Michael's analysis was back on track, and he was writing the technical section of the report in parallel with the actual work. There were blanks here and there to fill in when those portions of the analysis were concluded. He was taking no chances, backing up his work every day before leaving Haematite. The summary tactic they decided to follow was to pinpoint the level of transaction below which the Black Swans had diminishing effect. An additional point, which they called the break-even point, was the point at which Haematite would neither make nor lose money. To simplify matters, the actual expense of network deployment and operation were not included in the analysis. These would be included in a follow-up analysis if Haematite considered the profit on these small transactions to be worthwhile.

Nowhere in the report was there any speculation about the origin of the Black Swans. There was no statement that the Black Swans were coordinated, and not isolated, events. Nevertheless, Michael realized why the mere existence of such a report would make Man Duc very uncomfortable. No one thought much about the Swans because they were rare. The report demonstrated that these rare Swans were shuffling a lot of money around, right under everyone's nose, and their affect on the financial markets could be huge. No one had cared to investigate the Swans before, since no money was ever missing. It was just parked somewhere for anywhere from a few minutes to a few hours before it was sent to its destination.

Back at her laboratory, Sandra noticed a message on her transceiver screen to call Hal, the director who had protected their project from being summarily canceled at the review meeting. He had phoned only a few minutes beforehand, so Sandra was hopeful she would still catch him in his office and learn what he wanted. As typical, the ring-back number reached an assistant and not Hal directly, but since Sandra was returning his call, she was put through immediately.

"Sandra, happy you could respond so quickly. Just a quick request."

"Sure. Hope I can comply."

"I need a progress report on your project. I know your deadline for completion isn't for a few weeks, but I need to quiet some concerns."

One name immediately flashed into Sandra's mind.

"It's Jack, isn't it."

"Yes, how did you guess?" Hal laughed. "It would be easy if a Director only needed to manage his own people. Much of my time seems to involve managing the other Directors. It's all a competition for scarce resources. Well, to get back on topic, Jack heard you had some technical problems, and he thinks you'll miss the deadline. First, is that correct; and second, can you give me a few crumbs I can forward to him to demonstrate that you're still on track?"

Just as Michael predicted, Jack was starting to believe that his apparent operation to erase data on their computers had somehow gone amiss.

"Jack's right that there was a small computer problem. I told him about it a week ago. Although Michael is still part time until he defends his dissertation, he put in some extra effort when the problem was discovered. He's gotten things fixed and back on track. We'll still make the deadline."

"Good to hear!" Can you send me something I can forward to Jack?"

"I'll organize some of the more important data slides that will illustrate the level of effort. The conclusions will need to wait until the end."

“Sandra, that will be fine. Send along my appreciation to Michael for his work.”

Hal disconnected, and Sandra thought about calling Michael. Since it was close to the end of the day, she decided it could wait until morning. Michael intended to spend the night at his apartment to do some final Sterba tasks, so she wouldn't see him until then.

27 SNATCHED!

Michael had just finished punching the key code into the lock on his apartment door when he was surprised by a hand over his face. A brief smell of chloroform, and then he was out. Man Duc had decided to pay him a visit! He awoke seated on his couch. His ankles were lightly bound, but his hands were free. One of his assailants was seated next to him. When he noticed that Michael was awake, he looked at him squarely face-to-face and said, "Keep still, and there won't be any trouble."

As Michael's vision cleared, he could see another man seated at a table. It was the same man who had accessed Basil's computer, and now he was attempting to access Michael's computer! Michael was puzzled why his hands weren't bound. He was puzzled also as to why he wasn't kept unconscious, like Basil, until his assailants had finished with his computer. He gained the courage to speak.

"What's going on?"

The man at the computer stopped and turned towards Michael. He resembled Basil's photograph, but he didn't look all that sinister in real life. He was an older man, about fifty, nicely dressed, looking more like a businessman than a thug. Another gentleman thief.

"Sorry about our strong-arm tactics, but we didn't want you to raise an alarm. Some neighbor might have called the police, and that would have been bad for all of us. The chloroform might give you a slight headache, but we've been gentle. We've been instructed to treat you gently, as long as you behave and follow orders."

If their treatment of Michael up to that point was gentle, the image in their heads of not-so-gentle was something he didn't want to experience! Michael decided not to exercise his imagination. The gentleman thief continued.

"It's important for us to examine your recent computer files. We bound your feet just to remind you not to run. Now, it will help if you'll type in your password for me."

This was the reason Michael's hands weren't tied. Basil's computer was unlocked when they had gained access to his office, but here they needed Michael's password. Michael was not going to object. The computer was passed onto his lap and he entered his password. He was sorry he never implemented the multiple password trick Basil had taught him. One password for regular access where all files are visible; another password for restricted access where all files except marked files are visible; and a last doomsday password that erases marked files, all this activity happening stealthily so that observers are none the wiser.

As Michael returned the computer, he said, "I thought guys like you never needed passwords."

The gentleman thief ignored him, plugged a media stick into the computer and executed a program. It didn't appear that the man was especially skilled in computers, since the entire operation was labored. After a minute, the man pocketed the media stick. He didn't power-down the computer.

"I've transferred copies of your personal files to another location, and I've installed a program that will allow my associates to delete selected files. These will be just the files that they believe are sensitive to our operation. I was told that as a professional courtesy we were not to wipe your entire computer. By the time you return to this computer, certain files may have been erased, as will our program and all traces of it. Another team has been dispatched to the university for the same purpose. They're somewhat more expert, and I hear they don't need passwords."

Michael wondered how long these operations would take, since it appeared that they intended to keep him away from his computer until they were finished with their coordinated operation.

"Now, we're going for a ride. Soon, all your questions will be answered."

Michael was being taken for a ride. Bad connotations for that phrase existed in too many videos he had seen. But these men had been especially gentle, considering what they could have done, and Michael had been immediately cooperative in releasing his password. He was hoping that his gentleman thief theory followed through for the rest of the night.

28 MANUS DUCENS

The car stopped, and Michael was guided into a building where he was plopped into a chair. When his blindfold was removed, he found himself in front of a desk in a spacious office. The window shades were drawn, probably as a precaution against his identifying the location. He had been driven around for at least a half hour, but the drive could have been in circles, so Michael couldn't be sure how far he was from his apartment. A half hour's driving radius from his apartment, if that were correct, would include a huge part of the state, so he could be almost anywhere. At least no aircraft were involved. An air journey seemed more likely to be a one way affair.

A gray haired man in a finely tailored business suit sat at the desk. From Michael's observations to this point, it seemed as if Man Duc was staffed almost exclusively by gray haired men in business suits. The man behind the desk, like Michael's assailants, wore no mask. Michael suspected that everyone in the room could be using some sort of theatrical makeup to obscure their identities. Perhaps such Man Duc "business meetings" were so common that there were ready made masks that took just a minute to apply. More than likely, Michael's knowledge base, assembled from watching spy thriller videos, was flawed, and these men actually didn't care who recognized them.

And, in one corner of the office, seated in a chair nearly as overstuffed as its occupant, was Basil, who was contentedly munching cookies!

"Dr. Martelli, I'm happy to finally meet you. I hope our zeal in arranging this meeting hasn't frightened you. I apologize for your blindfold. It was a precaution in the event you may have escaped before our conversation and revealed our location. As you will find, our conversation will bring you considerable enlightenment. You will find that you will have no need to draw attention to us. Do not fear for your safety. We are all gentlemen here. You've noticed that we've also summoned your friend, Basil. Basil and I had a very long chat before you arrived. As you can see, Basil is quite content."

Most of this sounded like pure "B" movie script. If he wasn't so nervous, Michael would probably laugh. But the gray haired executive did make a point about Basil. Unless Basil was involved with Man Duc from the start, which was very unlikely, any fear of Man Duc that Basil may have had was erased by whatever this gray haired man revealed. Not only did Basil look relieved, he appeared elated; or, maybe it was just the quality of the cookies.

Michael answered, "A small correction. It's Mr. Martelli. My dissertation defense is still a few weeks away."

"As I hear, it's a mere formality in your case. You have been an exceptional student, and your skills as a Computerati have not escaped our attention. The computer skills of your friend, Basil, are exceptional as well. You two have penetrated to the heart of our operation. We consider that to be a considerable achievement in light of our penchant for secrecy, and our own computer people have learned much from your methods. You've actually rendered us a great service, since you've pointed out an unexpected vulnerability in our methods. They think that you're just an isolated case; but, as they say, forewarned is forearmed."

"Thanks for the compliment, but there was nothing too special in what we've done. I'm just an apprentice of no great skill, indentured to Haematite Corporation to do routine computer work. Basil and I are merely colleagues at East Wodenstumpf University doing academic work."

"A cut above mere, I would say. Your Haematite project engaged our attention early on, but it was your unorthodox handling of it that was quite alarming to us."

It was time for Michael to get some answers. At the least, he might confirm his suspicions.

"How is it that you know about my work at Haematite? The information isn't public. And what is it about the Haematite project that interests you?"

"We have people in many high places, and they feed us important information whenever they can. We've learned that you've been making some statistical inferences about stock trades. There are small discrepancies between theoretical predictions and your experimental finding. Scientists usually modify or abandon their theories at that point, but you persisted. And you enlisted the services of your friend, Basil, to get to the root cause of the matter. It's this persistence that caused us concern and led to this meeting."

Back to the "B" movie script.

"Am I to understand that these "small anomalies" are your doing?"

"Yes, most of them are, but I assure you that although the playing field is high finance, none of this is motivated by greed. As a professional courtesy, I'll tell you the purpose of the anomalies and the purpose of my organization. I ask that you not repeat any of this. If you do, you will bring much more trouble upon yourself than to us. However, after hearing our purpose, I'm sure that you, like your friend Basil, will find no need to cause us any further trouble."

This sounded like a small variation on, "I could tell you, but then I'd have to kill you." The variation being, "I'll tell you, but don't tell anyone else, or I'll kill you."

"Don't tell me anything I really shouldn't know," replied Michael. "I really don't want to be involved. As I said, I'm just an academic."

"But Mr. Martelli, you are involved, as is your friend, Basil. You will hear the full story. Basil already has, and he finds no problem with what we do."

It didn't appear that his abductors were armed. Perhaps he shouldn't let his imagination get the better of him. Then there was Basil, sitting in an overstuffed chair, quietly drinking coffee and munching on cookies. Basil must have heard a similar speech before Michael arrived, and he appeared to be quite comfortable. On the other hand, a tacit endorsement from Basil was hardly the *nihil obstat* Michael would prefer.

"OK. Shoot."

Bad choice of words!

"Have you studied history, Mr. Martelli? Specifically, the Italian Renaissance?"

"I have a general understanding of the topic, but I'm a Computerati. I'm not an historian."

"No problem. I'll be more descriptive in my explanation so that everything will be clear. The Italian Renaissance was a time of rapid cultural and economic change. As usual during those times, the Church was a chronic problem. The Church was limiting progress through outdated concepts, such as its idea that all forms of interest, no matter how small, constituted usury. The Italian merchants would dutifully haul their households to High Mass every Sunday, recite the Latin responses, and then plot against the Church hierarchy in their secret chambers. A clandestine group of intellectuals formed to devise a means of moderating the influence of the Church in such matters, and this monied class of merchants was generous in its support of their organization."

"Can I surmise," said Michael, "That the Reformation was your idea?"

"No, no. It is against our charter to undertake such concerted action against any one group, the Church, or otherwise. It would surely lead to a mutiny among some of our members, and a heated response by our enemies. Some of our members may have individually supported Luther, but we had no response as a group. Our strength was in the fact that we didn't take sides against particular groups. We took sides against particular ideas."

The gray-haired man sipped from a coffee mug and continued.

"Our main charter was to direct the economic progress of the world into appropriate directions. A secondary purpose, in furtherance of the others, was to limit any unfair economic advantage of one group over any another. We decided that greed was good, but not when taken to excess. It may not surprise you that Galileo and many other intellectuals were members of the group. Galileo's difficulties with the Church are written as if they involved his science, alone. His opposition extended much deeper."

"Can I presume that even if I were an historian, I would know nothing about this group?"

"You are correct. This was a secret society, bound by blood oaths, fear of the Inquisition, and the desire to do good in the world. Few knew of its existence. Their secret has remained to this day. I am a member of that society, the Manus Ducens, which is Latin for The Guiding Hand."

"Man Duc!" exclaimed Michael.

"Yes, we use that short form for most business matters."

OK. The "B" movie script was still operative. A secret society controlling the world, or at least trying to control it, for more than five hundred years? Michael remained silent.

"Secrecy was of utmost importance, since our lives depended on it, but we needed a way to act. Events themselves were hard to orchestrate and change. In those days you would need a standing army for most actions. We had no real power beyond our intellect and ability for analysis. Events themselves were hard to change, but the timing of events and their sequence often could be changed with little effort. Do you understand?"

"Time is money?"

"Close to the truth. Five hundred years ago, history was measured on the scale of months. All important matters, whether of church, state, or trade, were conducted along the highways of Europe. One would send a messenger with a sealed proposal. He would travel to his destination, present the proposal for consideration, and then return with the reply. The messenger, of course, might be delayed by bad weather; or he may bed down with a woman of easy virtue for a few nights. He might even be bribed to walk just a little more slowly, or shun a certain road for another, possibly because of rumors he had heard about bandits. We were the suppliers of many women, a few men, many bribes, and some disinformation."

"That doesn't sound very efficient."

"Efficient, no, but our objective was not near-term wealth, or abrupt changes of government or economy. Our hand guided over the decades. As the world progressed, our changes became evident in the rise of the intelligentsia, and what has come to be known as the Western Intellectual Tradition. All that was not an accident. We were like the Hand of God working for the betterment of man."

"Well, in my opinion, you failed quite badly in the last century."

"Yes, and we were ashamed, especially since the Second World War is seen by historians to be a direct result of economic conditions, the very things that we sought to control. Manus Ducens had become ineffective and was nearly dissolved. The problem was that the world began operating on a much faster time scale. Transactions were done in the course of hours; then minutes. The advent of the telegraph caused us some problems at first, but these were overcome by the use of repeaters. Are you familiar with repeaters?"

"In the modern context, they're circuits that accept signals and then pass them along unchanged, usually with higher amplitude."

"Our repeaters were somewhat different - they sometimes delayed the message. By modern standards, they were crude, almost laughable, but they were the only solution at the time. We would break the telegraph line. One operator would transcribe the messages, and then pass them to another who would retransmit. Messages we wished to delay would fall to the bottom of the pile. They would reach their final destination, but after an appropriate delay. Sometimes certain messages would be retransmitted in a different order, thereby giving one party an advantage over another. The advent of telephony ended our control of communications. Soon, it became impossible for us to intervene. We thought all was lost, but then the computer age was upon us."

Michael started to get the idea.

"You see, Mr. Martelli, the computer may have allowed for transactions on an even more rapid time scale, but it also allowed a very easy way for us to continue our purpose."

"In short, you're the ones responsible for the heavy tail in the transaction latency."

"I'm not a technical man, Mr. Martelli, but if you mean that we are the guiding hand in some financial transactions, you are correct."

"Why haven't you been caught? If a mere student Computerati can discover in a few weeks that there's something amiss, the government must know."

"We have friends in high places. As I said before, we don't target people, we target ideas. Manus Ducens has a policy not to give allegiance to any one government, but there are a few people in high places in all governments who realize that what we do is right, and they tacitly support us in many ways. Manus Ducens is the creator of the societies on which their governments are based, so they owe us a debt of gratitude. We intervene only in minimal ways, and we cause no real harm to anyone. We are not feared, since we are known to do the right thing, the right thing being what's best for humanity *in toto*. Your profession as a Computerati would not exist were it not for our shaping of culture and society throughout the centuries."

"The main problem with our present world and all of human history is that people want to govern themselves locally. In prehistoric times, humans were tribal, and it was tribe against tribe. As kingdoms and empires developed, it was the same thing, but on a much larger scale. In our modern age, it's the same thing, but now it's country against country. Yes, there are treaties in place, and agreements on climate and other environmental matters, that somewhat mitigate these adversarial tendencies. But, officially, there is no central authority, no guiding hand, to nudge humanity along a more civilized path. Unofficially, there is Manus Ducens."

He paused for a moment, then continued.

"This leads us to the problem at hand. Manus Ducens won't allow Haematite Corporation to meddle in the stock market. Our net effect on the market is not that large, since we are very selective in our interventions. However, Haematite's influence would distort the market to an extent that our interventions would be less effective."

The "B" movie script was finally writing Michael in as a character, albeit a minor character. He was now in a very low position in a cast of thousands.

"As you must know," said Michael, "I'm not even a full time employee of Haematite at this point. Even if I were, it would be impossible for me to sabotage their work undetected. I am powerless."

"Don't imagine yourself to be that powerless. The advice of a scientist is always taken seriously. That's what you're paid to do, offer advice. But in this case, it will be all too easy. Just as in the governments, we are not without influence in the business world. The Haematite management itself will decide to kill the project, summarily and without a final report. They will notify you and your colleagues, possibly as early as tomorrow, that you should focus your efforts on other interesting areas. But, there is another matter..."

"Although you are indentured to Haematite, I'm allowed to make you an offer of employment with the Manus Ducens. A similar offer has been made to your friend, Basil, and I'm happy to say that he's tentatively accepted. He would like to tour our technical facilities first, and talk with kindred souls in our organization, before making a final judgment. He thinks it will be enjoyable work, and I know that his Old World contacts will be very useful to us."

So, Basil has found his niche. It was almost as if the job was made for him. The gray haired man continued.

"Now that you understand our noble task, I hope you will consider. It is your choice, completely. Haematite will not hold you to your contract if you chose to join us, but you may remain with Haematite if you wish. Manus Ducens, is prepared to offer you a somewhat larger salary than you would make at Haematite. Manus Ducens, however, will insist on your silence in either case. You are a logical man.

Exposing us would bring you no reward, but it could bring inestimable woe upon your children, and their children."

The "B" movie credits were about to roll, and Michael found that he could either be edited from the film, or assume a supporting roll. He still didn't know who the lead characters were.

"I'm sorry to say that I don't have any children. I'm not even married, but I get your point. Thanks for the employment offer, but I'll decline. My computer interests span many broad areas, and I would feel too constrained focusing on just one idea for the rest of my career. Also, I wouldn't feel comfortable in a secret society, no matter how noble; plus, I'm starting to like things at Haematite. Most importantly, I think Basil is more the type of employee you would want, not me."

"Then I accept your decision on the matter," said the gray haired man. "Now, as to the matter of our secrecy. Do you believe my story and our need for secrecy?"

"Yes, your secret is safe with me; and pardon my saying it, if I did talk about your society, people would think I'm crazy. It would be a good idea for a book, though."

"I'm sorry I didn't convince you to join us. I'm sure you would have been an asset to our organization. Perhaps your friend, Basil, will be able to convince you in the future. As a show of our good will, we will let you leave without the blindfold. If you ever change your mind, you'll know where to find us."

The gray haired man rose to shake his hand, and Michael accepted his handshake. One of the toughs opened the office door and motioned Michael and Basil to leave. As they exited the office, Michael wondered whether this office was a permanent facility of Man Duc, or if it was appropriated just for the night. As he left the building with his two shadows and Basil, he noticed a sign on the building, M. Ducens & Cie. They were hiding in plain sight!

29 MUTUAL CONSENT

Michael finally had a chance to talk with Basil while they were being driven home by the Man Duc muscle men.

"Basil, how did they get you here? In my case, it started with a chloroform rag at my front door."

"Ah, the chloroform rag! Basil remembers it well! Basil was in his office, as usual. Basil's two friends here just walked in and asked Basil to go with them. Basil is not a fighting man, so Basil just went. Basil was more curious than nervous, and when Basil got the speech from Mister Big, it was all very exciting. Imagine, a job description that fits Basil perfectly! Not only that, but Man Duc does not restrict compensation based on advanced degrees. They are just interested in how useful you can be. Basil, without a Ph.D. will be treated as well as a full Computerati!"

"About the compensation part. From what we surmise, this is a powerful organization, possibly staffed with thousands of individuals in many countries. And their employees don't come cheap! Except..."

Michael lowered his voice so that only Basil could hear.

"Except for these muscle men, they must all be highly skilled people. Add on top of that this need for secrecy, and we're talking big money. They claim they don't steal any of the transaction money. Where does their money come from?"

"As Basil was told, they have a donor base that includes wealthy individuals and many governments. They wouldn't be able to operate if they didn't have such a power base. And these donations can be quite large! It seems that whatever is good for Man Duc is good for business in general. Some of these same donors may have been on the short end of Man Duc's scheme from time to time; but secrecy is tantamount, so they would never know. Perhaps just knowing of Man Duc's existence keeps most of them honest. Giving to Man Duc is like giving to your church, but in this case it's the secular church of finance. You feel good in doing the right thing, and you always believe that it's the other guy who's behaving badly."

Michael was hashing out various organizational schemes in his head.

"I guess you get a personal introduction to Man Duc from a respected elder in business or government. More gray hairs in business suits. That's the only way something like this could propagate and still be secret. There are probably infrequent caucuses among local members, disguised as business club meetings. I wonder if there's a secret handshake."

"Basil doesn't care about the handshake, as long as the hand has money in it!"

The trek back to Michael's apartment was just as long as the trip to Man Duc, so it was apparent that the Man Duc soldiers hadn't driven around in circles to confuse him. Michael said his goodbyes to Basil, and then tried to formulate a plan to tell Sandra about what had happened. It was too late to see her that night, but he decided to drive to her place early enough in the morning to brief her before work. If Man Duc was as efficient as he thought, there might be a message for her already that the project was canceled. He wondered whether they should launch a feint protest to keep the cover story in play.

The next morning, Michael arrived at Sandra's and briefed her while she prepared for work. She wondered why they had targeted Michael, and not her, until Michael explained that they likely believed that she was just a typical project manager, a titular head.

"At least they got the tit part right," said Michael as he swerved his head to narrowly avoid the towel thrown at him.

"Well, this makes our life that much less complicated. No more cloak and dagger and checking over our shoulder to see whether anyone is following us. And Basil, do you think he'll join Man Duc?"

"It's nearly the perfect career for someone like Basil. He's been effectively disenfranchised all these years because of his lack of an academic credential, and possibly because of his shady past. Basil's particular qualities are exactly what Man Duc needs to keep ahead of the game. The fact that he penetrated Man Duc's defenses is proof enough to them of his worth. I'm very happy for the guy."

"And they're just going to hope that you and I don't cause any problems for them?"

"I don't know anything specific about their process, but they claim their intentions are for the good of mankind, including my children and grandchildren. As far as I can see, they don't affect anything in my life directly, so I have no personal motive to expose them; and the downside risk in exposing them is that I might be responsible for the extinction of the human race. As far as I'm concerned, let sleeping dogs lie."

"What's that other dog analogy?" said Sandra. "When you lie down with dogs, you come up with fleas."

"Then, we need to take a flea bath and get on with our lives. At least we know what to buy Basil next Christmas."

The next morning, Sandra and Michael found an urgent meeting notice posted on their schedules. Arriving at the conference room at the appointed time, they found a sole occupant. It was their corporate nemesis, Jack. Jack motioned them to seats, closed the door and addressed Michael.

"Michael, some friends of mine mentioned they might talk with you last night. Did you have a nice conversation?"

All doubts about Jack's involvement with Man Duc were erased. Michael seemed to think that Jack didn't have any idea of Michael and Sandra's relationship, so he decided not to involve her in his answer.

"Yes. We had a pleasant conversation, and I was happy that they were able to speak with me. It's fortuitous that you called this meeting, which I assume was for an informal progress report."

"Exactly," said Jack. "So, how do things look?"

Jack was playing it cool. He appeared to address the question to Sandra, but he was hoping that Michael had taken the lead in winding down the project and devising a way to get Sandra's buy-in. Likewise, Sandra continued the act.

"Michael's taken most of the morning to convince me that we're at an impasse. On the basis of his data, I've agreed that the arbitrage idea we researched is too much of a risk for Haematite. We should end the project and move into other areas."

Jack gave an audible sigh of relief. The pressure on him may have been greater than any Michael and Sandra experienced. He turned to Michael.

"Michael, I'm well known at Haematite for my miserly traits. Perhaps that accounts for my longevity." Jack laughed, the first time Michael had heard him laugh. "Since your project is in such a specialty area, I don't really think a final report would be useful to anyone. You've likely learned a few computer tricks as a result of the project; but, I'm sure these would be useful only to you and Sandra, and you already have those files. Would you agree that preparing a final report would be a waste of your time and Haematite's money?"

So, this was going to be a consensus action, very neat and tidy. Jack keeps his cover, and he and Sandra keep their jobs. Michael realized why Man Duc had been so successful over its many centuries of existence. It was a shame that his Man Duc offer was an all-in or all-out choice. Michael could have learned a lot from these guys over the course of a short internship.

"I think that a final report won't be necessary." He turned to Sandra. "Sandra, do you agree?"

"Well, Jack has a convincing manner of addressing the value-added proposition. I agree that a final report would have no value to Haematite, since the lessons-learned on this project are valuable to only Michael and me."

Lessons-learned? Value-added proposition? Sandra speaks their language! Michael was impressed. He had a brief fantasy of Sandra in animal skins yelping at baboons in the jungle, and the baboons sitting in rapt attention.

Jack pushed himself away from the conference table and stood.

"Then it's agreed. The arbitrage idea is too risky for Haematite. I'll pass the word upstream, get you both gold stars for your thorough investigation, and look forward to your next interesting project. Sandra, what's next in the hopper?"

"I think we'll use Michael's mathematical expertise to make some incremental improvements in our existing systems."

Sandra opted for a safe harbor, at least for the near term, until a bigger fish presented itself. Compared with Man Duc, the next project would be like a paid vacation.

As they left the conference room, Michael was hoping that this was the last he saw of Jack. The revelation about Man Duc's mission moderated Michael's dislike of Jack somewhat, but Jack was still a dyed-in-the-wool manager, and Michael just didn't care for managers. Sandra's grasp of their language was worrisome. Was this just a small side effect of her rubbing elbows with these people all these years, or would she someday become a manager? Some thought this sort of thing was inevitable, the cream rising to the top. He made a note to ask her about her managerial aspirations when he had dug himself out of Mother Wode.

30 CERTIFIED COMPUTERATI

After the Man Duc fiasco, Michael was able to devote more of his time to tying the loose ends at Mother Wode before his dissertation defense. Basil would have just disappeared in the middle of the night if it weren't for Michael's arranging a going-away luncheon for him, appropriately at Miguel's. Basil had worked for so many people that nearly the entire building attended the luncheon, and there were quite a few speeches about his excellent performance on one project or another. When asked where he was going, Basil concocted a story about being invited to work at his mother university in the Old Country, where he could be close to family. He said his English skills would be important, if only for editing the professor's papers for submission to the more prestigious computer journals. Someone joked that he couldn't remember seeing anything remotely resembling English in any computer science papers he read.

Michael's dissertation defense was, as expected, a mere formality. The only wild card was the one professor on his examination committee who was from another department - A concession by the Guild to the university during the transition of degree-granting authority many years ago. This professor's only contribution to the defense was highlighting a few typographical errors in the text. As smart as they were, the automatic correcting features on document processing programs were not perfect. They had improved over the years with context-adapting algorithms, but technical documents were so far out of their ken that they were not too effective. The joke was that if you were to emulate human intelligence perfectly in a computer program, you would necessarily emulate human stupidity as well.

Now that Michael was full time at Haematite, he had a full paycheck and some laboratory space of his own. He didn't even consider encroaching on Sandra's space, since he knew that they each needed their working environments to be as separate as possible. It was a corollary of the "Absence makes the heart grow fonder" law handed down through the ages. Michael was given what had been an optical metrology laboratory at the time when you could still examine computer chips with light. The space was too cramped and not sufficiently vibration-isolated for the specialized nanoscale imaging equipment that were now needed, so the room had remained idle and used for storage over the course of quite a few years.

Most of the equipment in the room was discarded, since any item older than a few years was already obsolete. There was one item that caught Michael's eye, and he saved it from the dumpster. It was a traveling wave tube, once used not for its usual communications purpose, but to form a plasma in an analytical instrument. Michael had no idea whether it contained the platinum alloy magnets that Basil mentioned at the hub router, but Michael had it shipped to Basil. In any case, it would make a nice paperweight.

As it turned out, Sandra's safe harbor project after Man Duc was more important than either Michael or Sandra had thought. Michael had discovered that the traffic on Haematite's electrical futures arbitrage network could be divided into at least two tiers, one fast and the other slow, based on some filters and triggers. The increase in speed on the fast transactions translated quickly into real money for Haematite at no additional capital expense. Michael had quickly shown his worth to Haematite, and both he and Sandra were awarded a substantial year-end bonus.

Now that he was earning some real money, Michael was able to buy a better car. The extra income also got him thinking in other directions. Sandra had been promoted, and she and Michael no longer worked with each other. Their intimate relationship no longer needed to be kept a secret.

31 HITCHED

Michael thought he knew Sandra quite well when he proposed marriage to her. After all, they had been living together and working together for more than a year. More importantly, they had weathered the Man Duc affair together, and there's nothing like a little danger to cause people to cling to each other. However, there were gaps in Michael's knowledge base that he never suspected. Sandra turned out to be a traditional girl who wanted a church wedding. Not only that, but she was a Catholic girl.

"Michael, I never told you I went to a Catholic girl's high school?"

It was a test of his true love for her that he suffered through the meetings with a priest, and the seminars in which he and Sandra were thrust among couples barely out of their teens. The stated purpose of these seminars was to learn the secrets of living together harmoniously - As if most of them hadn't already lived together for years. It seemed to Michael that some of the girls were starting to show, but it was hard for him to judge, since he didn't want Sandra to catch him staring too long at younger women.

Basil was Michael's best man. He was paired with Sandra's younger sister as maid of honor, exposing another gap in Michael's knowledge base. Michael never knew that Sandra had a sister. Sandra's sister was a little unsure what to make of Basil, but Basil was great fun at a party, and she seemed to enjoy herself. Little did she realize that she was paired with what now passes as a secret agent in the electronic age. Another surprise was when Sandra invited Sterba to give her away at the ceremony. The two had met at Michael's post-defense party, and they seemed to enjoy each other's company. That Sandra was a Computerati from a top school, had connections to a large corporation, and was a beautiful young woman had not escaped Sterba's attention. Sandra, for her part, thought that Sterba deserved a little reward, since he was responsible for Michael's coming to Haematite and their consequential relationship. The old guy looked quite stately in his tuxedo.

Sandra was the beautiful bride that Michael anticipated her to be, the darkness of her hair contrasting nicely with the white dress and matching Michael's black tuxedo. The only major slip in an otherwise perfect day involved Michael's shoes. He was certain he had a pair of black dress shoes somewhere, but between living mostly at Sandra's and boxing his things for an official move, he wasn't able to find them. Fortunately, his old brown shoes, augmented with some creative use of a black marker, were an adequate substitute, and they were indistinguishable from the real thing in all the wedding photos.

After a year, Sandra and Michael bought their first house and two dogs. The dogs were appropriately named Manfred and Duke.

About the Author

Dev Gualtieri received his PhD in 1974 and had a thirty-five year research career in physics and materials science.

He is listed as an inventor on more than thirty US patents, and on numerous international patents. His eclectic research interests included superconductivity, chemical thermodynamics, magnetism, electronics and computer science. At one time, he was an internationally recognized expert in crystal growth.

Dr. Gualtieri is now retired, and he resides in Northern New Jersey with his wife, Anne. They have a son and daughter who reside with their spouses in Pennsylvania.